The Mississippi Boys

A Novel of the Civil War

Jane Bennett Gaddy

Jane Bennett Gaddy, Ph.D.

Oxford, MS.
May, 2013

iUniverse, Inc.
New York Bloomington

The Mississippi Boys
A Novel of the Civil War

Copyright © 2008 by Jane Bennett Gaddy

All rights reserved. No part of this book may be used or reproduced by any means, graphic, electronic, or mechanical, including photocopying, recording, taping or by any information storage retrieval system without the written permission of the publisher except in the case of brief quotations embodied in critical articles and reviews.

Certain characters in this work are historical figures, and certain events portrayed did take place. However, this is a work of fiction. All of the other characters, names, and events as well as all places, incidents, organizations, and dialogue in this novel are either the products of the author's imagination or are used fictitiously.

iUniverse books may be ordered through booksellers or by contacting:

iUniverse
1663 Liberty Drive
Bloomington, IN 47403
www.iuniverse.com
1-800-Authors (1-800-288-4677)

Because of the dynamic nature of the Internet, any Web addresses or links contained in this book may have changed since publication and may no longer be valid. The views expressed in this work are solely those of the author and do not necessarily reflect the views of the publisher, and the publisher hereby disclaims any responsibility for them.

ISBN: 978-0-595-52792-2 (pbk)
ISBN: 978-0-595-62846-9 (ebk)
ISBN: 978-0-595-51583-7 (cloth)

Printed in the United States of America

Also by Jane Bennett Gaddy

House Not Made With Hands

To the memory of my great great-grandfather, Captain Thomas Goode (T. G.) Clark, and his sons, Privates Jonathan and Albert Henry Clark, soldiers of the Mississippi Volunteer Army of Ten Thousand, Company F, 42nd Mississippi Infantry Regiment, Davis Brigade, A. P. Hill Corps, Heth Division, Army of Northern Virginia, General Robert E. Lee, Commander, Civil War heroes who fell at the Battle of Gettysburg, July 1 and 3, 1863.

And to the memory of Sergeant Marcellus Church, Company F, 42nd Mississippi Infantry Regiment, T. G. Clark's half brother, wounded at Gettysburg in the first day of battle and later died in a Federal prison at Point Lookout, Maryland.

They gave ... *the last full measure of devotion.*

The scene was not only magnificent to look upon, but the realization of what it meant was deeply impressive. Even in times of peace our sensibilities are stirred by the sight of a great army passing in review. How infinitely more thrilling in the dread moments before the battle to look upon two mighty armies upon the same plain, "beneath spread ensigns and bristling bayonets," waiting for the impending crash and sickening carnage!

General John B. Gordon
Of the Confederate Army
Reminiscences of the Civil War

Contents

Prologue	*Through Eyes of Faith*	xv

Part One — The Hills of Home

Chapter 1	*War Like a Whisper*	1
Chapter 2	*Twenty-Five Pound O' Flour*	9
Chapter 3	*Under the Shadow of the Almighty*	21
Chapter 4	*In This Valley*	23
Chapter 5	*The Glories of Winter*	27
Chapter 6	*The Christmas Tree*	33
Chapter 7	*Don't Cry, Mama*	41
Chapter 8	*Benjamin, My Son*	47
Chapter 9	*Albert Henry*	51
Chapter 10	*Yalobusha Wilderness*	55
Chapter 11	*Oil of Healing*	67
Chapter 12	*O, Day Most Dreaded!*	71
Chapter 13	*Not for Evil*	75
Chapter 14	*Far and Away*	79
Chapter 15	*Grenada*	85

Part Two — Mississippi Volunteer Army of Ten Thousand

Chapter 16	*Gentlemen of the South*	103
Chapter 17	*Off to Paducah*	107
Chapter 18	*Unsullied Courage*	117
Chapter 19	*Cause to Celebrate*	125
Chapter 20	*The Hornets' Nest*	129
Chapter 21	*I Shall Wish for the Same*	137
Chapter 22	*Stand in the Gap*	141
Chapter 23	*On Forbidden Ground*	147
Chapter 24	*In My Lonely Hour*	151
Chapter 25	*Restless One*	155

Part Three   The Bravest of Men

Chapter 26   *Fighting on the "Southern Side" of the Potomac* . 165
Chapter 27   *The Name is "Lee"* 177
Chapter 28   *Life is Uncertain, Death is Sure* 185
Chapter 29   *Fredericksburg* 191

Part Four   Gettysburg

Chapter 30   *Isaac, Go Home!* 197
Chapter 31   *The Bloody Trough* 201
Chapter 32   *Faithful Sons* 209
Chapter 33   *Infinitely More Precious* 219

Epilogue   *In Some Golden Age* 227

Notes 231

Thanks....

To my cousin, Charlie Clark, great-grandson of Thomas Goode Clark and most valuable keeper of the memories of our Clarks, who shared his memoirs and who edited the manuscript. I'll always remember the trip to "Isaac's House" in Calhoun County, Mississippi.

To my cousin, Betty Crocker Abdo, whose knowledge of the *Clark Family Genealogy* and our forefathers' march from Calhoun County, Mississippi, to Gettysburg, Pennsylvania, was most helpful in writing this story.

To my cousin and lifelong friend, Burlon Crocker, Mississippi born and bred, who willingly edited the manuscript in search of my geographic and cultural errors.

To the memory of Bill Stenhouse, a *most grace-filled man*, whose family, at his death, sent me his cherished book, *Life Work and Sermons of John L. Girardeau* (1916). A portion of Dr. Girardeau's address in memory of the Confederate dead is cited in the epilogue. To my friend, Barbara Massey, who presented me with that book and the following message: "May Bill's love for writing and for history of Christian faith inspire you in the writing of your next book." —It did.

To Pastor Decherd Stevens, a great Presbyterian preacher of the gospel, whose knowledge and admiration for Generals Stonewall Jackson and Robert E. Lee inspired me to know more and to imagine their connection to my great great-grandfather.

To the memory of my grandmother, Vallie Georgia Clark Smith, who first stirred me with remembrance of our Civil War heroes, her own grandfather and uncles, and who encouraged me to travel to Gettysburg to see the place where they gave their lives for the Confederacy.

To the memory of my loving mother, Lola Clytie Smith Bennett, who brought me into the world of such a wonderful family.

To all who read *House Not Made With Hands.* If you had not responded with such interest and affection, I may never have had the courage to write *The Mississippi Boys.*

To my own dear husband, the rarest soul I know, who put his needs on hold and made sure I had time and space to write this story on the heels of *House Not Made With Hands.*

Prologue
Through Eyes of Faith

All hastening onward… Most of us will admit we spend our days connecting with a generation that moves at break-neck speed—the sound of shuffling feet, the deafening clamor of people running to and fro living, moving, and having their being for whatever reason, but mostly in egotistical preoccupation. Shelley wrote in *The Triumph of Life* …*all hastening onward, yet none seemed to know whither he went, or whence he came.* The spiritual culture we grew up in shifts beneath our feet and we're left to tolerate an unkind world, wondering how we will exist, much less make a meaningful contribution.

Years ago, I began to journal. I wrote on everything. Note pads, lined paper, paper without lines, Bible margins, journal books. There came a day after my visit to the old plantation house where I grew up and where memories came back in waves that I returned to those journals, realizing my life's page was just about covered and I was writing on the margins. I spent fourteen years with the journals and my memories from the old plantation to get *House Not Made With Hands*, and letting it go was like saying good-bye to an old friend. I dared to believe this was my meaningful contribution and kindred spirits out there would take the journey with me.

After all was said and done, I couldn't bid farewell to certain characters in my story, so I opened a new one from a chapter so deep-rooted in my history that I had to peer through a glass darkly to get images of those about whom I wanted to write. Their heroic story consumed me, and I wrote, realizing my page was not yet full.

And this is it. Though historical fiction, I hope its dynamic will touch you in a way you never thought possible, for we each have an investment here. Our forefathers—yours, mine, Blue and Gray—left DNA on battlefields all over the South. Their blood was sprinkled—yea, freely poured out—from Shiloh to Fredericksburg to Chancellorsville to Antietam to Gettysburg.

☙

It was fall 1984, and in sacred privilege, I stood looking out over the Wheatfield. A mist of rain fell across my face and the Pennsylvania Battlefield. This was hallowed ground for reasons you will know all too soon. My great great-grandfather Thomas Goode (T. G.) Clark, and his sons, Jonathan, and Albert Henry spent invaluable time here. Just three days. Invaluable, nevertheless.

My grandmother, Vallie Georgia Clark Smith, told me parts of the story some years ago. She knew far more than she revealed to me but there would come a day when I would learn more of the story, for those Mississippi Boys wrote letters home to my great great-grandmother, Margery Brown Rogers Clark. The originals are archived in the Mississippi Room at the University of Mississippi in Oxford. Appropriately so, for they were Rebels of the most splendid sort. Confederate soldiers who gave it all—for the South.

They sat by lonely campfires in the mountains of Virginia, chilled to hurting, feet propped on fire logs for a measure of warmth, so tired and cold they could scarcely hold pen in hand, words emanating from a rare place, one where few have dared to go, one from which many nevermore returned. I read those letters some one hundred and forty-four years after the war, and I was inexorably attached to these men. My forefathers. I reckoned for myself why T. G. went to war at the age of forty-six when the maximum requirement age was forty-one. Jonathan, nineteen, and Albert Henry, seventeen, would have to go, and he could not let them go alone. The way I see it, he gave three times. Once for himself, once for the Confederacy, and once for his sons. He was a real hero, this Mississippian.

For the space of five years, Mississippi and ten other southern states were a country with a flag, a president, and with fearless men who, as Jefferson Davis said, just wanted to be left alone, but who, when pressed to the wall, became willing to fight defensively for their Confederate States, for their flag, and for their homes.

I've read the letters over and again, and I see these men through eyes of faith, but I've thought about how it will be when I see them face to face for the first time, and if it be in clouds of glory or by way of the grave, I will know them. They will know me. And, any way you view it, that's a wonderful declaration of truth.

For now we see through a glass, darkly; but then face to face: now I know in part; but then shall I know even as also I am known (I Corinthians 13:12).

Jane Bennett Gaddy, Ph.D.

Part One
The Hills of Home

Chapter 1
War Like a Whisper

In the year 1860, in the hills of Mississippi, summer lingered. September, then October, and October begrudgingly allowed an unforgettable autumn. Unforgettable because it would be the last for many of Mississippi's native sons. South Carolina was pulsing with talk of secession. For Mississippi—it was bound to happen. Whispers of war traveled on the breeze, across hills, from Corinth to Vicksburg, and over the flat cotton fields of the Delta. From Natchez to Pascagoula, whisper gave way to voice, deep and resonating, made full circle and returned to fall on every ear of the Mississippi hill folks. Men reached into the past and pulled forth their birthright, their blessing, a craving to protect. The right of southern men to fantasize—the right of all men to fantasize—a lust for war. *The words of their mouths were smoother than butter, but war was in their hearts, their swords drawn*, the biblical warrior had said. Soon the whisper was no longer a romantic, far-fetched melody played on a fine-tuned violin, but real, the sound of thunder—the bugler's call, the beat of the drum, beating faster still, pounding out a marching cadence. The Mississippians were destined to tramp their way to the Potomac River. The birthright was now a curse.

∽

The brooks rippled, rivaled by the shuffling sounds of the deer that cavorted on the banks, and the mocking birds stopped singing long enough to dip their beaks in the cold water. Cottonwoods, ash, and longleaf pine rose to meet a blue autumn sky, splashing colors of brown and green over the red clay slopes. Hillsides blistered with yellow and orange leaves and, except for those that covered the ground like a patchwork quilt in the making, they clung to the maples and oaks in a last effort to prolong autumn. The noon sun leaned toward the horizon, detained by nothing in a slow pass over the peaceful homestead in the valley.

Smoke rose from the chimney over the kitchen. The smell of side meat frying and crackling bread baking tantalized the two Payne boys.

"Mother knows how to call us in," Albert Henry said, taking one last fish off the line.

"Man!" said Jonathan. "When she cooks, it drives me crazy from afar. I'm starved. Let's go on now. We need a little time to clean the fish and drop them in cold water. Knowing her, she'll fry these up tonight."

"Here, Jon, grab the canes and I'll get the fish."

Jonathan and Albert Henry mounted their horses and rode. When they reached the top of the ridge, they stopped and waved to their mother in the valley below. She was predictable, but so were they. She waved both arms in response.

Rachel Payne was beautiful, refined. She was soft-spoken and smart, but unaffected. And she was of French descent. Long dark hair hung to her shoulders in tight curls pulled back from her face with a colorful ribbon, and a handmade cotton dress touched the tops of her bare feet. She dared to do it, breaking one of the rules of the chaste women of the South—until winter's chill forced her to put on warm woolen socks. She willingly submitted, in silence questioning why every inch of the body must be covered at all times, especially her feet. She needed freedom. But inside the cabin—the choice was hers. The wood floors, sanded free of splinters by her sons, were partially covered with Persian rugs her mother had given her years before, treasured pieces that brought back memories of days stashed in the corners of her mind. Better days if measured in dollars and cents, things you could put your hands on, but never so pleasurable as now. She had everything. Absolutely everything.

Rachel lifted the iron skillet from the wood-burning oven and turned the cornbread onto a plate, crusty side up. The boys liked it that way—crusty and crunchy. She cut large wedges and pushed it to the back iron burner plate to stay warm and put the second one in to bake. She always made two cakes of cornbread. The boys would devour both. Especially today, for she had added cracklings.

The stove was hot, and little beads of perspiration formed on her face. A wisp of hair fell to her forehead and she tucked it behind her ribbon. She brought the pot of beans that hung from the Dutch oven in the living room fireplace to the stovetop. Everything was done except for the second cake of bread, and it would be ready by the time the first one was gone.

Thomas Goode Payne was not himself these days. He looked and acted like a man much older than his forty-five years. It was the talk of war in town, at the sawmill, anywhere men gathered; and the simple fact was, he could break the news to Rachel any day. She expected it, but she refused to add to his anxiety by revealing her uneasiness because of it. Not now.

"Benjamin, run to the cellar and get a jar of peppers," she said. "And bring up some apple butter. I'll need it for the afternoon surprise."

"Yes, Mama. What is it?"

"Can't tell. If I did, it wouldn't be a surprise. You'll like it, though."

He scurried out the back door with visions of something warm and sweet from his mother's stove and took the eight steps down to the cool, mossy-smelling cellar where herbs and spices hung from the ceiling, adding their nuances to the earthy fragrance, and where dried apples and peaches dangled from the rafters in flour sacks.

Fruits, berries, and vegetables lined the shelves fastened to the walls of the cellar. Benjamin was familiar with every jar. He helped put them there, for Rachel and the boys had canned, preserved and pickled all summer. Just five paces beyond in the shade of the giant oaks and ash trees and facing the cellar was the door to the smokehouse. At the first hard frost, Thomas and the boys would slaughter another hog and add to the supply of pork that hung from the hooks in the rafters—two hams, a slab of bacon and several bags of sausage. That is, if the men were not off to war by then. Rachel was no stranger to reality. She and the boys would soon fend for themselves. And they would not touch the meat in the smokehouse until ... until the time came.

"Here, Mother," Ben said. "Are these okay? I got those cayenne peppers Papa loves."

"Perfect choice, son. Now, run get Isaac for me. Tell him to bring Samuel."

Isaac was thirteen, tall and lanky. He was mature beyond his years, and he loved everything about the hills of Mississippi. Ben knew where to find his brother. Using both hands, he dropped the latch and pulled the heavy plank gate open, fastened it behind him, and walked to the last stall where Isaac stood grooming his horse. Too small to see over the top rail of the stable gate, he peeked between the wide planks into the stall.

"Mother said come on in and get Sam for her. It's about time to eat."

"Okay, boy, I'll be right there. Five minutes. Tell Mother five minutes."

Isaac led Glory out of the stable and into the lot. He removed the bridle, hung it on the rough-hewn wall of the barn, and slapped the rump of his sorrel mare. She romped through the back gate to the pasture beyond, and Isaac headed for the cabin.

He found his two-year old brother entertaining himself with wood blocks Jonathan had cut and sanded for him. Ten-year-old Joab sat on the floor beside him, responsible for his brother's well being. Isaac reached down and scooped Samuel into his arms. He glared at Joab.

"You washed up yet?"

"No. Am I that dirty?"

Isaac gave him a side-glance that answered the question.

"Where's Ben?"

"Outside."

"Call him in and get on out to the back porch."

He drew fresh water from the deep cistern just beyond the steps, brought it up to the wash pan where Samuel waited like a little man, and he washed his brother's face and hands.

"Cold," said Samuel, shivering.

"I know, little brother."

He dried Samuel's face and hands with the towel from the nail, patted him on the seat of his overalls, and sent him off with instructions.

"Now get on in the house and don't get dirty before you go to the table."

Isaac dumped the water and drew fresh for Joab and Benjamin.

T.G. arrived from the sawmill, tied his chestnut mare to the hitching rail, and headed for the kitchen. He kissed Rachel and stepped out on the back porch to wash up before gathering with his family around the long, narrow parson's table made from pieces of lumber he salvaged from the mill years ago. Joab lugged Samuel over to his father, plopped him in his lap, and then took his place next to Ben and Isaac on one of the handmade benches. Jonathan and Albert Henry sat across the table on the other bench. Rachel's place was nearest the stove and T. G. sat at the head of the table holding Samuel on his lap. The boys bowed their heads and their father prayed the Lord's blessings on his family and the food. Rachel served their plates and passed around the hot crackling bread slices.

"How'd you do this morning, boys?"

Joab and Benjamin sat grinning. Cunningly, from ear to ear, caught in the moment if not the conversation. They knew better. But they had overheard talk. They weren't totally unmindful to what went on around them, and Joab, unable to hold back, dared to break into laughter and speak.

"We heard they could have done a lot better if Henry didn't yap so much about Cassie Walker."

"Well, where did you hear such a thing as that?" said Rachel, squelching her own laughter—not at Henry, but at her little boys who had obviously been eavesdropping.

Isaac ducked his head in time to stifle his own desire to guffaw.

"They were biting. We got a fair string of bream and perch," Henry said, attempting to avert the innuendo, considering the source.

"Are we to expect a good fish fry for dinner?" T. G. looked at Rachel with hopeful eyes, ignoring the conversation on purpose. If anyone knew about being in love, it was Thomas Payne. And as far as he was concerned, it was nothing to joke about.

"You never can tell," she said, teasing her husband.

"Not that we'll need it after this good food," he said, pushing back and sighing from satisfaction.

Rachel poured him a fresh cup of coffee. He leaned back on the sturdy legs of his cane-bottom chair and relaxed a few minutes before turning to his two older sons.

"We better drink our coffee and ride so's to take advantage of the daylight. We've got to make up for your fishing time this morning. There's a pile of new logs head high waiting for us."

"Yes, sir! Let's go," said Albert Henry stumbling over the bench and grabbing his hat. "We've got work to do."

He was crazy about Cassie Walker. Translated when he thought about her. No one could possibly understand the way he felt. He didn't understand it himself. In fact, when he thought about it, he was mortally terrified. Either this was really happening or it was a mockery of delight come to haunt him. When he closed his eyes he saw brown hair, like coffee with the slightest drop of cream, and blueberry eyes that smiled and cried at the same time. The stage of his life was set, its backdrop sapphire skies, mossy riverbanks, and peaceful waters; but the accompanying music, doleful—reminding him he would soon be courting storm clouds threatening death. If that be the case, he had earned temporary happiness. He was man enough to fight a war. He was man enough to fall in love. He dared to be joyous of heart when such a sad calamity hung over their heads. Anyway, try as they may, no one knew what he was thinking in this moment. He chose to believe it was really happening.

The Payne men rode silently to the mill.

☙

When Rachel had dried and put away the last dish, she called the children to the front room of the cabin where the once-blazing fire burned to glowing coals. The wind whispered through the barest of cracks in the log cabin, October's chill blending with the warmth of the dying embers to give the room a comfortable feel. Now cool, now warm. Samuel nodded and fell asleep beside his mother in the rocking chair. Rachel put him in the crib Thomas had made for Jonathan almost twenty years ago. Isaac, Joab, and Benjamin sat working at the mahogany table.

"Bring your books, and come closer. We'll read until the fire goes out."

Rachel was educated and clever, and teaching her children at home was far better than sending them off on the two-mile trek to the little one-room schoolhouse in Sarepta where the wood-stoked potbelly stove was either too hot or not warm enough in the winter, the room stifling hot and fly-filled in the summer, and all that aside to a teacher who didn't meet Rachel's expectations.

"You start, Ben, and read with feeling," she said. "*Pilgrim's Progress*, page seventy-four is where we left off yesterday."

"Almost five thousand years ago there were pilgrims walking to the Ce … "

"Celestial," said Rachel.

"Celestial City, as these two honest persons are; and Be … Be … "

"Beelzebub."

" … and Beelzebub, A … "

"Apollyon."

"Apollyon and Le … Le … gion, with their companions … "

Ben struggled with the absurd names. He rolled his eyes and sighed, turned the book over to Joab, who could do no better, and then Isaac read to the end of the chapter.

Finding it difficult to concentrate these days, Rachel muddled through for a couple of hours and said, "You can put them away, now. We'll work on arithmetic and language tomorrow. It's time to get your chores done, anyway. And … I have a splendid surprise for you when you come in."

Joab and Benjamin scurried outside. Ben filled a bushel basket with corn and sat down on the stump to shell it. When his pan was full, he walked around the chicken yard throwing out the corn. The young pullets flocked to his feet, pecking away. Joab gathered the eggs from the henhouse, careful to avoid the peck of a certain prideful hen that could draw blood sufficient for a transfusion. He handed the full basket to his mother at the back door, brought out the slop bucket and poured its contents into the hog trough. He washed the bucket with water from the cistern and returned it to the back porch.

The barn belonged to Isaac. The cows, the horses. Whatever it took in the keeping was his to do. Once a week he shoveled manure from the stable and piled it by the fence next to the gate to the pasture beyond, to be used for fertilizer later on. He took care of Glory as if she would transport royalty. When Jonathan, Albert Henry and their father returned from the sawmill at the end of the day, he was there to take their horses, brush them down and feed them, and that by the light of his lantern, obliged to do so for his tired father and brothers, the contribution of a young man coming of age. In fact, he would do anything to demonstrate his manhood. To prove himself worthy of consideration to fight a war alongside them should duty call. Though scarcely more than a boy in years, Isaac and his youthful friends had become men long before the appointed time. Political unrest and circumstances in the South had made it so.

Chapter 2
Twenty-Five Pound O' Flour

It was early yet. Isaac bridled the horse, threw a blanket over her back and mounted. He was strong and lithe, second only to Jonathan in height and weight, larger even than Albert Henry. He could run and mount with no saddle, never disturbing the blanket. He desperately wanted to be included with his two older brothers and their father, but Rachel said no. He was only thirteen. She didn't want him listening to radical war talk much less entertaining the idea of going if the time came. *When* the time came was more like it. She walked to the barn and called for him. He met her at the wood gate.

"Are you done with your chores?"

"Yes, ma'am."

"Then could you saddle up and ride to Sarepta? I need some thread from the Mercantile and a bag of flour from the gristmill. I'm going to run out if I make these apple fritters this afternoon."

"Of course," said Isaac. "Anything to get apple fritters."

He was always ready to ride into town, especially when there was enough time to see his friends or go by the square, more eager to do the latter than to eat apple fritters these days.

"Don't tell the boys, for I've promised them a surprise. Come right back, now. The sun can't make up its mind, and we may get a shower of rain. And son, I don't want you to go by the sawmill."

"Yes, Ma," he said, wondering why she could not have left off those last instructions.

His father and brothers were more apt to talk at the sawmill, but never much at home where they could be heard. And it was only minutes away from where he was going.

"Dang!" he said where his mother couldn't hear him. It was the only curse word he was allowed, but she didn't even like that one.

The sawmill belonged to Moses Church, T. G.'s stepfather. His own father had died many years before and his mother had married a good man. Having the family working together to keep the mill going had, through the years, been a pleasant experience for all of them. Isaac worked there when he was needed, and he knew the daily ritual of stacking the lumber after it passed through the milling. T. G.'s half brother, Marcellus Church, also worked for his father, Moses. Family ties were strong. Isaac was sure they spent endless hours discussing the state of the country, and blast it all, he was missing out on all the talk.

He wasn't planning to see his friends, Abe, Billy, and Cliff, but he did want to hear word about Harpers Ferry first hand. He would contrive a means to get that information from the old men in the square. Something happened late last year, but his father hadn't shared anything so's he could know, and he had not been able to find out in town. His father brought home local newspapers when he could, but they made their way to nothingness before he even laid eyes on them. He guessed his mother was responsible for that. But his curiosity was getting the best of him. It was an affliction—being on the fringe of manhood.

Rachel handed him the money and watched Isaac mount his saddled horse and ride away, proud of her son for his self-taught skills as a rider and hostler.

"He'ah!" he shouted and rode like William Barksdale, his shoulder length brown hair blowing in the wind, thoughts of the silver-haired Mississippi fire-eater dancing in his head.

He had tried to glean information from his brothers but at this point a good imagination was all he had to work with. He knew they were withholding on purpose, stifling his desires to go with them when the time came. They were doing what they were told. But just plain irritating is what it was. He wondered how on earth he was expected to know anything at all about the talk of seceding from the Union and Harpers Ferry and John Brown without some substantial inside information. He aimed to find out what happened when Colonel Robert E. Lee went to Harpers Ferry. Enough time had passed. Someone had to know, and he must conjure up the courage to ask.

As usual, the old men gathered at the town square, turning their faces toward the capricious afternoon sun for a measure of warmth. A couple of them, overcome by a lazy afternoon, keeled over on the grassy knoll, eyes closed for a quick snooze.

Isaac hitched Glory to the post, attempting to trade nonchalance for rapt contemplation. He would take at least fifteen minutes and listen for the latest word. It was difficult to understand even the gist of what they were saying, and he would not have asked, but before long the old men motioned him over. Just what he wanted.

They knew him. They knew his father and his brothers. After all, Isaac was near six feet tall, almost fourteen, and he looked like a grown man. They continued their intense talk of political unrest and the prospects of war, drawing Isaac into the conversation. He was exultant, but cautious about revealing how little he knew. He didn't want them to know he was a great deal out of the loop.

Sitting amongst the dippers and spitters—something his mother never allowed, least not in her presence, but he had to get clever about this situation—he laid aside his inhibitions and spoke.

"Can anybody tell me what happened at Harpers Ferry, Virginia?"

"Why, son, a few months ago, Robert E. Lee left his post in Texas to go home to Washington. He needed to see his wife. Word had it she was sick. Whilst he was there, John Brown pulled a big raid on Harpers Ferry. Lee was sent to Virginny to arrest 'im and bring law and order over there. He did the job and hightailed it on back to Texas. That's 'bout all I know."

"Well, has Colonel Lee come down on a side yet?"

"We ain't had no further word, really."

"Guess it's too early to tell," Isaac said.

"Wellsir, now, rumor has it South Carolina's talkin' 'bout see-cedin' from the Union. Fact is, that's a-bein' talked up all over the South. Lee's a Colonel in the United States Army, a good man. He don't favor see-cession, and neither do most Mississippians. And Lee don't like slavery, and we ain't got many slaves around here, so we don't rightfully care one way or the other. They're mostly over in the Delta on the big plantations or down at Jackson, Vicksburg, Natchez. Well, son, you know. Yer ma's folks have a fair number of slaves. They're the one's needs 'em with all those big plantations to run."

"Yessir," Isaac said.

"Freein' the slaves is a-bein' talked about, but that's not the only thing."

The old man continued, pulling out all the stops for Isaac.

"That raid on Harpers Ferry is still a-causin' a lot of commotion between the North and South. You just wait, there'll come a day when we'll have to make some decisions and take a stand. When we take a stand, we'll be takin' sides. With the South, of course. Mississippi will stand for states' rights like South Carolina, if I have anything to do with it. I don't know 'bout see-cedin' from the Union. That sounds farfetched, but it could happen the way things is a-linin' up. Yessir, it could happen," he said.

He leaned back on the wood-framed bench with a far away look on his face.

Isaac wasn't sure he understood all the talk about states' rights and secession and what was behind it all. He ventured to ask the question he had pondered.

"Just who is this John Brown, anyway?"

Isaac was respectful to the old gentlemen, but embarrassed that he knew so little. He wanted to know, and he wanted to get the events straight in his head. In the right chronology. Right now, everything was jumbled.

"*Was* is a better word for old John Brown. He was a radical abolitionist who was a-tryin' to stir up the slaves, and he thought he could git what he needed from the arsenal in Virginny to help 'im lead an attack on the South. But what he went and done got several folks killed, and he had already caused a heap o' trouble out in Kansas, so we heerd. He was a murderer. An outlaw who got a lot of sympathy I guess from the northerners. He and a gang of 'is men laid hold on the arsenal back in October. The militia closed up Brown, with 'is men that were dead or wounded and some prisoners he took, in the arsenal, and that's when Robert E. Lee commenced to take over. He and 'is men forced the arsenal open and took Brown to trial. They said he was convicted of treason, and they hanged 'im in early December last year. They done the right thing."

The old man was confident about his information, and he stopped talking just long enough to spit snuff into the brown Skeet and Garrett jar and move the sweet gum brush he chewed from one corner of his mouth to the other. Isaac marveled that he could do both at once, never losing his train of thought. He would have to try it sometimes, but never mind that, his mother would never let him have snuff. Not in a million years.

"He had no business a-causin' all that trouble," the old man continued.

He leaned forward on the bench, securing his snuff jar on the ground beside him.

Isaac was attentive and dared not interrupt, for soon he would have to be on his way, and he wanted the old gentleman to talk, and talk fast.

"He 'as a-tryin' to make a name for hisself. You just wait, hit ain't over. He stirred up a hornets' nest 'mongst the northerners, a-tryin' to git their support. And he got some of the slaves in the South all riled up. They said 'is men murdered five proslavery settlers in Kansas."

"Hmm," said Isaac.

"He may 'uv had the right idea 'bout slavery, but the way he went 'bout what he done was just plain wrong. A-killin' all those people. Lee knowed what to do, though. Makes no difference the cause, if y' don't go 'bout it the right way and accordin' to the law, y' gonna have a man like Lee come down hard on y'. Some of 'em from the North tried to get 'im declared insane but Lee wouldn't hear nary bit o' that. The law wouldn't hear of it. The man was guilty of murder and treason and wound up a-danglin' from a hangman's rope. Son, I hope this ain't too gruesome fer sich young ears."

"No … no, sir. I was anxious to know why there's such rumblings of war and what's behind it all. Everybody seems to be on edge these days."

"Well, ain't that the truth."

The old men who had not succumbed to the afternoon nap nodded and agreed.

"Robert E. Lee must be a prince of a man," Isaac said, visualizing the colonel's skill in handling military crimes.

"Yessiree," said the old man. "They say he's honest, alert, and intellygent, a Christian man. Gradiated with honors from West Point. He's dignyfied and calm no matter what. He proved that at Harpers Ferry. I seen a photygraph of 'im once a-sittin' on 'is steed. He calls 'im Traveller."

Isaac wanted to linger, but he had stayed more minutes than he could spare and might have to do some explaining to his mother. He bid good day to the old gentlemen and thanked them for including him in their conversation. He purchased the thread at the Mercantile on the square and headed for the mill.

"Twenty-five pound o' flour," he told the grinder.

"I just bagged about twelve of those twenty-five pounders, Isaac. You go ahead and get you one of those, and I'll write up your ticket."

Splendid, thought Isaac. No waiting. A good ten minutes saved.

"Much obliged, Mr. Parker."

"You be careful, now, Isaac."

"Yessir. You tell Jethro I was here, asking how he's doing."

"Oh, Jethro's fine. About all he can talk about is what's goin' on between the North and the South. I'm afraid a storm's a-brewin', son."

"You're probably right, Mr. Parker. I'll be seeing you."

He mounted with the bag under his arm, secured it behind him in the saddle, and rode fast, kicking up a trail of dust. He had the two items his mother requested, and much more. At last he understood what happened at Harpers Ferry, and he had a good handle on how the old men were sizing up what was developing between the North and the South … and Jethro Parker's pa thinks a storms a-brewin'.

When Isaac reached the ridge, he slowed Glory. His mother could see him coming if she had a mind to step out on the porch. But his wits were turning slowly, deliberately, like the wheel at Mr. Parker's gristmill. He could fight if war were declared. He was strong and alert. Submissive, though he had to admit there were times when his father called him to task. He was a sharpshooter, had no idea how to brandish a saber, but he would learn if he could get his hands on one. And he could ride. He had everything it takes to be a good soldier. His mother needed him at home, but the way he viewed the situation, he was a man now. It would come down to what his father would let him do, and he would never give up trying to convince him he could fight when the time came.

He nudged Glory to pick up speed. His mother needed the flour.

☙

Rachel thanked her son, looking him in the eye. She had visions of him sitting in the square or pulling up close to the old philosophers—and these elders had the unaffected story, revealing the events of each day with a calmness that Isaac's generation needed to hear, realistically, not romantically— but she would not embarrass him by asking. She didn't blame him. He deserved to know what was going on, but she wasn't willing to let go of him. Not just yet. Isaac didn't avoid his mother's look, for he would face the music if need be. In fact, he wanted to talk about it. But Rachel didn't mention it. She resented the way boys became men so soon these days. She would not fan the flame that was already burning.

He took the bag of flour to the kitchen, cut the first thread, and unraveled the top for his mother. He poured half of the flour into the bin, rolled the sack down, and tied it with the string he had removed. When the bag was empty, Rachel would turn the flour sack into a dishtowel or polishing cloth to be stored away in the window seat.

In no time, the pastry was ready. She spooned the stewed apples onto each square and folded the pastry over. She pressed the edges with a fork and dropped them into the hot lard on the stove. When they rose to the top and were crusty brown, she dipped them onto a plate and rolled them in sugar while they were hot.

"Mother, those fritters are tempting my taste buds, and I can't wait to have some. Do you want me to put the coffee on?" Isaac asked.

He was happy to have made his trip to town, gather information, and return for such a treat as apple fritters all in the same afternoon.

"Would you, please? Here, taste this for me."

"Happy to."

Isaac popped the hot pastry into his mouth and drooled.

"Superb! As usual."

"I thought so."

He reached for the blue speckled coffeepot on the shelf over the stove, spooned in the coffee, filled the pot with cold water he drew from the cistern, and placed it on the hot grate of the wood cook stove. He pictured himself sitting on a log by some blazing campfire on the hillsides of Virginia, somewhere with the brave army of the South, brewing coffee for soldiers like himself.

By the time the cold water boiled, the coffee was just right. He poured off the top for the younger boys. He and Rachel would drink the stronger from the bottom. He put the mugs on a tray and took them to the big room.

The mahogany drop leaf table Madeleine Beauregard had given her daughter sat near the fireplace in the living room. Rachel took out a white linen cloth and spread it over the table, laid out the napkins, and took some small plates from the cupboard. She placed the platter of piping hot fritters rolled in granules of sugar on a wood block in the center of the table, opened the jar of apple butter, and served the coffee from the tray Isaac brought in. She poured fresh cream a-plenty into Benjamin and Joab's cups. Isaac could add cream to his liking. A lump or two of sugar, and they were ready to partake of the afternoon treat.

∽

She washed the cups and saucers, brushed the crumbs from the cloth, folded it, and put it in the window seat. Returning the lantern to its place in the center of the table, she thought about how pleased the children were with afternoon coffee and fritters, a rare treat, and as far as they knew, she did it for no apparent reason. Isaac, on the other hand, was on to Rachel, for he knew the situation. Times were changing, and one day they would evolve to the extent they would nevermore be the same. The little boys had no idea. But Rachel wanted them to always remember the good days, and she wracked her brain for special times like these.

Rain threatened. It was bound to happen. The fickle sun hid for most of the late afternoon. In one last brilliant revelation, it broke through the clouds and like a giant peeled peach it began to drop, leaving muted rays in spots. Gray clouds hovered in others. When time came for it to disappear behind the ridge, there was nothing left to show for it except sufficient daylight for the children to do the last chores of the day while Rachel started supper.

Isaac's low fire sparked and popped on the hearth. Perfect until after the evening meal. Later he would take it up with four or five big logs that would blaze and crackle to keep the house warm all night.

Apples were plentiful, the trees loaded and the ground covered. Rachel peeled more and put them on to stew with a little sugar and a dust of grated cinnamon. When they were tender, she gave them a slight stir and, leaving the top off the Dutch oven, carried it to the fireplace and hung it high over the burning logs. They simmered, the fragrance wafting through the cabin.

With a dot of fresh creamy butter, the hot apples would be sufficient for a little something sweet following their meal.

The screen door slammed. Joab scuffed into the kitchen and hugged his mother, something he did at least seven times a day, Rachel cherishing each hug.

"Where's Isaac?"

"Milking. He's almost done."

"Good. Want to bring the lanterns up?"

"Yes, ma'am. Should I trim the wicks first?"

"Yes, I fear they need it by now. They're beginning to smoke up the globes, so clean those before you do anything else."

"With what?"

"I'll bring some paper."

Joab wiped the black soot from the globes with the newspaper his mother brought. She was careful not to get anything of importance and stuck the rest of it back in the edge of the quilt box. He trimmed the burnt edges off the wicks and rounded them, lit each one, fastened the clean glass chimneys to the lamps, and returned his mother's scissors to the nail on the hearth.

"You do that well," she said.

Joab grinned, proud that his mother allowed him to stick the long splintered piece of wood into the stove and use it for a lighting stick.

Isaac lugged two buckets of milk in and poured them into the churn next to the stove. He laid a flour sack over it and gently topped it with the pottery lid. When the milk clabbered, the boys would each take a turn with the dasher until the butter formed.

He put the lamps in their places. Two in the kitchen and three on the mantle. The cabin took on a nice glow, one that could be seen by the Payne men from a distance. At seven o'clock they would top the ridge.

Rachel stirred the creamy yellow grits, made the hushpuppy batter, and set it aside. When the fish were fried, she dropped the hushpuppies in the hot lard behind them. Supper was ready. She stepped out on the back porch to look for Thomas and the boys. A drizzle of rain began to fall, and soon it was pouring off the side of the house. She walked back into the warm kitchen.

"Isaac, it's raining. Better be ready to grab the horses and get them to the barn."

She chided herself and begged his pardon for saying it. Rain or shine, Isaac never had to be reminded to take care of the horses. The rain pelted the tin roof. Something she loved. A comforting sound unless her men were out in it.

"That's okay, Mama," he said. "I hear them now. Don't wait supper for me. I've got to dry the horses down a bit."

"I'll keep something hot for you."

Isaac met the men at the hitching rail and took their horses to the barn in the pouring rain. T. G. and the boys ran to the back porch, removed their muddy shoes, and scurried into the warm kitchen. Rachel handed them dry work clothes from the stack on the quilt box and laid Isaac's by the stove to warm.

"You're soaking wet, Thomas."

"Aw, it's all right, Rachel," he said. "Besides, we need the rain."

He reached inside his coat, pulled out the newspaper and handed it to Rachel. She hid it in the edge of the quilt box.

"Well, get changed and hurry, the fish are hot and ready for you. Isaac said not to wait for him. He'll be in when he gets the horses down."

"That boy is worth his weight in gold when it comes to taking care of the animals."

"I don't know what I would ever do without him," Rachel said. "For so many reasons. Sometimes I think I ask too much of him."

☙

Thomas pushed back from the table and reached for the fresh cup of black coffee Rachel poured.

"You laid out a mighty good spread tonight, my dear."

"Oh, it was nothing," she said teasing her husband, though she had gone to great lengths to make sure everything was prepared just right.

"Anyway, the boys did the hard part. They caught and cleaned the fish. Oh, here's my Isaac, soaked to the bone. Sit with him, Thomas, and drink your coffee. Benjamin and I will clear the table."

Isaac slicked his wet hair back with the comb on the shelf and dried his face at the washstand on the porch, ignorant of how he looked. It was dark out there. He hid behind the quilt box and pulled on the dry overalls and a red flannel shirt his mother laid out for him, picked up his plate from the stove, and sat down beside his father, hoping he would start a conversation about what was a-brewin' out there, but he just brought Isaac up to date on the mill happenings. No gossip. None at all. Neither did Isaac share what he had discussed with the old men earlier in the afternoon.

Rachel washed and rinsed, and Ben dried, leaving the dishes on the table. He couldn't reach the cupboard. He was still a little boy, seven years old, and so much like Albert Henry. They favored. And Ben had already taken on Henry's temperament.

"Joab, I'm done," he called.

Rachel swept the kitchen as Joab put the last of the dishes in the cupboard. There were no leftovers to deal with. Hungry boys and men had scarfed it all down, and now it was time for them to take their places about the hearth.

※

Madeleine Beauregard had given each of them a violin on their sixth birthday, desiring that her grandchildren be exposed to a measure of culture. There would not be much of that in Calhoun County, not that she knew about. The boys rosined their bows and waited for all the family to gather round.

Madeleine never wanted her only daughter to marry outside her social standing. Rachel was raised with the best of everything. In a pompous white mansion buttressed with marble columns. It stood under the massive moss-draped oaks in Natchez, perched high on a bluff overlooking the Mississippi River. Her father, Jonathan Henry Beauregard, a wealthy planter, had been pleased to pay for an education of the finest sort at Mississippi College in Clinton.

Rachel had everything money could buy, but all she wanted was happiness and contentment; and in a summer's visit with her cousin in Houston, she met Thomas Goode Payne at a frolic. In a barn. She danced with him that night and fell in love. The touch of his strong hand on her shoulder, his kind voice and genteel behavior sparked the fires of romance and she vowed that night she would see him again. That was twenty-one years ago.

Thomas built the cabin with his hands and carried his young bride across the threshold of an empty house. They slept on blankets made by the Choctaw Indians that night. Together they filled the cabin with love, laughter, and handmade furniture with the exception of the things her mother had given them. The Persian rugs, tapestry curtains, the mahogany table and chairs and five priceless paintings that hung from the low ceiling on gold cords were wedding gifts, family heirlooms that cast cultural light over the primitive cabin. Her mother had given her china, crystal and silver, the pieces handsomely displayed in the cupboard and hutch Thomas made.

Rachel held back nothing, raising her sons not only to appreciate the finer things, but to love and respect the country atmosphere of the low hills of Mississippi. The hard work ethic and love of family and community came from Thomas; Rachel had imbibed the riches of his noble contribution, embracing them as her own. Two cultures kissed—the elaborate and the simplistic—creating beauty and warmth unsurpassed.

※

Isaac's logs blazed. Rachel loved a cold October evening, a dancing fire, and the warmth of family around her. If there were anything finer, it would be the pouring rain that slowed to a drizzle, stopped, and dripped incessantly from the eaves of the cabin.

Chapter 3
Under the Shadow of the Almighty

Benjamin had practiced, and tonight he ventured into a swelling crescendo that faded into a lonesome whine. He glanced at his mother and winked. She smiled and nodded approval. Madeleine Beauregard would have applauded and shed tears of happiness over her grandson's splendid achievement.

Rachel pulled Samuel close and wrapped the flannel blanket about his legs. She had a feeling he was her last. He snuggled there a few minutes, listening to the lonesome sounds of the music and drifted off.

She taught the boys well, and once they knew the basics, they learned to embellish and share their own ideas. Now they played in fine harmony. Jonathan could play as well as the others, but his violin lay on a shelf in its case, rarely opened. Rachel was not sure why, but he had not played it in five years. He was quiet, always in the back, but it was his own choosing. He was more like Thomas. Hard working, as if something were driving him in a contest with time, and even more so in the past few months. He was six feet, two inches, and powerfully built. He hunted with a bow and carried a long bowie knife. Never a rifle, though he was a sharpshooter. She worried about him—it was hers to worry—but she knew he was clever enough to take care of himself.

Rachel closed her eyes and breathed in the balsam wood fragrance of the fire and the apples cooking in the kettle. She rocked Samuel. Like the rain dripping off the eaves, the music was soothing, lonesome, touching the soul, songs she had learned at Mississippi College years before and passed on to them. Jonathan leaned against the wall sharpening his bowie knife, but watching the children, listening to their music. He loved them with passion and would be their protector at all hazards.

They played the last notes and laid their fiddles aside. Thomas opened his timeworn black leather Bible and began to read from Psalm 91.

He that dwelleth in the secret place of the Most High shall abide under the shadow of the Almighty. I will say of the Lord, He is my refuge and my fortress: my God; in him will I trust. Surely he shall deliver thee from the snare of the fowler, and from the noisome pestilence. He shall cover thee with his feathers, and under his wings shall thou trust: his truth shall be thy shield and buckler. Thou shalt not be afraid for the terror by night; nor for the arrow that flieth by day; nor for the pestilence that walketh in the darkness; nor for the destruction that wasteth at noonday.

Rachel silently enjoyed the presence of God, her eyes still closed. She prayed for strength to endure the inevitable. For protection for Thomas and for Jonathan and Henry, who would always stay beside their father. For Isaac who would be left behind.

Thomas read on.

For he shall give his angels charge over thee, to keep thee in all thy ways. They shall bear thee up in their hands, lest thou dash thy foot against a stone.

"They shall bear thee up in their hands."

Rachel repeated the words under her breath, still rocking Samuel with her eyes closed. Scripture was giving her courage, though she struggled in her attempt to release her men into the hands of a loving Lord. She must get to that place.

Rachel and Thomas had instructed their sons in spiritual matters. And, one by one, they confessed their faith in Christ their Savior. Blessed consolation, this childlike faith, but war loomed on the horizon, and the intensity of her personal faith, when tried, was found wanting these days.

Albert Henry, Isaac, Joab, and Benjamin sleepily shuffled to the bunkroom. The long and tiring day was over.

"Goodnight, boys. Don't forget to pray before you fall asleep. Papa loves you."

Thomas wrapped his arms around Rachel and Samuel, kissed them goodnight and retreated to his room.

Chapter 4
In This Valley

Rachel followed her husband, laid Samuel in his crib, and covered him with a soft homemade quilt. Jonathan stood in the doorway of his parents' room, but as Rachel turned to say goodnight, she could see he had something on his mind, and pulling the door to, she followed him back to the fire.

"Mother, I know you're tired, but can we talk?"

"Of course, son."

"Would it chill you to ride up on the ridge? The rain's over. I'll saddle the horses."

"By the time you've saddled up, I'll have my boots on. I'll tell your father and meet you in the stable."

"No, wait on the porch and I'll bring the horses out. The lot's muddy. Put your heavy cape on."

"I will."

The night air was cold, but the ride warmed them. Besides, they were both burning with thoughts. Thoughts of war rumors. Thoughts of the ones leaving and those who would be left behind. And Jonathan needed to be on comfortable turf to talk. It was dark, but the clouds parted and where the sky cleared, the stars and a harvest moon broke through to light the evening.

They rode hard to the top of the ridge and dismounted. The cabin lights flickered and glowed in the valley. Their valley. All six of the boys were born in this valley. They romped the hills when there was nothing but wilderness. It was not much more than that now, but Thomas and the boys had cut a fair number of trees on the slope leading to the top tree line, leaving only the tallest oaks. One stood in prominence on the side of the hill, its branches casting lanky shadows across the landscape. An October wind blew through the limbs, now sparse of leaves. Rain drenched and heavy, they moved like a giant quill dipped in black ink, writing a melancholy story of things to come across a dark southern sky.

Jonathan took a blanket made by his Choctaw friends from his saddlebag. He folded it twice, spread it on the damp ground for his mother, and sat down beside her. He hardly knew where to start. They sat without speaking, breathing the cold night air, each waiting for the right moment to share thoughts when Jonathan broke the silence.

"Mother, you know we'll be going soon. Pa, Albert Henry and me. Pa's been trying to keep the talk down at home for the sake of the boys, especially Isaac, but everybody's talking about it—all over the place. Things are happening out there that I won't even try to explain, but you've got to know it will come soon, and when it does, we'll be gone."

Rachel cringed, clinching her teeth as if by so doing she could prevent change. Hold back time. She gaped at the tiny lights that glittered in the distance. Familiar lamps that had faithfully given light every night for over twenty years. She had not been subject to change when it concerned her family. She was comfortable the way things were. And now, Jonathan was reminding her that change would come. Soon. And they would be gone.

"We'll muster in at Grenada, I figure, where we'll get uniforms and provisions. We'll ride our horses, and Isaac and Joab will have to ride with us to bring all the horses back. The war will be fought on foot, I suppose. Only the generals and the colonels and cavalry will ride about on horses. Besides, you'll need at least two of the horses for the buckboard and the others to ride for emergencies. Pa's going to have a long talk with Isaac. He wants him to work at the sawmill in our place, and Joab can stack lumber. That way they'll be together. Isaac doesn't need to be alone lest he get ideas about running off to join us. They can ride two of the horses in, and that'll leave you with two here at the homestead while the boys are at the sawmill.

"Mother, I know this is hard for you. You'll have your hands full with the boys and the garden and livestock, but you're strong. You can do it. Just until we come home. And there's always grandfather and grandmother. If things get too hard, you can lock up the place and go live with them."

"I will never do that," she said. "I'll stay right here with my face pressed to the windowpane, waiting for you to return. And you will come home. Home to the hills of Mississippi. Not to Natchez. And Grandma and Grandpa Church are close by. They'll be here for us. We'll be here for them. You're not to worry about us."

Tears ran hot warming Rachel's cold cheeks, as she sought to embrace the peace and courage God had promised in Psalm 91.

Jonathan paused before going further in conversation, fearing he was heaping too much on his mother at one time, but he wanted to get everything said tonight. Rachel knew he was speaking for his father, trying somehow to soften the blow before Thomas told her everything.

"Mother, you know Albert Henry is in love with Cassie Walker?"

"She's a lovely girl, but she's only sixteen."

"She's almost seventeen, a beautiful woman, and very much in love with Henry. And she's all he talks about lately."

"I gathered as much."

Rachel smiled, remembering the conversation at the table.

And in a more hushed tone, he added, "I'm just sorry I didn't find her first."

"Why, I've never heard you talk like that. It gives me hope you may one day seek out a bride for yourself."

It was against his nature to open up about intimate things. He would never say he had a liking for his brother's girl. Not to his mother. He didn't know that he did, really. Not until the words came from his lips. In this moment. They were on the edge of war, a possible explanation for what had possessed him to say such a thing aloud.

Jonathan was silent, not uncommon for him. Rachel sat mulling the situation over, still gazing at the familiar flickering cabin lights below.

"And you wish you had found her first?"

She glanced at Jonathan, but he didn't return the look. She had repeated what he said and what she supposed he was thinking, but Jonathan was holding those thoughts close to the vest.

Rachel continued, stoking the conversation, "Or better still, you wish she'd found you."

"I was only kidding, Ma. Albert Henry—he wants to marry her, and she wants to be with him as his wife now. Before we have to leave. I know he's going to tell you all of this, but I might as well tell everything I know tonight so you'll be prepared. I figure you don't need any surprises. There will be plenty of those soon—soon enough."

"I'll talk to your father about you boys finishing out the attic over the bunkroom so they'll have some privacy. We can make a little home for them in no time. Maybe Cassie has some things in her hope chest. Don't you suppose she does?"

"You're amazing, Mother."

"If they do marry, I want her to stay with us if you boys leave. Do you think she would? It would be comforting to have another woman in the house, especially if she belongs to Henry."

"I have a feeling that's exactly what'll take place."

"Let's just pray it doesn't happen soon. The war, that is."

Jonathan folded up the blanket and laid it behind his saddle. He helped Rachel onto her horse, and they rode home beneath the stars, the cold night wind chilling only their faces.

Rachel was comforted. Jonathan had spoken what he was thinking, something he seldom did. And she knew in this moment his wisdom exceeded his eighteen years.

Chapter 5
The Glories of Winter

Mid-December 1860

Snow lay deep, piled to the top of the bricks that under girded the front porch of the cabin. Winter had arrived with a vengeance. The snowbirds flitted about, decorating the white world crimson red. They landed then flew away in frenzy, returned to entertain the small world at the Payne homestead, and flew away again. Rachel watched the playful activity from the window seat wishing they would light and allow more time for enjoyment.

She spent the early hours of the morning and late evenings knitting socks and mending the boys' long johns and overalls. Her mother had sent wool, cotton, flannel pieces, and thread. Thankful her Negro servant had taught her to sew years ago, Rachel made flannel shirts and wool scarves for each of them, including Thomas. Their Christmas.

Her mind wandered with thoughts of her childhood, and imagining herself sitting amongst plush velvet cushions in a window seat of another time—another place, the sewing room that overlooked the Mississippi River—she could hear Sally's voice.

"Now, Miss Rachel, you's gonna have ta rip out dat seam. It ain't gonna work de way you got it sewed. Heah baby, let me help ya."

"Oh, Sally, I'm not good at this, am I?"

"You's gonna be jes' fine, honey. Jes' fine. Let's git it all ripped out and stah't ovah. Now, heah's how it work. Jes' snip dis one thread and pull. See how it unravel, dahlin'? Now, git it back on da machine and peddle. Dat's it, baby. Jes' keep peddlin' and keep yo cloth straight."

Rachel pondered what might become of Sally and Ned and all the other Negroes on her father's plantation. Sally and Ned were getting old now. They were the kind of servants, who, if you set them free, would chain themselves to your kitchen table. They wouldn't leave the Beauregard house. Not for any reason. They had a nice cabin just a few paces through the garden out back of the mansion with plenty of firewood, food, and clothes. Everything they needed and many things they wanted. Mediocrity never paid a visit to the big house. There was always something frivolous going on, and Sally and Ned were right in the middle of it.

☙

The days came and went with talk of war forbidden inside the four walls of the Payne home for the sake of the children, but Rachel gathered time was running out. When he could get his hands on one, Thomas brought home a local newspaper, and after reading it from the headlines to the last page, he handed it to Rachel. When the chores were done she retrieved the latest one from the edge of the quilt box and retreated to the window seat, her favorite place. She propped herself on a pillow, pulled her bare feet under her skirts, opened and read the headlines aloud: "December 20, 1860. *South Carolina Secedes from the Union.*"

Oh, my soul, she thought. No wonder Thomas read with discretion the night before, making no comments when he finished. He and the boys had a colorful conversation on the way to the mill this morning. She was certain of that.

She cringed, clinching her teeth. Mississippi would be right behind South Carolina, and as much as she favored state sovereignty and free trade, she was smart enough to know what decisions like these meant. The flag of the United States was still flying over the South. But that would soon end if states started to break away.

The war talk was not all about slavery, though the North would have you believe it. There were other issues. Lingering issues from decades past. The North and the South failed to reach compromise time and again. A lot of it had to do with the two worlds that existed—the industrialized North and the agrarian South. And they remained worlds apart, an enigma few understood. In Rachel's opinion they needed each other—the North and the South—but far be it from her to try and figure it out. She couldn't see how war would solve anything. It would take men and boys from both sides, ripping a mother's young son from her arms, a husband from her heart. Rachel had six sons but not one she wanted to give up. And she couldn't bear to lose Thomas. Their grandfathers had fought in the Revolutionary War. And they had won independence. This should not be happening all over again.

☙

She sat in the windows, her mind wandering. Ten years before, Stephen Douglas had proposed a bill that would set up a new territorial government for the land between the Missouri River and the Rocky Mountains. The Kansas-Nebraska Act, they called it. Things got chaotic as a result, ending up in the new Republican Party. Kansas became a political theatre and a bloody battlefield where the abolitionist fanatic John Brown was out there harassing pro-slavery people. In May of 1856, Brown, his sons, and a small group kidnapped five pro-slavery men from their cabins in Pottawatomie Creek, Kansas, and murdered them in cold blood. The newspapers said they split their skulls open with swords.

Rachel shivered at the thought. She hopped down from her comfortable place, scurried to the trunk where she kept her old history books and notes from college days and returned to the window seat to read. South Carolina had supported states' rights and just as strongly opposed federal tariffs, for their economy depended on free trade in and out of Europe. Same as Mississippi, she mused. When the Depression hit in 1819, South Carolina blamed federal tariffs for economic problems, and in less than ten years, the tariffs had gone even higher. So bad they called it the *tariff of abominations.* That's when Vice President John Calhoun got involved. He wrote a document declaring that, if a state deemed a federal law to be unconstitutional, the state should not be bound by that federal law.

She scanned her notes to recall more of South Carolina's involvement, for all of that was relevant now. *Nullification! Nullification*—and what was that? South Carolina had adopted the *Ordinance of Nullification*, having to do with the tariff acts. It declared them null and void. That happened long about 1832. She recalled there had been a dispute between the North and the South about whether slavery should be allowed in parts of the West, and South Carolina had threatened secession back then. That was ten years ago.

When Abraham Lincoln was elected president on November 6, it was the straw that broke the camel's back, for South Carolina was afraid the northern Republican would use his power to abolish slavery, and they had seceded from the Union just less than two months later.

To say nothing of curiosity, her intellectual bent led to a desire to stay informed. Her maternal instincts, however, begged a clear mind, and she would leave the politics to Thomas for the time being. Besides, she had no control over these things, and continuing down this path was making her crazy. She laid the paper and her history notes aside. She must think about her sons, especially Henry, who would soon say vows to the woman he loved.

⁕

Not as tall and big as Jonathan and Isaac, Henry was every bit as handsome, and he had a heart full of love for the family. He treated his father with highest respect and when he or his mother entered the room, Albert Henry stood. He was a southern gentleman. No doubt about that. No wonder Cassie Walker loved him. The younger boys watched every move he made and were beginning to follow his example. That pleased Rachel. Jonathan likely would have stood in the presence of his parents, but he was always standing anyway. He seldom sat. Too energetic and watchful. Like the things she'd heard about Colonel Robert E. Lee, a bit militaristic. He would make a fine soldier, and whether Isaac ever thought about it or not, he was just like Jonathan.

Deliver me from these ruminations of war, she begged!

She gazed out the frosted windows, forcing herself to abandon thoughts of secession and politics for the moment. She searched the branches for the snowbirds. Oh, yes! Back to Albert Henry and Cassie. Remembering the fabric she had purchased a couple of years ago and never used, ostensibly saving it for something special, she forsook her pondering place, ran to the closet and took out the two rolls of cloth. A blue one and one of gauzy white. Tomorrow. She would start tomorrow.

⁕

She sewed in her spare time during the day and late into the nights, and in two weeks she had finished the fluffy white see-through curtains and the blue quilted coverlet. Sally would be proud of her. That colorful patchwork quilt of pink and blue in the quilt box will be perfect at the foot of the bed, she thought. Sally made it years ago. She would have no problem making it clear. If Albert Henry and Cassie left, the quilt stayed.

Meanwhile, Thomas and the boys spent their evenings working over the bunkroom.

Zzzt. Creak. Bang! Zzzt. Creak. Bang! Bang! Bang!

Saws and hammers, obviously. Laughter, shouts of horror. Someone's finger under the hammer.

Ouch! Great Lord A' mighty help me! Hold that end up, Joab! Get it straight now, Isaac!

Henry was not allowed up there. He listened to their hoopla, grinning from ear to ear, trying to imagine what they were doing from the noise and bizarre hints. He wished he could join them.

The day came. Time for Rachel to climb the ladder to view their finished work and to clean up. The windowpanes were from an old abandoned house over in Chickasaw County. Thomas had brought a cord of firewood in exchange for them. He and the boys framed out the windows across the back wall floor to ceiling and inserted the panes. The attic was long and narrow like the bunkroom below where all the boys slept except Samuel. It had been a daunting task to set the windows on the slant, but he had done it with the help of three of his sons.

She washed the windows and swept up the sawdust, and on hands and knees, she oiled the floor and shined it with flour sacks. Thomas and Isaac brought up the bed and bureau. A chair, a lantern, a primitive table, an old wardrobe freshly stained, and that was it. All they had. Cassie would, no doubt, bring some things to the marriage room. Maybe a woven rug. Anything for warmth. The floor was icy cold to the bare feet, thanks to all those windows, but beauty must suffice for comfort.

Rachel brought up the gauzy white curtains, a feather bed, goose down pillows, the comforter and some quilts. Scanning the room, she admired their handiwork and thought about her own wedding night. Splendid! Cassie … well, Rachel cried at the thought of how Cassie was going to take this. Henry had told her nothing about the room, not even that it was there.

Daylight faded and Rachel lit the lantern, running the wick up. The light flickered on the icy windowpanes, casting a soft white glow about the room. She pushed the curtains apart and pressed her face against the coldness. The view from the loft was new to her. The snow-covered hills of home and the ice on the pines. The glories of winter stared back, the snow reflecting light of its own with the help of the moon, enough so she could see the line of pines at the top of the hill and the giant oak halfway up the ridge, its lanky, snow-covered limbs, bare of leaves, moving about mysteriously.

There was a special place up the hill in the distance. She couldn't see it from where she stood, but it was there. The Secret Grove—a place that sheltered the altar faithfully frequented by Rachel and Thomas, sometimes separately, sometimes together, but always invoking the presence of Almighty God. For over twenty years they had approached the throne of grace from this enigmatic place Thomas called the Secret Grove.

The moon glimmered and the stars winked their approval of the bridal room. She turned and looked from the other direction. Her men had taken something rough hewn and made it beautiful. She set the lamp on the table, blew it out, and lowered the wick.

If life could always be this good, she pined.

Chapter 6
The Christmas Tree

Mid-afternoon, December 21, 1860

It was cold. So cold Rachel's wash froze to the wires. There was no worry the wind would blow them away, for they were stuck there. Twelve pairs of overalls and twelve flannel shirts. Green, blue, red plaid. Poor Isaac had just about frozen trying to spread them on the wires. The ground was covered with snow that had stayed for over three days when another one came. The boys were bored, and Rachel searched her wits for ways to dissuade cabin fever. If she let them spend too much time outside, they would come down with pneumonia.

"Isaac, let's get the wash off the lines and into the house where it's warm if we can. They're not completely dry, but we've got to thaw them out somehow."

"Yes ma'am. Then what? The boys are driving me crazy. They need something to do."

"I have an idea," she said. "When we get the clothes down, bring the boys to the kitchen and I'll tell you."

Rachel and Isaac spread the overalls and shirts around. Over the chairs, across the table, on the quilt box until every inch of the kitchen was covered with work clothes. When they were finished, Isaac brought Joab and Ben to the kitchen. Sam toddled alongside, obviously wishing to join his brothers.

"Boys, it's time to go to the woods and cut a Christmas tree. You go. Sam and I will stay and bake some cookies and make a big kettle of hot apple cider. Take your sled and get the biggest one you can find. Remember, who uses the hatchet around here?"

"Only Isaac," said Joab and Benjamin in unison, ecstatic, for surely a tree meant presents on Christmas Eve.

"That's right, and no exceptions. Isaac, make sure you trim off as much as possible before you bring it in. Get a good full cedar tree. Go on, now, and come back soon. You'll want to eat those cookies while they're warm. Above all, do not stay past sundown."

"Don't worry, Mother. I know just where to find us a tree. I've had my eye on a couple already," Isaac said with confidence.

"Okay. Be careful about the creek. I'm sure it's frozen over, but stay away from it."

"Yes ma'am."

The boys grabbed their coats from the pegs on the wall and wrapped scarves around their necks. They were full of excitement when they left, pulling the empty sled behind them.

When they had gone a few yards, Isaac came to an abrupt halt and threw up his hands as if to say, "What am I thinking?"

He put Joab and Benjamin on and began to pull as fast as he could up the hill. Rachel stood at the window, watching as Ben threw his head back, laughter ringing across the hills. Oh, how she loved that little voice. What a great idea, this sled ride!

She mixed the sugar, butter, eggs and grated vanilla bean to start the cookie dough and then added raisins, walnuts, and a little coconut to the flour. Soon, enough cookies to feed her small army lay cooling on the table. She tidied up and checked on Samuel who was playing with his wood blocks in the big room. She was nervous. Something was keeping the boys. They had been gone too long. Now she was beginning to worry she had done the wrong thing by sending them out alone. But this was not the first time they had been out on such a venture. She could trust Isaac. She arranged the cookies in the tin box. Cider steamed in the Dutch oven.

She folded the overalls and shirts and stacked them on the quilt box and went back to the windows hoping to see them coming over the hill, but they were not at the tree line. There was nothing she could do but wait until Thomas and the boys got home, for leaving Sam was out of the question. She pulled on her boots and stepped out on the front porch.

It was almost seven o'clock. In the light of the moon against the white snow, she could see the silhouette of her men riding in from one direction, but they were just at the top of the ridge, not yet off the main road and still a good distance from the house. And then, the boys came flying over the hill from the other direction, Joab running out ahead, screaming to the top of his lungs. He stumbled and fell in the snow, regained his footing, and half ran, half tumbled down the hill. Rachel grabbed her cape and ran toward him.

"Ma! Ma!" he screamed.

Joab was crying. Something awful—

Rachel yelled back. "Joab ... Joab, what on earth?"

"Benjamin fell in the creek and Isaac jumped in after him. He almost never got him out. He drifted down the stream holding onto a broken limb, all the time Isaac was trying to get to him. It was an accident, Ma. We got him out."

"Where's Benjamin?" Rachel was panic-stricken.

"He's on the sled with the Christmas tree, wrapped up in our coats. Hurry, Ma!"

"Run to the house and watch Samuel. Keep him away from the fire."

Rachel ran up the hill toward Isaac who was pulling the sled, crying so hard he could scarcely see.

"Son, what happened?"

"I don't know. It took a while to find the tree. I cut it down and Joab was holding it when I looked around toward the creek just in time to see Ben go down. I think he ventured too close and slipped on the ice. I jumped in and pulled him out. He's freezing. We're all freezing. We got the tree, Ma! But Benjamin ... he could have drowned!"

"Oh, my babies! Pull, Isaac, pull! We've got to get Ben out of these wet clothes."

Rachel jerked off her cape and added it to the boys' coats draped over the little body, not knowing if Ben was conscious. He looked lifeless lying on top of the Christmas tree. She ran ahead to put two big kettles of water on the stove.

⁂

The men dismounted, giving their horses over to Isaac who waited on the porch for them.

"Pa, Ben fell in the creek. We pulled him out, but I think he's in shock. Ma's working with him. I'll take the horses to the barn. Go help Ma."

"No, we'll take care of the horses," said Albert Henry. "You go get out of those wet clothes. Hurry up, now. You'll catch pneumonia. Get some fire for the lantern, Jon, and meet me in the barn."

Thomas Payne took two long strides to the front door of the cabin and rushed to the kitchen where Rachel sat near the stove with Benjamin on her lap. He was still shaking and his wet clothes lay in a little heap on the floor. She bathed the small frame with warm, soapy water, rinsed and dried him. Long johns lay draped across a chair, warming by the stove. Rachel pulled them over his chilled body, flannel pajamas over those, wrapped him in a quilt, and handed him to his father.

"Go, sit close by the fire with him, Thomas. I'll be right there with some lemon and honey tea. Shall I put in a drop of whiskey?"

"Won't hurt. Might help him settle down so's he can sleep," he said. "Heavy on the lemon and honey, Rachel."

"Isaac, get those wet clothes off and jump in this tub of hot water and warm yourself. You're soaking wet, too," his mother said. "I'll bring you some dry clothes and a blanket."

Isaac sat in the hot tub of water, tears still falling down his cheeks. He hated when he felt this way. More of a boy. Less of a man. But Benjamin was his little brother, and if anything happened to him, he would never forgive himself. He stepped out of the tub, dried off, draped himself in the blanket, and went to the fire with the clothes his mother brought. He wanted to see Ben for himself.

The other boys gathered in the big room by the fireplace and things began to settle down. Thomas held his son close to his chest, rocking back and forth and talking to him in whispers.

In all the commotion, Rachel had not prepared supper. She got out her dough bowl and wooden board and in no time she was cutting out biscuits. While they were browning, she scrambled a dozen eggs and warmed some slices of country ham from the slab. She layered the eggs and ham onto the biscuits, placed them on a platter, and took a tray to the living room. Joab brought out a tray of coffee, Albert Henry prayed, and the family sat silently around the fire, eating supper, all but Isaac. The thought of food made him sick.

"Isaac, you must eat something," Rachel said.

"No thanks, Mother. I'm not hungry."

"But son—"

"I'll be fine. Just can't eat right now."

❧

Ben tossed and turned most of the night. Too restless to sleep herself, Rachel got up. She stoked the fire, heaped on some logs, and rocked him until the early hours of the morning. When Thomas got up, she took Ben to her bed, piled on the quilts, and joined her husband in the kitchen.

"I'll stop and see Doc Malone on the way to the sawmill," he said.

"Yes, I'll feel much better if he looks at Ben," said Rachel. "His ears and throat hurt during the night, and he hardly slept at all. The creek episode disturbed him."

Doc Malone came during the day while the men were at the mill.

"Well, Rachel, he's got fever, but I think he's going to be all right. I don't hear any sound of pneumonia in his lungs. Keep him in for a week or two and close to the fire. I'm leaving something for the croup in case he commences to cough, and he will, for his throat is scarlet. But don't give it to him yet. I'll be back the day after Christmas to check on him. If you need me before then, send one of the boys to fetch me."

Rachel helped the old doctor with his overcoat and wrapped the scarf around his neck. Isaac saw him to his buckboard and covered his legs with one of Jonathan's Indian blankets.

"Do you want me to come with you, Doc?"

"Thanks, Isaac, but that won't be necessary. I'll be fine."

"Just stay in the ruts and don't get on the ice. I'd really hate it if something happened to you, too."

"Good advice, son, but don't worry about me. Nellie will see me safely home. And Isaac—"

"Yessir, Doc Malone."

"Don't be too hard on yourself."

Isaac nodded and waved as the old doctor pulled away. He secretly wished that Doc had consented for him to ride along. For right now he would like to get on Glory and ride, never to return.

≈

Rachel had things to do for Christmas, and to be close to Benjamin until he fully recovered, she brought the gifts to her bedroom where he lay wrapped in a flannel blanket. Reaching in the top drawer of her bureau, she pulled out some brown paper, a skein of red yarn and one of green. She folded and wrapped the scarves, socks, and flannel shirts she had made the boys and Thomas, wrapping Ben's when he was not looking, then took all the wrapped packages to the living room and laid them beneath the tree, grateful that her mother had sent the fabric and thread. Without them, there would be no gifts for the tree.

"Isaac, I need nine hooks across the mantle board."

"Oh, I can have that done in a jiffy."

"If you can't find hooks, some small nails will do. Space them evenly all the way across. There'll be plenty of room."

"I think it will have to be nails."

"I'll hand them to you, Isaac," said Joab. "Ben's asleep now, and I'm not having a lot of fun."

Rachel sewed scarlet ribbon to the tops of the woolen socks she had knitted and hung each one of them on a nail. On Christmas Eve she would fill them with nuts and a piece of fruit and bring out the jelly bucket filled with peanut brittle, which for the time being was safely hidden in the cupboard.

Isaac took pieces of cedar he had cut from the bottom of the Christmas tree, interspersed them with pine branches and cones, and layered them across the mantle. He lit the three lanterns and arranged them in the evergreens. The warmth from the fire on the hearth and the lanterns on the mantle ignited a Christmas fragrance that permeated the cabin. Now anxious for Christmas to arrive, Rachel's boys were quite willing to do anything she asked.

☙

Ben's lack of appetite concerned Rachel. The coughing started the evening after the creek episode, and his fever hung on until Christmas Eve, when he began to feel better.

"Isaac, I need you to kill two chickens off the yard, but get the washpot going first. Stoke the fire under it. The water needs to be real hot, you know. I'll send Joab to take the feathers off after you dip them. Be careful, son."

Isaac muttered something under his breath, but not so's his mother could hear. The gist was that wringing a chicken's neck was not his favorite pastime, though he was quite skilled in so doing.

He picked up the hatchet and strolled to the barn. For the sheer thrill of it and because he could, Isaac whirled the hatchet into the air; it circled three times, and when it fell, he skillfully caught the handle. He laid the blade hard into the stump of a tree left for the purpose. Shelling a double handful of corn, he began to drop it around his feet until the young chickens surrounded him. He reached down and grabbed two by the neck, one in each hand. He wrung the necks simultaneously and left them under a washtub until they stopped flopping, then he took the hatchet and finished the job on the stump. Holding the chickens by the feet, he dipped them several times in the boiling water to soften the feathers. When that was done, he laid them on the bottom of the washtub he turned upside down. He called for Joab, who plucked them clean.

Isaac shoved the washpot off the fire with his foot and held the chickens high over the flame to singe off any remaining feathers.

Done.

In half an hour he handed the plucked chickens to Rachel and went back outside to kill the fire and clean up the mess. He returned the washpot to its place.

"Now, that was not so bad, was it?"

"Mother, did you hear me complaining?"

"Of course not, Isaac." Rachel laughed at her son.

He left the kitchen before his mother asked him to perform another repugnant duty.

She cut up the chickens and removed the gizzards.

"What are you doing?" asked Joab.

"Scraping the gravel out of the gizzards. Look here," she said, pulling open the gizzard that was full of tiny gravel.

"Aw, that's dreadful."

"Well, just think about the fascinating way a chicken grinds its food."

"How?"

"These little pieces of gravel are their grinders. They peck around outside and when they swallow the gravel, it grinds their food and goes to the gizzard. It's like a second stomach. Have you ever seen a chicken with teeth?"

"Oh, Mama, you're so funny!"

She washed the giblets and put them in one pot and the chicken in another. The giblets were for her gravy tomorrow. But right now, Ben needed chicken soup.

"Son would you go to the cellar and get me some sage? It's hanging from the ceiling. Do you know what it looks like?"

"Yes, ma'am. I know what it smells like."

"I only need a few small sprigs. Take the scissors, and please be careful when you climb up on the stool. Don't fall. And don't stab yourself with the scissors."

Rachel shivered thinking that something so dreadful could happen and another of her sons would be hurting. Hush, now! she thought. It's Christmas Eve, and I need help.

The screen door slammed and Joab jumped the four steps to the ground. In a few minutes he was handing the scissors and the sage to Rachel. She crushed it and dropped it in the stock, added salt and pepper, and let the chicken boil until it was tender.

She took a bowl of the broth with finely chopped chicken to the fire, where Ben sat in the rocking chair, and made sure he ate it all. It was his first solid food in two days, and he was getting thin. He drank weak tea with honey and no lemon. She had used her last one.

"Now, go get on my bed and cover up with your flannel blanket," she said, motioning for Joab to follow.

"Take your boots off, son. Climb up there and entertain your brother. I have things to do in the kitchen."

"I know what you're getting for Christmas," Ben said.

"Don't tell me. I want it to be a surprise."

"Joab, I wouldn't tell you if you begged me to." Ben chuckled.

"I think you're getting to be a spoiled brat," said Joab.

Rachel could hear them from the kitchen and smiled. Ben felt better, able to argue with his brother, using the last measure of his energy to do so.

She added a jar of creamy corn from the cellar and some sweet cream to the chicken broth, cut the chicken in chunks, and returned it to the liquid to simmer until some good chicken corn soup emerged. A little more salt and some cracked pepper, and it was savory. With a skillet of hot crusty cornbread, they could sit down to a fine Christmas Eve supper. Tomorrow was Christmas Day, and she would do even better.

Making pies posed no problem, for she had pumpkin, nuts of all kinds, eggs from the hens, butter, and lard the boys rendered. Jonathan stalked and downed a wild turkey, and she had purchased celery at the General Store for cornbread dressing. All of this and her canned vegetables would make a fine Christmas feast. Thomas and the older boys would help with the preparation after the supper dishes were done and Joab, Benjamin, and Samuel were in bed for the night.

Rachel set the mahogany table with cloth and napkins, fine china, crystal and silver, beautiful candelabra in the center, and on one side a big tureen of chicken corn soup; on the other, the sliced cornbread. The mill was closed by now, for it was Christmas Eve, and her men would top the ridge at any moment. She was ready for them.

✎

They handed the reins to Isaac, and he devotedly led the tired animals to the barn, fed them, and returned to join the family around the table. The light from the lanterns on the mantle danced about the festive room; the fire beneath it blazed and sparked. Rachel dared not think that this could be the last and most splendid Christmas Eve for a long, long time. Maybe ever.

Chapter 7
Don't Cry, Mama

Christmas 1860

Ben struggled to recover, but on Christmas Day he felt better. Rachel was glad, for making merry would be difficult this year. For many reasons.

Albert Henry brought Cassie over from Houston, and Rachel scurried around to find a gift for her amongst her own things. This is it, she thought. A lovely piece of jewelry her mother had given her years before. She wrapped the cameo brooch in a piece of white linen from her scrap box, tied it with scarlet ribbon, and placed it under the tree with the other gifts, pleased to share something she loved with someone she would soon come to love as her own. She hung another sock on Henry's nail and filled it for Cassie. The family gathered around the tree in the early evening.

Henry, Isaac and Joab rosined their bows. Ben, still wrapped in his flannels, guarding his sock filled with nuts and fruit, whispered something to his mother, and she brought him his violin. From the chair, he struck a chord, *Sing sweet and low your lullaby while angels say 'Amen.' A mother tonight is rocking a cradle in Bethlehem.*

Cassie sat beside Henry on the rug near the hearth. It was her first visit to the Payne home, and she was not only in love with Albert Henry, but the entire family. Tears glistened in her dark blue eyes as she watched Ben play his violin. He was frail. His music, enchanting. The boys stood and joined him, playing their favorite Christmas carols. Rachel glanced at Cassie, the tears now dropping to her cheeks as she looked at Henry. He laid aside his violin, sat down beside her, and took her hand in both of his.

Rachel whispered to Thomas, "I'm dying to show her the attic room."

"No, Rachel, you mustn't. It's got to be a surprise."

"Oh, all right."

She would wait. Another surprise for another day, Their wedding day.

Rachel glanced at Jonathan, who stood against the wall on the far side of the room, one foot on the rough-hewn boards, his head down. She wondered if Cassie's presence bothered him. Her heart ached for her eldest son, for what he might be experiencing in these desperate days, remembering what he had said to her the night they rode up on the ridge.

❧

Threshold of a new year, 1861

Ben made some progress, but the croup persisted, the cough getting deeper. His fever soared on the first day of the New Year, and in spite of everything Rachel tried, she could not bring it down. The medicine Doc Malone left for him was almost gone. He was restless all night, and the next morning after the men left for work, Rachel sat on the bed beside him. He flailed about, the fever going out of control. She cooled his face with fresh snow, dried it, and pulled the flannel blanket around him. In a few minutes he was calm again.

"Mama," Ben said, from parched lips.

"Yes, son."

"Mama … tell me about heaven. About those angels Papa says will bear us up."

Rachel eased off the side of the bed, knelt beside him, and touched his scarlet lips with melted snow.

"Why do you want to know about the angels?"

Tears welled, and she fought crying aloud.

"I just wondered if one of those angels will bear me up to heaven when it's time to go."

Rachel groaned in her spirit, making no audible sound, wondering if this was going to be the hard part and how on earth she would answer the question.

"Oh, Ben, there's going to be a whole band of angels to bear you up when the time comes, but that won't be for a long, long time."

"No, Mama. It won't be long. I saw one of those angels while I was sleeping."

Rachel took her apron and wiped the perspiration from Ben's face then wiped the tears from her own eyes.

"That was just a dream, son."

"But it was a … a good dream. I was afraid, but now … now I'm not any more. I feel … I feel fine. Don't cry … don't cry, now, Mama."

Ben was speaking in staccato voice, shaking from time to time. Rachel added a blanket and he settled down again. She tried hard to suppress the sounds that were bound to follow her tears.

"Where's my Christmas sock?"

She found it under the covers and tucked it under his arm.

"Do you want to eat your orange?"

"No, ma'am. I want you to tell me about heaven. Now, Mama. Now. Tell me about heaven."

She swallowed hard determined to speak where he could hear and understand every word. She would tell him everything she knew about heaven.

"It's … heaven is a beautiful place. Why, the streets are pure gold, so pure you can see right through them. And the gates are of pearl. You know that little pearl handled knife of Jonathan's? They're just like that, only big. Real big. The little children play on the riverbank—lots of little children. And there's a pure river of water, clear as crystal. It comes out of the throne of God and the Lamb. You know who the Lamb is, don't you?"

"Yes, Mama … it's … it's Jesus. He's the … he's the Lamb."

"And the tree of life is there."

"What's it for?"

"The leaves on the tree are for the healing of the nations."

"Does that … does that mean we won't be … be sick in heaven?"

"You will never be sick again."

"Then why … why wouldn't we all want to … to go there?"

Ben was shaking again.

"We do, baby. We do."

The more Rachel talked, the easier it became.

"You know you will not need to light a candle or bring up the lanterns in heaven when evening falls, for it never gets dark there. And even in the daytime, you won't need the sun. The light of the city is Jesus, and he's all that is needed to dispel the darkness."

"Mama … Mama … I'm thirsty. I want to drink from the dipper … like … like Papa."

Ben licked his parched lips and fidgeted incessantly. His fever was soaring again.

"Where's Papa? I'd like to see Papa."

Rachel called for Isaac to bring some cold water from the cistern. She lifted Ben's head. He drank then pushed the dipper away. She laid him back on the pillow and stroked his head until he fell asleep. His breathing was labored.

She left the room and called for Isaac again.

"Ride and get your father and the boys. Try not to alarm them, but tell them Ben has taken a turn for the worse."

"But Mother, he looks so calm and he's sleeping peacefully now. He's just having trouble breathing because of the croup."

"Yes, I know, son, but … just tell them to get home. One of you boys needs to go by Doc Malone's and bring him."

Isaac reached for his coat and scarf and grabbed his hat.

"Mother, this is my fault. I should never have taken my eyes off Ben the day we went for the tree."

"Isaac, don't. It's easy to place blame and if we do, it would go right back to me. I'm the one who sent you out to cut the tree. If anyone's to blame, it's me."

"No, Mother."

"Then stop blaming yourself, son. Don't ever let me hear you say those words again. Don't even think them."

༄

January's wind blew cold and harsh across Isaac's face as he rode hard to the sawmill, hot tears streaming down. He pulled his scarf around his nose and mouth and tightened it to keep the tears from freezing on his face. The sides of the road were iced over and a foggy haze hovered close on the snow-covered slopes. Isaac felt the gloom inside and out. He urged Glory on, climbing the last of the hills before reaching the mill.

Thomas heard the hard clopping of hoofs, and in the distance, he saw his son rounding the bend.

"Boys, saddle up, quick! Something's wrong!"

"Ben's in trouble," Isaac yelled, turning Glory around in the road. "Ma said to come on home as soon as you can and somebody needs to fetch Doc Malone. I'll ride over and get him, Pa. I can be there in five minutes."

"Okay, son. Bring him at all hazards. But first, get over there and tell your Grandpa or Marcellus what's happening. Let's ride, boys."

In twenty minutes they were hitching their horses to the rail. Thomas jumped the steps and dashed inside the cabin, Jonathan and Albert Henry behind him.

"Joab, where's your ma?"

"She's in your bedroom. With Benjamin."

"You stay in here with Sam. Watch him carefully. Don't let him go near the fireplace. Isaac will be here soon with Doc Malone."

"Yes, sir."

Once again Joab was left to wonder why the commotion. Appeared a lot of stuff was going on that he didn't understand, and this time it was Benjamin again. But he thought Ben was getting well. He wished they would at least let him know what was happening.

"Rachel, what's wrong?"

"His fever went way high." Rachel spoke softly. "I got it down some, but he was delirious for a while. When his fever broke, he started asking me questions about heaven, and he said he saw an angel. Thomas, he's going to die, isn't he?"

"No, Rachel, no!"

"It's all right."

"How can it be all right? What makes you say he's going to die?"

"Remember the night you read Psalm 91 to us?"

"Yes."

"The part where God gives his angels charge over us to bear us up?"

"Yes—My Lord! Rachel!"

"He wanted to know if an angel would be there to bear him up when it's time to go. I told him a whole band of angels would be there. He knows he's leaving us. I didn't know if I could bear it, but while I was talking to him about heaven, the Lord gave me peace. I never wanted to lose a single one of my children."

"Of course not, Rachel."

Thomas broke. He went limp and his body shook. He wept like nothing Rachel had ever seen.

"God has shown us favor to let us have them if only for a short time. I know they belong to him and he has made a way for us to see them again. Does it make sense that God has given me this kind of peace?"

"Yes, Rachel, but right now I don't have it. My God in heaven! How will we live without Benjamin?"

"There's only one way we can, Thomas. God will help us."

Isaac arrived, Doc Malone following in his buckboard. The old doctor flung off his overcoat and scarf and reached for his bag. The boys moved to the sides of the room and stood still. Rachel sat on the bed, holding Ben with her arms. She laid him back on the pillow and moved aside so the old family physician could get to him.

"The pneumonia. It's deep in his lungs, I fear. Doesn't sound good. Not good at all."

"Is he going to—?"

"T. G., I'm sorry. I'm really sorry."

"No!" Thomas choked. "There's something you can do! Do something!"

"There's nothing else to do, T. G.," said Doc Malone softly. "He's peaceful. It's hard for him to breathe, but he's uncommonly peaceful."

With great effort, his eyes still closed, and in a raspy little voice Ben whispered his last words, "Papa, you came. I love you Papa."

"Papa loves you, Ben," he said, choking back the tears.

Isaac left the room and came back with Joab and Samuel. Jonathan lifted Samuel into his arms, and they stood over the bed where their brother lay, all but Jonathan weeping as Ben took his last breath. No struggle. And he was lifted from this life. Lifted out by angels that bore him up in their hands. To the water from the throne and the Lamb and where the little children play on the riverbank.

Thomas and Rachel sat holding their son, holding each other, rocking back and forth. Doc Malone left the room, and the boys surrounded their parents and Benjamin.

Rachel sobbed in spite of her son's instructions that she was not to cry. A cold, gray winter's gloom hovered about the cabin, and a little body lay still in his parents' arms.

Joab fell to his mother's feet, crying and hugging her about the legs. Rachel wept bitterly for her son.

Chapter 8
Benjamin, My Son

January 3, 1861

A foot of snow lay untouched on the cold hills under a gray and hazy winter sky; a pair of snowbirds sang cheerfully and hopped from one snowy pine branch to another, unaware of the pain around them. Jonathan, Albert Henry, Isaac, and Joab, with shovels thrown over their shoulders, trudged side by side halfway up the hill and dug a fresh grave, the only grave on the hillside. In a little flat place under the giant oak tree. Doc Malone had stayed the night and rose early to take Ben's body to Calhoun City to prepare it for burial. T. G. went with him. Rachel was alone with Samuel. She took him in her arms and sat rocking, staring dry-eyed into the roaring fire the boys had made when they first got up.

༄

January 4, 1861

Thomas and Rachel Payne and their six boys gathered in the little one-room frame meetinghouse. It was the only meetinghouse on their end of Calhoun County, whitewashed year in and year out by the Baptists. Friends and family, one by one, slipped into the seats, there to grieve and mourn with the Payne family.

This was the last time they would all be together, Ben with them in body only, but Rachel was certain he was panting with delight at the gates of pearl and the streets of gold. He lay in the little pine box in his Christmas shirt and scarf, the socks his mother knitted him for Christmas on his little feet.

Rachel cried.

"Oh, my son, Benjamin."

Thomas tightened his grip on her hand, wiping tears that were falling non-stop from his own eyes. She was glad Ben wanted to have the conversation about heaven. It helped her far more than it did him, for at the time they talked he was just moments from waking up to the reality. She looked down the pew at her five remaining sons, thinking about the brevity of life and the fact that she may have a short time to spend with each of them. She dared not extend her thoughts to the war and the cold, hard fact that it would take her husband and sons from her, and they may nevermore return. She could not bear to lose another son or her husband. Moment by moment, she thought. *Sufficient unto the day is the evil thereof.* Jesus said it in Matthew's gospel. He knew best.

Madeleine and Jonathan Henry Beauregard sat at the far end of the pew on the other side of their grandsons. When the last of their friends and relatives were seated, Ned and Sally, dressed in their Sunday best, took a seat alone on the back row of the church. Rachel whispered something to Thomas and he slipped out. When he came back, Ned and Sally were following him. He seated them directly behind Rachel.

"Thank you, Thomas. It feels right to have Sally and Ned close by. They comfort me."

"I know, Rachel. Me, too."

When the service ended, Ned and Sally drove the Beauregards in a fine carriage to the place where the family gathered with their friends and neighbors.

Leading a sad procession, Thomas and Rachel with Joab and Samuel seated between them, rode the buckboard to the hillside. The pine box holding the body of their beloved Benjamin lay behind them on the floor of the wagon. The older boys followed on their horses—Albert Henry riding to the right of the makeshift hearse, Isaac to the left, and Jonathan to the rear. Thomas stopped the horses at the bottom of the hill, and Jonathan, Albert Henry, Isaac, and Joab lifted the little pine box to their shoulders, and with faces pressed to the coffin, they carried it up the hill and placed it in the red clay, tears pouring from every eye except Jonathan's.

He walked back down the hill before his father started to read, lifted two items out of the wagon and came close to the grave with them tucked under his arm. He laid them both on the ground at his feet.

Their friends and family drew near, and Thomas took out his black leather Bible and read from First Thessalonians, chapter four.

> *For this we say unto you by the word of the Lord, that we which are alive and remain unto the coming of the Lord shall not prevent them which are asleep. For the Lord himself shall descend from heaven with a shout, with the voice of the archangel, and with the trump of God; and the dead in Christ shall rise first: Then we which are alive and remain shall be caught up together with them in the clouds, to meet the Lord in the air: and so shall we ever be with the Lord. Wherefore comfort one another with these words.*

And from Job chapter 1, he read:

> *… the Lord gave and the Lord hath taken away; blessed be the name of the Lord.*

Thomas closed his Bible and pulled Rachel close to his side. Jonathan opened one of the cases and took out Benjamin's violin. He played in beautiful strains that drifted across the hills of Mississippi an old hymn his mother taught them years before. *There's a land that is fairer than day, and by faith we can see it afar, for the Father waits over the way to prepare us a dwelling place there.*

Sally and Ned stood at a distance by the side of the Beauregard carriage, mopping tears.

Sally, unable to suppress her desire to mourn and wail, waved her white handkerchief and shouted, "Umm, thank you, Lawd Jesus! Oh, thank you, Jesus!"

For Ben had gone to the land that is fairer than day.

"Sally's gonna meet you there, baby boy! Umm, hallelujah!"

Jonathan, remembering the night Ben performed the swelling crescendo for the family and winked at his mother, pulled down on the bow until strong hands, calloused by rough-hewn wood and wilderness experience, yet as tender as soft petals fall from a rose, reached that same lonesome whine and finished the song with the refrain, *In the Sweet By and By, we shall meet on that beautiful shore.* The music swelled then disappeared on the wind. Benjamin's little body rested in the red clay, but Rachel imagined him getting his wish. Surely there had been angels all around, and a whole band to bear him up.

And Sally stood on the hill waving her white handkerchief, crying and shouting.

The boys covered the coffin and packed the dirt down. Jonathan took his own violin, and in a sacrificial moment he secured the beautiful instrument inside the case and placed it on the ground. It would mark Ben's grave until he could carve out a wood marker. He tucked his brother's violin under his arm and mounted his horse.

Thomas put Rachel and Samuel in the wagon and climbed in beside them. Rachel turned around and looked back on the gravesite. The night she stood in the window of the bridal room she watched the lanky limbs of the old oak tree moving about mysteriously hovering over this spot. She did not intend to enshrine the place, for she knew Ben was not there. He had reached destined perfection. But the giant oak would shelter the ground where his body lay, and in all seasons for time immemorial, its branches would blow gently in a summer breeze, lay a blanket of color in the fall, and droop low and snow-covered in the winter, a constant reminder of her little boy.

The wagon moved out with Albert Henry and Isaac riding to the sides, Jonathan following close behind with Joab riding in the saddle with him. And the Paynes mourned their greatest loss.

Chapter 9
Albert Henry

Rachel had no trouble identifying the grief on Henry's face. Just two days until his wedding, and they had buried Benjamin the week before.

"How are you holding up, son?"

"I don't know how to express my feelings. On the one hand I'm happy because I'm marrying the most wonderful girl in the world. That is, besides you, Mother."

"But you're grieving over Benjamin?"

"You always said he was just like me."

"From the day he was born, he reminded me of you."

"I can't believe he's gone and it happened so fast. Life was just too short for the little man. I miss him. I miss him bad. And I can't seem to get past it. What am I going to do, Mother? Should I postpone my wedding until I can get over this?"

"Son, it's easy for mothers to give advice—that part of our job we don't get paid for," she said, smiling.

"First of all, you'll never get over it. None of us will. But we can go beyond it and do all the things Ben would have wanted us to do. You go ahead and marry Cassie. She will be your greatest comfort. She'll laugh with you and cry with you. You're going to need that. It would be the best gift you could give Ben—in this life, be happy. He's where he wanted to be. I know. I had a conversation with him just hours before he died. He wanted to go to heaven. Somehow the little one knew how ill he was. He had information we weren't privy to. I can't begrudge that, and I can't live like I don't understand it, though it's hard. God has given me peace, and I want that for all of you boys and your father."

"Thank you, Mother. That's a great comfort to me. And you're right about Cassie. She has already helped in my grief just by being there for me. She's warm and honest and she says the right things without denying me the right to my moments."

"Then shall we go ahead as planned?"

"Yes, indeed," he said. "It's the right thing to do."

❦

As if life were not full of trials enough, the threatening breath of war blew hot over the hills of Calhoun County. On January 9, 1861, Mississippi seceded from the Union, and the next day, on Albert Henry and Cassie's wedding day, Florida seceded.

The long day ended, the wedding and festivities in Houston were over, and the Payne family left for home in the darkness of a cold January evening, Thomas, Rachel, Isaac, and Samuel riding on the buckboard. Joab rode in the saddle with Jonathan, and Albert Henry and his young bride rode together. Laughter rang across the hills of Mississippi as the Payne side of the wedding party made their way home to Calhoun County with the new addition to their family.

❦

Rachel and Thomas climbed the ladder to the marriage room and lit the lantern. The bitter wind whipped through the cracks of the icy cold loft room and Rachel shivered.

"Hope I have enough quilts on this bed," she said. "I'd give anything if there were a fireplace up here."

"That would be nice, and one day, I'm going to make that happen."

"I know, dear. You gave this room everything but a fireplace, and it's wonderful. In the meantime, these hot smoothing irons will help."

Turning the massive stack of quilts back at the foot of the bed, they laid in irons warmed in the hot coals of the fireplace and wrapped in flannel pieces. Glancing around once more and reassuring each other that everything was perfect, they returned to the family.

Isaac, now skilled in decorating the mantle board, had added fresh evergreen, and Rachel had beautifully set the mahogany table with her finest. Light from the candles on the table, the lanterns on the mantle, and the blazing fire danced about the cabin. The family sat chatting around the table, indulging in large pieces of Rachel's pound cake, drinking hot spiced tea, and getting to know the newest member of their family—a girl of seventeen with warm brown hair and dark blue eyes that glistened when she smiled and talked. Cassie was beautiful. No doubt Henry had chosen her for many reasons.

When everyone was stuffed and they were no longer able to control the desire to reveal the surprise, Rachel hurried the young couple to the attic, the whole family climbing up behind them, anxious to see their faces. Cassie paused to look around and then burst into tears.

"Why, this is the most beautiful place on earth," she said.

"Splendid!" Henry said, echoing her excitement.

That was all the Payne family needed to know. She loved it. Henry loved it. They stood looking at each other as though they were just handed the keys to one of those stately mansions over in Holly Springs.

The newlyweds stayed and the family returned to the lower part of the cabin. Rachel was satisfied there was a measure of happiness in the Payne home in spite of the grief that cast an oppressive shadow.

"Goodnight, boys," Rachel said. She left the door to the bunkroom open so heat from the blazing fire could rise to the attic. At least she hoped it would.

"Goodnight, Mother." Joab never failed.

She lay quietly listening to Thomas breathing as he fell asleep and Samuel humming as he always did before he drifted off. One day he would play a great violin.

Chapter 10
Yalobusha Wilderness

It was yet cold and wintry when Georgia seceded from the Union on January 29. Texas followed on February 1. On the seventh, the Choctaw Indian Nation declared their allegiance to the South, no surprise to the Mississippians, who were thankful for their faithfulness at such a time as this. On February 9, Jeff Davis of Mississippi was elected the first president of the Confederacy, Alexander Stephens of Georgia, his vice president. And on March 4, the flag of the Confederate States of America was raised over Mississippi and the other states that had seceded. T. G. Payne and his family were living in a new era, a new country, under a new flag, and under threats of war with the North.

Early March 1861

Rachel and Jonathan walked out on the porch of the cabin and sat on the swing. It was cold. The wind blew fiercely out of the north and just as quickly stopped. The lanterns flickered through the windowpanes lighting the otherwise dark evening. The sweet fragrance of jasmine and jonquils filled the air unencumbered by the dark or the cold. Crocuses, both purple and cloth-of-gold, pushed through the reluctant soil in a bouquet that made a promise. Spring was coming.

"Mother, I'm leaving early in the morning. Pa knows. I'll be back before sundown on Saturday."

"Where will you go, son?"

"Yalobusha County," he said.

"Oh. You don't usually go that far, do you?"

"No, not usually, but I've been before. Lots of times. It's where the Yocona flows into the Yalobusha, about twenty miles as the crow flies from

Coffeeville. There's nothing but wilderness. I need to think about some things."

Rachel dreaded going further with this conversation. Jonathan's thoughts concerned the war, and the least said to her right now, the better. And, too, his brother and best friend had just married a beautiful woman, yet Jonathan was the elder son. She wondered if he resented that. If so, no one would ever know. There was another reason for this retreat. Jonathan had not said as much, but he had pent-up grief over Benjamin. He had to find a way to make it more bearable. Rachel knew it, and this was her opportunity to say what had been on her mind since the funeral, something that might help lessen the burden.

"I'll never forget what you did at the graveside when you played Benjamin's violin. It soothed us that day, more than you know. Your father said as much. I believed you would never play again, and when you drew the bow down on that violin ... well, I can't tell you how I felt. I saw your grandmother smiling through tears. She so loves you, Jonathan."

"I know, Mother. I love her. When this war's over ... and it hasn't yet begun ... well, when this war's over ... a lot of things, right?"

Reluctant to rehash what she and Jonathan had already said on the hill that night, Rachel deliberately returned to the conversation about Ben.

"While you were playing Ben's violin, Sally was on the hill shouting. If I know her, she could see him romping and playing on the hillsides of Glory."

They stood, Jonathan towering over his mother. He hugged her, and she walked back into the house leaving him alone with his thoughts. Leaning against the hitching rail, he thought about Sally, wishing he could throw himself on the sure mercies of God and respond like she had. His body fought the rigors of grief. Not now, he thought. Not here.

He walked up the hill to the oak tree. Just beneath it, the body of his little brother lay in the cold Mississippi ground. No tears. Just memories rushing in. He fell to his knees and touched the earth, then stretching his long arms and callused hands across the grave, he silently mourned for Benjamin.

❧

Early the next morning Rachel woke and went to the bunkroom. Jonathan was gone, likely having left after a few hours of sleep, or maybe he had not slept at all. Thomas was already up with a fresh fire going in the fireplace and one in the kitchen stove. He made coffee.

She touched Isaac and he jumped awake, groaning, remembering he had to go to the mill in Jonathan's place for the next two days.

"Get dressed and come on out to the kitchen. Breakfast will be ready soon."

She called Albert Henry from the ladder that led to the loft.

"Time to wake up, son."

He left Cassie in the warm bed and descended the ladder to the bunkroom below where the younger boys slept. With boots and woolen socks in hand, he headed for the warmth of the kitchen where his father sat with a cup of black coffee. Rachel made biscuits.

"We're going to take the buckboard to the sawmill. Jonathan has Glory and Jackson, and he won't be back until Saturday late. We'll just all ride together."

"Gonna strap a buck to old Glory, huh?" Albert Henry said.

"Yes, if I know Jonathan, that's exactly what he's going to do."

Isaac joined them, expressing his concern about his horse.

"Hope he can get a small one. Poor Glory will cave under the load of a big buck."

Rachel handed Isaac a plate of brown-topped biscuits.

"Butter some of these while they're hot," she said, lifting the bacon to a plate and spooning scrambled eggs into a bowl.

"How does this look?"

"There's nothing I love better," he said, squeezing his mother across the shoulders.

He leaned down and kissed her hair. Rachel turned and hugged him. She was certain there was nothing better than a house full of boys.

They sat around the breakfast table in the small hours before daybreak, enjoying each other's company, drinking the last of the coffee. Reluctant to leave the warmth of wife and mother, the Payne men boarded the wagon and headed down the trail toward the main dirt road to the sawmill.

༄

Night fell on the Yalobusha wilderness. Jonathan fished until dusk. A decent string of bream and perch flopped in the edge of the water. His father loved a good fish fry. Besides, anything he brought now would extend the longevity of the smokehouse pieces.

He laid a huge fire at his campsite, careful to dig a sizeable trench around it, not wanting the fire to spread when he fell asleep. The snow was gone. Completely melted. And the ground was fairly dry, thanks to the March winds that blew cold out of the north.

He pan fried one of the perch and made a pot of coffee. His mother had slipped a jar of honey and some leftover biscuits into his saddlebags with his other supplies the night before. He ate the fish and washed out the skillet in water from the river, put it back on the burning wood, and laid in two biscuits to warm. When they were hot, he lifted them out and drizzled on the honey. Something about honey was comforting and healing, and his mother knew he needed both.

He ate the biscuits and honey, leaned back on his saddle, and did what he came to do. To be sure he would do the physical. He would get the fish and the deer and whatever else came his way. But he came for another purpose.

The events of the past two months weighed heavily on him. He thought of the bitter and the sweet. Of Benjamin. It was hard for him to believe he was dead and buried on the hill. He could still hear his laughter, a sweet voice. He saw his frail little body lying on the bed, saying last words to his papa. Dear God, how he missed him. He thought of his mother and father and the hurt they would take to their graves. Of the new Confederacy they found themselves living in because of civil unrest, and he thought of the coming war. It was close. He could feel it. And there was Albert Henry with a new wife he would have to leave behind. And the boys. Isaac would be left to take care of his mother and the little ones. The responsibility could be overwhelming. And he knew Isaac well enough to believe he was already contriving a way to do the things men do in times like these. He hoped he was mistaken about this. He would like to beat some sense into him now before it was too late, but that was mean spirited, something Isaac didn't deserve. It had just fallen his lot to be at that ridiculous age—between youth and manhood—and if he went out and got himself killed, it would drive another nail in his mother's coffin.

Jonathan sat with his eyes glued to the flames, his thoughts uncontrollable. Darkness surrounded him inside and out, until suddenly his wits collapsed under the trauma of memory and circumstance, leaving him heaving and gasping for breath. Tears fell like rain. He couldn't stop them. Yet neither could he make a sound. He choked with the surge of remembrance, and in a moment of panic he lunged for the ground, rolled over on his hands and knees and began to crawl around in the dirt away from the fire. Try as he may, he couldn't yell in a gruesome attempt to pour out all this grief. He was a wilderness boy. He grew up with physical pain. His hands were callused and his body was stout. He sat up, extended his arms in an effort to force sound from his lungs, and with fists clinched, he pounded on his stomach until it tightened, but to no avail. He half crawled, half walked to the edge of the water, the flicker from the campfire and the moon over the Yalobusha half-heartedly lighting his way. He snagged one of his hands on something sharp, and the pain was excruciating. The calluses. He had ripped the calluses off and his bleeding skin throbbed and burned. It didn't matter. They were just calluses. They would heal. But he wasn't sure if he could ever grow calloused to these feelings, to this war that was raging inside and out.

It was dark where he lay in the shadow of the trees. Cold and damp. He moved to all fours, heaved until his stomach throbbed from emptiness, and still crawling around on burning hands and knees, gruesome sounds began to emanate from his throat. He wailed aloud, the sounds erupting to join the tears—finally. He cried until all the anguish surfaced and relief penetrated the armored plate that protected his emotions. To his gratification the pain was gone. At the river's edge, he lay down and the tightness in his chest subsided, his throat relaxed. He knelt in the water and washed his face and hands. He was cleansed, a necessary exercise before he could move on in preparation for impending war. He could ill afford to take pent-up feelings to a battlefield.

He lay motionless on the slope, watching the moon over the Yalobusha cast its long rays of light as far as he could see to the right and to the left. The light moved with every gentle ripple of the water, dancing, curving to form a thousand smiling faces just for him. He sat up on the bank. The tiny new green leaves on the weeping willows rustled in the March wind, guarded by the stately cypress trees that grew in the edge of the water. The frogs and the crickets sang in rounds and the dry brown leaves and twigs on the ground rustled as a rabbit made his way home for the night. An owl hooty-hoo'd somewhere in the top of a tree—all reassuring Jonathan he was at home, protected by the wild. This was his wilderness—sometimes ruthless, thoughtless, but always his beloved Mississippi.

When he was sure there was nothing left within him, he climbed the hill to his fire, and in the warmth of the glowing embers, Jonathan Edward Payne leaned against his saddle and slept, bowie knife strapped to his side, faithful steed, Jackson, and Isaac's sorrel mare, Glory, tied to the tree beside him.

*

Jonathan woke at daybreak. He felt better. In fact, he was better. He pulled the charred chunks of the dead fire together and piled on fresh wood. Not too much. He had deer hunting to do. If he saw a buck, it would be his. No doubt about that. He would love to down a thirteen-point, but no. Glory couldn't take the weight. He hoped for a three point. A small buck dressed out would be sufficient for several meals and some to share with Grandma and Grandpa Church and Marcellus and his family. He would bring meat to the table now and leave the pork in the smokehouse for when he, Albert Henry, and their father were gone.

When the fire was hot, Jonathan made coffee. He was hungry—a good sign, and he pulled out another of his mother's biscuits and the jar of honey.

He leaned back on his saddle and sat beside the fire for a couple of hours, drinking coffee and thinking. Thinking about how and where they would muster in—likely Harrisburg, or maybe Grenada—and where they would go and with what regiment. His father would take care of that. He had talked with friends and relatives for months, pulling together a company of Calhoun County men. They were ready. Ready and waiting. He wondered what they would be able to take with them. He had a lot of questions, but no answers. He just knew he couldn't wait until the last minute to think about some of these things. He could almost hear the tramping of feet and the clanking of sabers, and suddenly he looked forward to defending the South.

It was mid afternoon but Jonathan sat still a few more minutes watching the peaceful gliding of the river and listening to the crackle of the fire, not wanting to start his deer hunt too early. He drank the last of the coffee, smothered the fire, and walked down to the river to wash his face and hands.

He took the bow and one arrow from the quiver that was strapped to Jackson. That should do it. Leaving Jackson and Glory tied to the tree, he walked a quarter of a mile into the woods. There was always an abundance of deer in the Yalobusha Wilderness. This time would be no exception. His was somewhere out there.

He moved far enough into the woods so the horses wouldn't spook the deer, crouched in a thicket, and waited. Patiently. A whole ten minutes he waited, and a huge buck with a weighty rack schlepped by him within six feet. Can't do it, he said to himself. Think about Glory. He counted the points, nine, ten, eleven. He would love to down the old gentleman, but he sat quietly. He could see where the deer, maybe a herd, had time and again broken through the thicket on either side of him, leaving a slick trail, making their way down to the river to drink. Not less keenly aware than the wilderness animals he stalked, Jonathan waited. Time was on his side, and the old big one had a smaller friend.

He stood still, aiming squarely for the neck for there it was, passing within easy shooting distance not twelve yards away. Pull hard and shoot straight. A slight popping sound and like the power of an eagle screaming its way to the eye of a storm, the arrow flew straight to the neck and he was down. Jonathan waited a moment and came close. The perfect three-point buck lay dead on the ground. He pulled out the arrow and wiped off the blood, then walked back to get Glory.

He told his mother he would return by sundown on Saturday, but he would have to leave early in the morning now that he had the deer. He mounted Glory bareback and rode into the woods. It was a struggle, but he threw the young deer over the horse and led him to the camp. He wouldn't be able to sleep tonight for fear of losing it to the vultures. That didn't matter. He had slept like a baby the night before.

When he reached his camp, Jonathan lifted the deer from Glory's back and secured him across two logs he pulled together. Not too close to the fire. It was cold in the late evenings and the nights were frosty. Cold enough to keep the deer, and he would head home early in the morning. He stationed Glory nearby. She would alert him to any night predator.

Scouting through the dry brush close to his campsite, Jonathan lifted four of the biggest logs he could find and brought them up. He skillfully stacked the dry pieces of wood and started the fire. Night fell, and soon the flames and blazing sparks dispelled the darkness around him. He dug in his saddlebag for any remaining biscuits and found two with salt-cured ham at the bottom of the cloth bag his mother had tucked in for him. She was one jewel of a woman, and he loved her, especially tonight when he was so hungry.

He finished his coffee, walked down to the river and washed up, taking a moment to soak in the glory of the evening. A full moon hung over the water, an eagle flew to his perch for the night, and the frogs croaked inexorably on a hollow log in the water.

He hesitated a moment, getting an uneasy feeling. Something was wrong. He sensed it. He knew it. He slowly climbed the bank toward his campfire, not more than twenty yards from the water. Now the horses whinnied and thrashed about. Jackson broke loose, then Glory, and they both bolted into the woods. Jonathan had to get to the far side of his fire. To his saddle. To the hatchet. He pulled his bowie knife from the sheath on his side, ready to use it at the first need. Jackson was gone with his bow and arrows. He wondered what spooked them so much that they would break loose and run. A bobcat, maybe.

Cautiously he inched closer to the fire, and in the flickering light, he saw it. At least eight feet of fur and hundreds of pounds of black bear standing, his body fully extended on hind legs between the fire and the saddles. The bear had spotted him coming up the hill. He roared in a thunderous throaty growl, pawing the air, reaching for Jonathan, hind legs solid to the ground. The bear would have to cross the fire to get to him, or go around it, which meant he would have to lower his body to all fours, something he was not willing to do—he would not take his eyes off Jonathan unless he absolutely had to. He had found favorable fare, and he aimed to get it. For the first time in his life, Jonathan was terrified. The monster let out another intimidating snarl, throwing his head back, growling, and thrashing back and forth, flailing his front paws, hind feet still planted between the saddles and the fire.

Jonathan collected his wits and took a moment to think of how to handle the dilemma. Likely the bear would handle him; then all his worries would be over, for there would be nothing left.

The smell of fresh blood had drawn the bear toward the campsite. He was after the deer, but he had not gotten that far when he spotted Jonathan. He needed to trade places with the monster and cunningly plotted a scheme that would get him there. He clinched his knife, to be used only if he had to. It wouldn't do enough damage to relieve him of the havoc the bear could wreak on him, but he felt more comfortable with it in his hand. His hands—he had snagged the calluses on a sharp piece of wood the night before, crawling around on the ground, but he would have to suffer that pain right now. His hungry opponent raged, stifling the silence of the night, pawing the air, epitomizing the harsher face of the wilderness.

Jonathan inched closer to the fire, hoping to urge the bear to the other side away from his saddle. The monster would have to go around the fire. He would never go through it. Jonathan moved in one direction, faking to get him in motion, and then turned. As he moved, the bear grudgingly fell to all fours and started around the fire behind him. Without the luxury of a running start and from where he stood with strength astounding even to himself, Jonathan jumped the fire, cleared it, and lunged for his saddle and the hatchet that lay beside it. He turned to face his opponent. The giant moved closer to the fire, and in a thoughtless desire for revenge, reached out with front leg extended and dragged a paw across Jonathan's face. Blood streamed, pouring into his eyes. In madness, Jonathan took a step backward and wiped the sleeve of his shirt across his face, attempting to get the blood out of his eyes so he could see, but to no avail. Blood was gushing from his forehead to his chin, faster than he could wipe it away.

The bear was in a fit of anger, outwitted by a mere human, and the fire blazed between him and Jonathan. He reared back and roared with an intimidating fierceness that penetrated the night. It echoed across the river and came back to fall on Jonathan's ears like a death gurgle. But the monster was now poised to receive what Jonathan had for him—a blade between the eyes. Jonathan quickly squatted and wiped his hand through the dirt. If he tried to throw the hatchet with blood on his hand, it could slip and that would be it for him. The dirt would afford him a better grip. He took another split second to think. To aim. To lay speed and force behind the hatchet that would take the bear down to his death. He only had one chance to do the job. If he missed and hit the bear with the handle, it would anger him, and Jonathan would no longer have a fighting chance.

He took a step backward between the saddles. With uncanny precision, he threw the hatchet by the light of the fire. It sailed through the night air with lightning speed and in a split second, lodged deep between the old bear's eyes. Jonathan moved from the path of the falling monster, who roared in one last painful defiance and fell forward into several feet of fire, scattering the hot burning wood. When he hit the ground there was the sound of thunder and the earth moved.

Fearful he may not have completed the job, Jonathan moved toward the trees. He had only the bowie knife to protect himself. But the bear lay across the hot coals of the fire, unable to regain footing, thrashing about, clawing at the hatchet that was not going anywhere.

Jonathan stepped away from the gruesome scene and into the edge of the woods then circled back around to where the bear lay on the fire. He jumped hard onto his back, straddling his shoulders, reached down with his left hand and took hold of the hatchet that was wedged tight in his skull, pushed in, and pulled his head back with no intention of removing the hatchet. The bear offered no resistance, though Jonathan could feel the pulse beating against his legs. With bowie knife in his right hand, he rammed it into the left side of the bear's neck and laid it open, pulling from left to right, blood spewing straight out. Jonathan let go of the hatchet and the monster's head dropped to the ground. He had tapped into the vein of the wild, feeling the pulse of nature. The old bear yielded to the speechless, smothering silence of the wilderness. The weary Jonathan was exultant, and with an earned air of haughtiness, he stepped away from his conquered enemy.

He ran around the river's edge for a quarter of a mile calling for Jackson. His faithful steed rushed at the sound of his voice, Glory right behind him. Everything had happened so fast, and Jonathan's head was spinning. First instincts were to get on Jackson, grab Glory, and ride out of the Yalobusha. Caution had replaced the carelessness of youth, but the desire to see the nightmare to an end pulled rank. Besides, he couldn't leave his saddles.

His quiver was intact. Jonathan lifted the bow and pulled out an arrow. He knew the bear was dead, but he was taking no chances with what he might find when he got back to the fire. The closer he got, the more distinct the smell of burning fur and animal flesh and blood. The bear lay motionless across the logs, his massive body smothering the fire.

Jonathan saddled Jackson and Glory. He tied the hind legs with a rope, wrapped one end around the horn of his saddle and one to Glory's and pulled the bear off the fire. He had not only saved his own skin, but he had a wedding gift for Albert Henry and Cassie—a rug for that cold wood floor in the attic.

He spent the night skinning the bear, his face burning intensely. He considered longing to be home, sitting by the fire, his mother slathering on the healing and soothing lard, but instead he thought of impending war and decided if it were anything like this, he was grateful for the experience and for the lessons learned—a keen awareness of danger, a split second to think, a plan hastily devised, a steady hand, swift execution with no pity for the adversary, and a fatal blow that took the enemy down and himself out of danger. When he mulled everything over, the pain was less excruciating, more tolerable.

Jonathan cut loose the last piece of hide and pulled the new bear rug away. Careful to leave as much of the fat as possible, he cut part of one shank off and wrapped it with pine branches, the best he could do and all he could carry with him. His mother would be pleased to render it for lard. She found many uses for bear lard. He visualized a low fire with leaves and a scaffold with the bearskin stretched over it. It would take several weeks to dry the skin. If they left soon, Isaac would teach Cassie how to scrape it until it was cured. It would mean more to her and she would proudly show it off when the boys came home from war.

He mounted Jackson, and took Glory's bridle. Together man and beasts pulled the carcass to the edge of the woods near the river and left it for the vultures and bobcats to enjoy at the first break of dawn. But before he left it, Jonathan had a thought, a plan that would play out in the months, maybe years, to come. He cut the fur away from the upper part of the paw in a perfect square. Then the other three. He cut each into two pieces and rolled the fur so the eight pieces fit snugly into his saddlebags. He had to remember to take them out when he got home. They would need to be cured.

He tied the horses, walked down to the river, and washed the blood from his knife and the hatchet, laid them aside and washed his hands with mud silt from the edge of the river then rinsed them in the clear water of the Yalobusha. Wading out a little deeper, he stood with the cold March wind blowing hard against him, bent over, and washed his burning face. In the moment it felt good, but it had been a long, tiring night, and he had not realized how cold it was until all the work was done. Chilled from the water and the cold night air, he walked back up the hill to his dreadful looking campsite, took a minute to clean it up, and laid a small fire to warm himself. He pulled a log close to the fire and spread his trousers across hoping they would dry out.

∾

Morning broke the eastern sky, and Jonathan lay still, wrapped in one Choctaw Indian blanket, lying on another, watching the vultures assemble above, getting ready to descend, to perform nature's chores, the cleanup, and he was satisfied. The experience had given him confidence beyond which most boys of eighteen could only dream.

He had not unsaddled the horses. Jonathan reconsidered the weight of the bearskin and the deer, and instead of Glory, he threw the skin across Jackson, fur side down and laid the deer on top of it. Just right. He tied down the deer and the bear meat with the rope and walked down to the river. He slipped the fish from the string and threw them back. He had no place for them.

The fire had long since died, leaving nothing to do but mount and ride. He returned the unused arrow to the quiver, flung the saddlebags across Glory and slowly rode out of the woods, leading Jackson.

The wind blew across his burning face. It felt good. His spirit was no longer broken, but lifted to the hilt. Tears shed. Binding fetters of grief unshackled. In this moment, there was nothing better. Though he had not counted on it—he would never have dreamed it—it had fallen his lot to face unthinkable danger and he won the battle. He had walked through the fire, and a burning flame was kindled within—the craving to defend his southern heritage, to fight fearlessly with his countrymen and to come home to his beloved hills of Mississippi. When the time came, he would willingly go. The warrior was ready.

Chapter 11
Oil of Healing

She stood in the windows gazing at the tree line at the top of the ridge though Jonathan would not return until sundown. He loved the wilderness, and he knew every hill and hollow in three counties, but when he was out there, Rachel worried. He was a prince. Tall, muscular and flawlessly handsome. His eyes were as blue as the skies over Mississippi, his hair as brown as the young deer he chased across the hills. She loved him no more than any of the others, but he was her eldest and a lot had fallen on his young shoulders. Not out of necessity. That was the way he wanted it.

༄

It was a Saturday afternoon no different from all others. The men were home from the mill, having left at noon. Chores were done, baths and hair washing were finished, and sitting around the low fire, Isaac and Joab played games they made up as they went along. Samuel lay napping in the crib. Albert Henry and Cassie were in their room upstairs. Thomas glared at the old newspapers he had read over and again, wishing the news could have been different.
"Rachel, come sit with me," he said.
"I know he's not supposed to be here until evening, but I have this feeling he'll be home sooner. I don't know why. I hope he's all right."
"He knows what he's doing."
"I know, but I have this feeling—"
"You're always having those feelings, Rachel."
"Don't you ever have a feeling something is not just right?"
"Not as much as you."

"What does that mean, Thomas? Are you saying it's because I'm a woman?"

"Yes, that's what I'm saying, Rachel Madeleine Beauregard Payne. You're a woman and a mother. Now, stop worrying. How many times has Jonathan been to the Yalobusha alone? He always comes back unscathed."

Rachel curled up beside her husband on the brown leather sofa her parents had given them on their twentieth anniversary, a wonderful gift. For years they sat on hard chairs. She treasured this piece of furniture, but right now she found it hard to relax. She pulled the handmade afghan over her skirts, making an effort. And then she heard something.

"Thomas, did you hear that?"

"No, it's your imagination. Or the wind whistling through the cracks of the cabin."

"No, it's not."

She jumped up and ran to the window.

"It's Jonathan! He's home!"

"Well, you're right, Rachel," he said, following her. "He's early. And looks like there's a deer across Jackson's back. Let's get out there and help him, boys. And, Rachel—I beg your pardon. I must have been wrong!"

As Jonathan came closer, Rachel saw his face and ran toward him. It was a mess. Dry blood covered deep gashes from his forehead to his chin on one side. His clothes were filthy, bloody.

"Jonathan, what monster did this?" She burst into tears.

"Mother, I'm fine," he said, dismounting Glory and tying both horses to the rail.

"No, you're not!"

"Well, if you think I look bad, you should see the monster. That's what's left of him," said Jonathan, pointing to the bearskin draped across Jackson's back, only partially covered by the small buck.

"It's just a little wedding present for Henry and Cassie. You said they needed a rug."

He lifted the deer to the ground with Albert Henry's help, and they brought the bearskin to the porch and spread it out.

"We'll need to cut off the burnt place and work on that little piece between his eyes, but the best part of the skin is not damaged at all, ready to be cured."

"Jonathan Payne, you are something else," his brother said. "How in the world did you do this alone?"

"Oh, I had Jackson and Glory," he said modestly. And out of hearing range of his mother, he whispered, "One day, on a battlefield somewhere in Virginia, I'll tell you all about it, Henry."

The two boys cut the horns from the deer's head and took the animal to the slaughter stand and hung it by the feet. They dressed it out, and Thomas cut the venison in pieces.

Rachel had visions of Jonathan in the wilderness alone, fighting the bear, and she had no care for the deer and definitely none for the wretched monster that had clawed her son. She put on two big kettles of water to boil and sent Isaac for the bathing tub. He sat it by the stove in the kitchen and Rachel poured the boiling hot water in with the cold, closed the door, and left her son alone by the warmth of the cook stove.

Jonathan undressed, stepped into the hot tub of water, and picked up the round of homemade soap his mother had left. He washed the deep furrows drawn by the old black bear, laid the hot cloth across his burning face, and sat there soaking for half an hour, thinking about how much he loved the comforts of home. He dried off, pulled on the long johns his mother left on a chair for him, and slipped on clean trousers.

ॐ

Rachel returned to the kitchen, poured in the healing oil, and slathered on the ointment. She gave her son a big mug of tea with honey and a drop of whiskey to kill the pain. He basked in the moment, but quickly shifted his thoughts. His mother would be nowhere around when they went to war.

Chapter 12
O, Day Most Dreaded!

Friday, April 12, 1861, Calhoun County, Mississippi

Jonquils bloomed in thick patches and the forsythia spread their lanky branches across the corners of the porch. Peach and apple trees blossomed and in the April breeze scattered pink and white flowers in blankets on the ground beneath. Tiny leaves appeared en masse on the giant oak tree on the hill. And though the snowbirds had spread their wings and flown away, the mockingbirds sang once again and the barn wrens made their nests. The sun warmed their world, and the harshness of winter kissed the earth and left for a season. Rachel was glad.

☙

Thomas and the boys left the sawmill at their regular hour, slowing the gait of their horses so they could talk freely before they got home.

Jonathan knew his father had gone into Sarepta late in the day to hear the latest scuttlebutt from the old men in the square, but they had not had time to talk until now.

"Did you get any details on what happened at Fort Sumter? The grapevine was working overtime at the sawmill."

"Well, that's the truth. There was such a noise about it, I thought I better get on over there and try to get a paper. I've got it in my saddlebag, although I think I may have gotten the last one. By the time I got there, people were swarming all over the square, reading over the shoulders of those who were able to get one. I'll tell you what I heard in town, and you two can go to

Henry's room and take the paper when we get home. I want you to read every word of it, but send Cassie downstairs first.

"We're at war, boys. The South was accused of insulting the flag of the country today when they—when we, that is—fired on it at Sumter. And the old men said the newspapers from New York to Philadelphia were full of insults to the South. Things like *Annihilation to Traitors! Down with the Rebels!* Now a cry to arms will go out all across the land from both sides. For all the rhetoric over the years that's led to this dreadful day, it will soon be known the South meant what it said. And, in turn, the North had best be ready to defend all its accusations.

"Now, I don't know how this will line up in the minds of the northerners, but all the Dred Scott decision did was stir up more trouble for the slaves and create discontent in the free black states. And not one good thing came from John Brown's deal for he wreaked havoc at Harpers Ferry and before that in Kansas. And you remember what preacher Henry Ward Beecher said at Brown's death. Well, he said it, but he was speaking purely from an abolitionist's standpoint, 'What is average citizenship when a lunatic is a hero?' How suitably stated and insulting to the intelligence of supporters of the reprobate abolitionist, though that's not why he said it. Truth be known, all of this has stoked the fire that's been burning hot in the South.

"And Lincoln made threats about all Federal property, when all he could possibly be concerned with was Fort Sumter. All this time, South Carolina's been trying to get Lincoln to stop occupying such an important port in the Confederacy. Why, the United States flag was still flying over Sumter until today, and South Carolina was the first to secede, for goodness sakes! Obviously, Lincoln has not yet read the Constitution; at least his decisions would make you wonder. Nor does he understand states rights.

"Anyway, he out-waited the South, stirring the pot, and whether he owns up to it matters not at this point. The fact is, he said Fort Sumter in Charleston's harbor belonged to the Union, and he declared he would keep it in the Union. Just eight days ago, he signed an order for an expedition to take food to Fort Sumter. Only food, mind you. No ammunition. This put the South in a bind, and Jeff Davis had to make a quick decision. He knew that firing on Sumter would be the shot heard from Charleston Harbor to Washington. It would mean war, a war that Lincoln would commence by forcing the issue, by sending relief to Sumter with no ammunition. Nothing good can come of this, boys. This is a dreadful day. Dreadful."

The boys had never heard their father speak so rapidly or with such intensity. And he had said they were at war. All his pent-up feelings, all the newspaper articles he had read over the last few months, everything that came to his mind surfaced and came spewing out.

"Pa, what about Tennessee and the other southern states that have not seceded? And the Border States? What will they do?" Albert Henry asked.

"The paper should tell. If it's not in there, I think we'll know, maybe by tomorrow, what they've decided to do. I'm sure they'll get the picture, understanding that Lincoln was the aggressor, and they'll gladly join their brothers and fight for the South now that it has come to that."

Jonathan and Albert Henry slipped up to the attic and sent Cassie down.

She willingly left them alone, fear gripping her insides as she descended the steps. The only reason they would send her down would be so they could talk about whatever was in that paper. Right now, she was satisfied to know as little as possible.

They read every article headlining war. The re-supplying ship with no artillery arrived at 4:30 a.m., aggravating an already boiling state of affairs, and at President Davis' orders to General Beauregard, he commanded fire-eater Edmund Ruffin to commence with the first shot. From forty-seven artillery pieces—cannons, howitzers, and mortars—his men fired. Four thousand shots, it was. Smoke rose up high, thick, and black between the fort and Charleston harbor, so dense the men in the harbor could scarcely see the fort.

"Here it is, brother," Jonathan said. "The first shot was fired by what Lincoln calls the rebellious states. In that case, I guess we're Rebels, Henry. And the other southern states—Virginia, Arkansas, North Carolina and Tennessee—immediately joined the Confederacy."

"That's good news," Albert Henry said.

"Yep, just what we wanted to hear. Let's go tell Pa it's in the paper. He needs to hear some good news. Do you want this wick lowered, Henry?"

"Shut it down. Save the wick. I'll light it when we come back up. Poor Cassie, she's a nervous wreck. It's likely she'll burn that lamp all night."

"I understand," said Jonathan.

ᴄᴏ

There was an immense imbalance in people, military power, manufactured goods, and transportation system. The South had railroads, but no way to keep them up. They would ordinarily get their parts from the North. Not any more. But the South had one huge advantage. They would fight at home. They didn't realize, at the time, that advantage would turn to devastation of their land, their farms, their wilderness, their towns; but they would fight regardless to defend what belonged to them. And the South had Jeff Davis who would roll out a plan that would reveal the patience and endurance of southern gentlemen and the skill of the South's remarkable generals, many of whom left the United States Army to join their beloved South.

Time and again, Lincoln tried the competence and fortitude of men—his men—and found them unfit for the task. He had no general he could count on, for most of them had gone with the Confederacy, and when he attempted in his own piteous efforts to strategize, his less than apt generals ridiculed him. Then came Ulysses S. Grant, Lincoln's ace in the hole. And behind him William Tecumseh Sherman, the cursing, cigar chewing monster with his march north through the Carolinas. Blockade the Navy. Divide the Confederacy. Gain control of the Mississippi River. Get Chattanooga. And devastate what remained of the Confederacy with his march through Georgia, wreaking havoc, crushing, killing, cursing, bringing down fire and brimstone on a hungry, ragged, hurting southern army.

That's what Lincoln would allow in time.

Meanwhile, the South would not be told they could be defeated, for they could not. They would not. Their love for family, home, and country, albeit southern states only, now, would keep them going through every atrocity that could be committed against them in the days, months, and years to come. They had a fresh Cause—not the right to own slaves—but the proud duty to defend the very soil upon which they fought.

Chapter 13
Not for Evil

It was a steamy hot summer at the Payne homestead, unusual for the hills. Time was drawing to a close. The Mississippians would soon lay down the saws at the mill, the plows in the fields, pack their gear, reach for their rifles from the rack over the mantle, and leave the beloved hills of home. The sawmill was buzzing with talk. A lot of the men had already left. Mostly those who didn't have families. They wanted to muster in before they were conscripted. There was something sacred about joining up before being drafted. T. G. would make a decision before safe travel became impossible. He wanted to get his farm in good shape for Rachel and Isaac, and he needed to bring in as much money as possible before he left the mill. They would need it. He wasn't sure how, what, or if the army would pay.

By summer's end, Rachel and Cassie had finished the canning and stored the jars in the cellar. They filled a portion of the barn loft with potatoes and onions, covering them with a thin layer of hay that would keep them dry and prevent freezing later on. Thomas and the boys stacked baled hay on the other end. They had planted extra corn in the early spring. Some to can, but most of it was for the livestock. When the stalks crackled to the touch, Isaac and Joab pulled the last of it, shelled a good supply and filled the bin for the chickens, and shucked whole ears for the hogs. At last, all the bins were full.

༄

Thomas and Rachel talked freely after they went to bed each night. He told her the truth as he knew it. They would soon be gone—he, Jonathan, and Albert Henry.

They lay arm in arm, whispering thoughts that must be verbalized now before it was too late. Samuel slept peacefully in the crib nearby.

"Thomas, I need to tell you how much I love you and how sorely I will miss you when you're gone."

"And I you, Rachel," he whispered back. "And the boys—why, Samuel is still a baby toddling about. Joab needs me. And Isaac—what on earth will Isaac do? How can I say goodbye to all of you?"

Rachel touched his face, wiping the tears that burned his cheeks.

"You'll be back. This war can't last long. We have no business fighting one another in this country. It's shameful, the whole conundrum, political. It has little to do with slavery. The North has made it so. Why, we're scarcely touched with slavery here in this part of the South. That's what makes it so hard to understand. I know why you and the boys are going—to defend our home place. I just hope I don't get too bitter against the North for taking my family from me.

"And Cassie—poor, young and bewildered Cassie. We've been talking a lot. I'm trying to prepare her as much as possible, knowing all the time I'm the one who needs to be prepared."

"How is she taking it?"

"She's way young to give up her husband and stay in her right mind. That's why I'm glad to have her here. We will comfort each other. But Albert Henry doesn't need to go off to war knowing how she feels about it. I hope she can keep her true feelings from him."

"I'm afraid this war will change us all, Rachel."

"We must let it change us for good and not for evil, lest we never get through it. You're a strong, godly man, Thomas. I could not let you go otherwise."

⁓

September nights, 1861

T. G. Payne and his friends, neighbors, and kin met in their little hometown of Sarepta night after night, organizing a company of fighting men with their sons of conscription age, for Lincoln had called for seventy-five thousand men to fight for the Union. They mustn't let grass grow under their feet, for soon the South would need them out there. The Border States were hanging in the balances with decisions to make. Most of them had an uncanny lean toward the South, finding the Union despicable. Their governors poignantly and openly declared refusal to send their native sons to fight for the North, and none dared entertain the thought that brother would fight against brother. Rachel read the governors' declarations one by one as they appeared in the newspapers.

"It is illegal, unconstitutional, revolutionary, inhuman, diabolical, and cannot be complied with," said Missouri's governor.

"Kentucky will furnish no troops for the wicked purpose of subduing her sister Southern States."

"Tennessee will not furnish a single man for coercion, but fifty thousand, if necessary, for the defense of our rights and those of our brethren."

"I can be no party to the wicked violation of the laws of the country and to the war upon the liberties of a free people. You can get no troops from North Carolina."

Plain and simple. The governors were in, but their states suffered at the hands of Union leaders within. There were strong Federal factions in Western North Carolina and Tennessee, albeit both states had joined the Confederacy, and those in the Border States who did not favor secession stirred up a lot of trouble. Each side determined to know who would align with the North and who would align with the South, an issue that was never fully settled in some states.

༄

The cause of state sovereignty grew less significant for the South, in time. They were now fighting for military advantage. In defense of their homeland. The seat of the Confederate Government had long since been moved from Montgomery to Richmond, a much more tactical location.

Closer to Washington.

Closer to *hope*.

Chapter 14
Far and Away

November's end, 1861

An early snow lay deep in the valley, and from the oak tree where Ben was buried to the top of the ridge the earth was untouched by human footprints. The ice on the pines brought the boughs low to the ground. A family of deer frolicked at the top of the ridge, and the old eagle soared in the gray winter sky, winging her way back to the nest in the tallest tree on the ridge, flying high, dipping, soaring, vanishing out of sight in the last rays of sun, for no mere mortal must know the exact location of her wilderness home. Decembers had come and gone for over twenty years, and the southern scene was etched in Rachel's mind, memories more poignant now because Ben was buried on that hill. And when the boys did go to war, she would no longer watch the horizon for them to appear. They would be gone—far and away—stirring yet another plethora of memories.

༄

A week passed. It was cold, though the snow had melted, and the road to the Payne cabin was once again dry and hard packed. Rachel worked at the wood stove in the cozy, warm kitchen, preparing supper for her men and boys, and as usual, Cassie began setting the table when Rachel stopped her.

"Cassie, let's have supper at the mahogany table tonight in front of the fire. I want this to be one of those special evenings."

"Of course, Rachel," she said. "Do you want me to use the good china?"

"Yes, let's do. And get that white cloth from the window seat."

Rachel brought the roasted turkey and cornbread dressing to the center of the table and surrounded it with rutabaga, sweet potatoes, green beans, and gravy. A pitcher of cold fresh cream, to top the stewed peaches for dessert, rested in a tub of icicles on the back porch. Isaac had pulled them from the eaves of the house. Coffee simmered in the blue speckled pot on the back burner of the stove.

"What's the occasion, Rachel?" Cassie asked.

"Why, I really don't know why I did this, Cassie. I just think every day is going to be the last one before the men leave, and for some reason I've felt more strongly about it today. It's in the air, and we've been able to hold onto our men far longer than most, but now the war is getting stoked hotter every day. It won't be long, I can assure you."

"Oh, Rachel, I can't bear to think about it. I've tried to hide my feelings from Albert Henry, but I don't know how successful I've been. The fact is my young husband will be going off to fight in a war that I deem utterly senseless at this point."

"I know, Cassie. I couldn't agree more, but it's reality. We must hold up for them."

"But it's so hard."

"Yes, it is, but we will comfort one another, and God will bear us up," she said, reminded of Benjamin.

"You always know what to say. I'm such a girl compared to you. You're this godly woman that I long to be like, Rachel. When Henry comes back from the war, he'll likely not be able to tell his wife from his mother, for I will watch every move you make, hoping that some of it will rub off on me."

Rachel laughed

"Don't look at me, for I'll disappoint you. Not meaning to. But I'll gladly teach you everything I know about being a wife and a mother. Things I've learned the hard way. For one day you'll be a mother. And a good one, at that."

"I hope so," Cassie said, harboring her secret.

ↄ

T. G. Payne and his sons rode hard to the cabin on the dirt road, leaving a dusty trail behind. Isaac met them at the barn. They were home earlier than usual.

"Son, I want you to let the horses cool down. Then you know what to do—only this time, make them all look like Glory. They need to shine. Feed them in their stalls and leave them in there tonight. Don't let them out in the lot. My pride's getting the best of me."

"What's happening? Is it time?"

"Yes, son, it's time for us to go. We'll leave early in the morning."

Isaac wasted no time, imploring his father in one last effort.

"Pa, is there any way I can go with you and Jon and Henry?"

Tears filled his deep blue eyes. Tears, yet no inkling of cowardice. No doubt his fourteen-year-old son was a man now, having reached maturity far too soon. Boys just older than Isaac would ride off to war with their fathers. He prayed Isaac would not grow bitter for being left behind and that he wouldn't try something foolish. Rachel needed him.

"Son, I know how much you want to go, but you must stay with your ma and the boys. I've got to have the assurance you're here taking care of things. You're the man, now. I'm counting on you."

"I don't want to stay behind, but I know you need me here. I'll gladly take care of things until you come home. You will come home, won't you?"

Isaac no longer fought the tears that streamed down his youthful face, and the suppressed sounds burst uncontrollably from his throat. He hung his head in the presence of his father.

Thomas went inside, wishing he could answer that question for Isaac. Besides, he couldn't look on his son right now. He was having trouble controlling his own emotions.

Jonathan and Albert Henry had said nothing to their mother. They waited silently for their father to join them in the house; he would handle this. But they were both aware that she knew this was it, and they were more concerned about leaving her behind than about going.

The fire crackled and loose sparks danced on the hearth, cheerful in spite of the gloom that hung over the cabin. The family gathered about the mahogany table and Thomas prayed for the Lord to bless the food and his family. He asked for a night of joy, peace, and laughter around his table, and when he said amen, forced delight and the usual chattering of the boys began to neutralize the otherwise poignant moment.

༄

Thomas followed Rachel about the cabin as she gathered up a few articles of clothing for him and the boys, some rounds of soap, combs, his Bible—she hated to part with his Bible. She had one of her own, but they'd always used his for reading each night. Oh, how she would miss those times. Thomas walked in his wife's footsteps, Samuel clinging to his father's pant leg, as if he knew some singular moment in time was about to turn his little world upside down.

"Rachel—"

Holding onto Samuel, Thomas took his beloved wife in his arms and began to weep.

"How can I do this? After all the talk of war, I'm ready to go and fight, but not to leave you. I never prepared myself for this. There are no words of wisdom to leave with you, for you are the wisest woman I know, and your love and compassion are unsurpassed. Knowing that you love me and are praying for me will keep me going until I come back home to you. But, Rachel, if I should nevermore return, you must remember how much I love you and our boys. You are the joy of my life."

Rachel choked. She tried desperately to suppress the desire to cry out. She clung to him for the longest and then pushed him back, tears flooding her eyes. She swallowed hard and looked at his handsome face, wanting never to forget every line, every little tired wrinkle, the gleam in his eye when she was in his presence. His slightly graying dark brown hair and the little scar on his cheek. Finally she spoke.

"Thomas, we have had a full life these twenty-two years. You've loved your boys and me passionately. I could not have asked for more. God has been gracious to us all, and I will pray every day that you're away. I'll pray for your protection from the enemy, for comfort, for food and a warm campfire. I'll pray those angels will *bear you up in their hands, lest you dash your foot against a stone.* I'll love you forever, Thomas Payne."

It was late when Samuel fell asleep. Thomas took him to bed, embracing the opportunity to tuck him in one last time before he left to fight a war. Jonathan, Isaac, and Joab sat on the floor by the fire talking in whispers. Albert Henry and Cassie said goodnight and climbed the steps to their attic retreat. Rachel dared not think of the conversation they would be having on Henry's last night home, but they had married knowing he would go when the time came. Poor Cassie.

॰

Morning had not yet broken, and Jonathan, Isaac, and Joab lay asleep on the floor in front of a hearth that bordered a dead heap of ashes. Rachel had piled Indian blankets on them during the night. The room was cold and Jonathan jumped up, pulled on his boots and grabbed his coat. It was still dark outside when he brought in a load of firewood from the porch, scooped out the vestiges from the night before, and started a blazing fire before taking the ashes outside.

The wind blew fiercely, chilling him to the core. When he came back in, he went to his parents' room and touched his mother's face with a cold hand. She woke to his touch and put her arms around him. He walked out and she reluctantly awakened Thomas. He held her in his arms, wishing this moment had not come, that war had never been declared, and that he didn't have to leave Rachel and the boys. But it was too late. Life as they had known it in the peaceful valley was coming to a close.

Rachel fed her clan a large farewell breakfast. It could be well into the evening before they would eat again, depending on the activity at the mustering station and the number of men enrolling in the army today. Without a word, Isaac got up from the table, walked in the darkness to the stables, and saddled the four horses for the journey. He and Joab would ride together.

Albert Henry said his last goodbyes to Cassie. Samuel stood on the porch clinging to his father and Jonathan. Rachel made every effort not to cry, but the look on her face rendered Thomas speechless. It was a sad day. The saddest Calhoun County, Mississippi, had ever known. A dark gray cloud hung over the Payne cabin on December 6,1861, and the Mississippi men rode off to fight the war they had both anticipated and dreaded for well over a year.

Rachel, Cassie and Samuel ran behind them, waving the Confederate flag Rachel had sewn, cheering them through tears. They ran the length of the dirt road to the main road, and turned around, slowly walking back to begin the longest years of their lives.

Thomas and the boys turned their horses in the road and pulled back on the reins. The horses snorted and Rachel, Cassie and Samuel turned around. One last look. One last good-bye before the curtain fell. Thomas turned his chestnut mare twice around and tightened the reins again, his horse blowing and snorting in a parade-like performance, entering into the farewell occasion with his master. He waved a final goodbye to Rachel and turned toward the main road, the boys right behind him.

The little diminished family stepped up on the porch of the cabin, the cold, clammy fingers of helplessness tightening around Rachel and Cassie. No longer able to touch the faces of their loved ones, they were left with oppressive lonesomeness with not the slightest promise of remedy. Not now. Not ever. They had said goodbye.

Rachel closed the door. She fell to her knees and laid her head on the floor, moaning, crying aloud, refusing to be comforted. Foreboding clouds hovered, stifling hope. This was it. Thomas was gone. Her first and second-born sons were gone. She had been strong for them, but now—now it was different. The thoughts she had held deep inside for months, the despair that she had squelched for the sake of Thomas and the boys suddenly erupted, and she lay prostrate on the floor, tears falling wet on the Persian rug beneath her body.

Cassie took Samuel to the kitchen and sat him at the table with milk and the teacakes she had made the night before. Made for the men—she had made them and hid them in their knapsacks. She didn't want to cry in Samuel's presence. He wouldn't understand. She choked back the tears, trying to suppress the sobs that were building. Fear and anxiety gripped her and the reality of a war that had just robbed her of a young husband shrouded her like a burial garment, sending her to a place she had never been—an unkind, merciless place. When she could stand it no longer, she lifted Samuel and held him close to her body, burying her face against him to stifle the sounds that were starting to emanate from her throat, and then it came like a flood.

"Oh, Jesus … Jesus help me!" she wailed. "Henry's gone. He's gone, and I may never see him again. What on earth will I do?"

Cassie had depended on Rachel for strength, and now she was on the floor, heartbroken, groaning and sobbing. She had just given three men herself. How could Cassie draw strength from her? Still clinging to Samuel, she lay down beside Rachel, and the three of them, side by side, lamented until the long shadows of evening fell across the cabin.

❧

Samuel and Cassie had long since cried themselves to sleep when Rachel got up from the floor. The fire had gone out and the house was cold, the epitome of loneliness. Frost lay stacked in little rows on the windowsills. Rachel stepped out on the front porch and brought in several logs, started a blazing fire, and lit the lanterns. When the room was warm again, she touched Cassie, only to awaken her to memories. She started to cry as if sleep had been the only interruption for tears.

"Dry those eyes and let's fix a bit of supper. We need strength. Isaac and Joab will be back soon, and they will cheer us. Each day will get a little better."

"Yes. Thank God for the boys!"

Cassie put her arms around her mother-in-law. Her source of strength had rallied, and in a pitiful moment they stood there drawing comfort from each other, both knowing Isaac and Joab would not be the least bit cheerful when they returned.

Chapter 15
Grenada

Before the men reached Calhoun City, the dirt road was crowded with stoic faces. Faces of men and boys riding to war—to fight for the Cause—the Greater Cause. By now, one that had little to do with slavery as far as they were concerned. It was the fight for Southern Independence. The fight to protect what belonged to them. And the fight just to be left alone, as Jeff Davis had begged.

With every man came his sons of fighting age and young riders like Isaac and Joab who would take the horses back home, except for those who would ride with the cavalry. But most of their grandfathers, fathers, and brothers were already fighting this war on foot. Thousands of Mississippians would fight before it was over, and they would all die a thousand deaths before the end came, many never returning to the hills of Mississippi.

It was a strange phenomenon, horses clopping on the hard-packed dirt road, effecting thunderous sounds that could be heard for a country mile. Faithful dogs running alongside their masters, barked fiercely, as if they knew something was inordinately wrong. They soon wearied and turned back, heads drooping, saddened by such great loss.

༄

Grenada, a little low hill town on the south bank of the Yalobusha River, was crowded and noisy, especially around the courthouse. Its residents milled about, proudly hosting the young soldiers mustering in. Confederate flags blew in the cold December wind, a beautiful sight, though sobering. Young women made large pots of coffee and cider on the open fires and served it in tin mugs, their contribution to the war effort.

The Yalobusha, a hundred and sixty-five miles long, flowed into the Yazoo River down the Mississippi to the Gulf of Mexico, and men came for miles on the river to arrive at an enlisting station. Thousands had already joined, and thousands would yet come that way. Fires blazed from one end of the river town to the other, allowing warmth for those who shivered in the cold. When night fell, the fires would serve a dual purpose, lighting the paths for the young soldiers who marshaled.

Before they got into the mustering line, Thomas took Isaac and Joab to the booths where the uniforms were issued so they could visualize their Confederate soldiers fully clothed and geared. He showed them the haversacks, knapsacks, the army issue of underclothing, blankets, the oilcloths, rifles and other weapons, explaining each piece to his boys. They would feel the romance of war, never to know the hideous reality of it. He hoped not anyway. He didn't realize that Isaac was taking it all in, not forgetting the minutest detail, for he would pass this way again—Isaac Payne would pass this way again.

T. G. returned to the muster line to inquire of the aid.

"Can you tell me the duration of our time here in Grenada?"

"Oh, mustering in—and all that goes along with it—usually takes a week."

"And how will we travel from here?"

"You'll go by foot, probably to someplace in Tennessee where you'll take the cars to the next destination. I can't say where or exactly when that will be, sir, but count on miles and miles of marching and some tired, sore feet."

"Thank you," T. G. said, and returned to the boys.

"Isaac, you can tell your mother that we'll be in Grenada about a week. I'll send word where we'll be going. There'll be folks we know here in Grenada who can get the word back to you until we understand how the mail works for the army. You're going to have to depend on the grapevine for a lot of information, so listen to everything at the mill and in town. Keep your mother informed. That'll be the next best thing to being with us."

"Yes, sir," Isaac said, trying to hide his feelings.

"Oh, and Isaac, you have my permission to sit with the old men in the square. They will know a right smart about what's going on, and you know how they love to share their information. But Isaac, please, no snuff dipping."

"Yes, sir."

Isaac forced a grin, but struggled, still torn between his desires and his responsibilities. The boy of fourteen knew his mother needed him, but he had a lust for war like the other youthful sons. Tears filled his eyes as he said goodbye to his father and brothers, at this parting questioning if he would ever see them again. Joab hugged his brothers and clung to his father, then standing with his arms dangling to his sides and his head bent, he cried. His heart was breaking.

The boys mounted and started back home from Grenada riding Glory and Jackson and leading the other two mares, joined by young sons and daughters and friends taking horses back to homesteads across several counties. They turned in the road and pulled back on the reins until the horses reared and snorted, and waving a final good-bye to their father and brothers, they rode out of sight. It was a lonesome, sad ride home, though Isaac and Joab were among proud friends and relatives of the men of the Mississippi Volunteer Army of Ten Thousand.

༄

The cry for volunteers went out for mounted men and foot soldiers. Calhoun County's magnificent Magnolia Guards, men of the Seventeenth Regiment, assembled in their representation of the cavalry, mounted on their steeds or mares. Though Mississippi's men worked, lived and had their being on horseback, those in the infantry dismounted at mustering stations. It was a sad condescension to a man who had not been raised on the plantations where other more substantial means of transportation were afforded, but he affectionately patted his horse, said farewell in the ear of a faithful old friend, and sent him back home by some trusted neighbor or relative.

In the corners of his mind, Isaac had tucked away the idea of joining the Magnolia Guards. He could ride and shoot better than most, and he entertained visions of saber clanking across war-torn Virginia with Mississippi's finest.

The Court House fast filled to overflowing. The place was noisy with the shuffle of nervous feet and stifled voices.

"Men over here, boys at the far end of the room for some instructions," a uniformed aid shouted. His voice thundered across the grand holding room so that all could hear.

"You'll be able to get back with your folks to muster in."

Since April 12, men mustered, women cried, children cowered, tugging at their mothers' skirts, struggling to understand why the sudden change and why they were waving goodbye to all the men in their lives. The call to arms rang out all across the South until every able-bodied man and every boy of fighting age devotedly donned the Confederate uniform.

"I wish, now, I had brought your mother and the boys and Cassie to Grenada to see us off."

"I know, Pa, but don't you think it would have been even harder to send them back home?"

"No doubt about that, but I miss them already. A few more minutes with them would have been splendid."

Henry turned his back on his father, not wanting him to see the tears that were starting. Not being with Cassie was going to take a lot of getting used to. He was hurting more than his father and Jonathan could imagine, and he would make sure they never knew.

෴

Eleven states were now fighting with the Confederate South—those that first seceded and Virginia, North Carolina, Tennessee, and Arkansas. Twenty-three supported the northern army. Border States brought heartache and pain to families, their sons divided in loyalty; some went with the North; some went with the South. When all was said and done, many from both sides would be the losers in this war.

T. G., Jonathan, and Albert Henry waited in line to muster in with over two thousand other men. They stood close, bound to each other by blood and determination, not wanting anything to separate them. They would stay together through this war if T. G. had his way.

Talk in the lines was cheap, most of it hearsay, but they would be remiss if they didn't listen. Some information, regardless of its authenticity, might help. The war had commenced just seven months before when Lincoln outwitted the South, refusing to fire the first shot that would start it. It was that simple. He out-waited and outwitted. Everybody who could read a newspaper understood that. The South fired the first shot; but John Brown committed his atrocities in Kansas and at Harpers Ferry, and Lincoln's scheme to keep himself clean of the first shot all led to the South defending itself. His orders to re-supply the fort but not to bring in additional ammunition ignited the short fuse at Fort Sumter. States seceding—still new to both North and South—the forming of the Confederacy, and the election of Jefferson Davis of Mississippi was on every lip. It all happened so quickly, and all Davis ever wanted was for the South to be left alone. His love for Mississippi could well have outweighed his love for the South, but at this point, he had enough love for them all—all the states that seceded, and those that did not, yet had pledged to align with the South, because they *were* the South. They were flying the new flag of the Confederacy, the stars and the bars, the first unfurled in early March.

The line moved slowly as the men received their issue. Uniforms were scarce at first, and the South's ragtag army started out just that—ragged. But now, eight months later, the army could issue uniforms, at least for a while. They would all proudly wear the Gray.

The young men revved with talk of skirmishes and hard-fought pitched battles. Some the Payne men knew about, some was news to them, still some was gossip. The Border States had suffered indecision. Kentucky tried to force secession in November, an exercise in futility, for Grant now had his claws in Kentucky. Missouri, too, was divided and gave sons to both sides, as did Maryland. In the opening hours of the war, Kentucky, Missouri and Maryland gave way to the Union, and by now, the commanders of the Confederate armies knew what they were up against.

The South had one distinct advantage—its generals. Many of them left the United States Army because they were married to southern women. The North still had the majority of army officers on active duty at the onset of the war, but the South had the most strategic. And the South had maintained its militia, something the North had not done. The North would come to hate those ragged sharpshooters hidden in the hills of Northern Virginia.

The Confederate side had its strong advantages, though they fell far short in the number of men and boys in comparison to the North. They were compelled to fight three times harder. Emotions ran high on both sides following the first shots at Fort Sumter.

By now, early December, the war had picked up steam and the northern army had come alive. Thomas had read every newspaper he could get his hands on since April 12, and now that he and the boys were in the company of many they knew from Calhoun County, they could intelligently compare accounts of the skirmishes that had taken place since the war started.

Some familiar faces stood in line directly across from the Payne men. T. G. shook hands with Duncan Jamison and inquired as to his welfare and that of his family. He had known Duncan for many years. They shared fellowship at the same meetinghouse in the small town of Sarepta.

"Well, here we are, Duncan," T. G. said.

"Yessir."

Looking at Duncan was depressing. His countenance drooped to the floor.

"Guess it was foreseeable we would meet in Grenada to muster in and to consummate the organization of our company. I was hoping it would never come to this, but it has, and we will do our part."

"Yessir."

Duncan found it difficult to have a decent conversation.

"I believe we've got a good company. I know we do. We're all hard-working men who've studied the war from every angle before and after April 12. I'm satisfied. How about you?" T. G. asked, trying to lift his spirits and get him past the homesickness he knew Duncan was already experiencing.

"Yessir. I've known it since our first meeting, and I'm sure proud to be attached to such a fine company of men," he said, perking up a bit.

"How was it with Rachel and the boys when you left, T. G.?"

"About as sad a day as you can imagine. I shudder to think what went on after we left this morning. I just pray we'll see them again. We're only in for sixty days, so that shouldn't be too bad. Why, that's hardly enough time to get some training, that is, if we're going to get any. There's talk we'll be going to some camp in Kentucky for artillery training. What about Jessie and the girls, Duncan? Did you get somebody to stay with them?"

T. G. knew this would prompt a pitiful response, but Duncan needed to face facts, buck up, and start this journey out on a more positive note.

"They just about died when I left, and they'll be staying alone for the time being. I couldn't find a man or boy left that could help much."

"I'll get word back to Isaac to check in on them from time to time. He can cut firewood and feed the animals."

"I'd be much obliged, T. G."

"And Duncan?"

"Yessir, T. G."

"The boys and me—we'll be right beside you all the way. You know that."

"Yessir. Thank you, sir."

Jonathan and Albert Henry stood with their father as he talked to their friends one by one.

"Pa, there's Rev. Eli Davis over there with Mr. Jim Stewart. Do you think he's joined up?" Henry asked.

"As a matter of fact, I think he has, son. I heard he was going to. Hold our place in line, Henry. I want to speak to Eli. Come with me, Jon."

T. G. walked to the next line over and extended his hand.

"Rev. Davis. Jim."

"Why, hello. It's good to see you, T. G., Jonathan. Ah, well—maybe not under these circumstances, though."

"You're right about that. Are you going with us?"

"Yes. I couldn't stay home with all of you boys going off to fight. You're not leaving me behind."

"But Eli, we need you here with our families," said T. G.

"That's what I was just telling him," said Jim Stewart.

"I left young Douglas Banks to preach and take care of the flock while I'm away. However, he may be conscripted before this is over. Then the women will be alone except for the old men, who will help. I figure they'll be just fine, doing a lot of praying for all of us."

"That was a good choice. He's a fine young preacher."

"Well, we may have joined up at a good time, T. G. It's dead of winter, and hopefully Lincoln's men are quartered somewhere until the weather breaks. I hear there's been a fair amount of skirmishing, though."

"I sure hope they don't come out until we get prepared, albeit Jonathan and Henry can handle a rifle, and they'll need very little training. They're both sharpshooters. And Jonathan can wreak havoc with that long bowie knife of his, though he's never tried it out on a Yank. Preacher, can you believe we're talking like this?"

"Well, we've had almost eight months to read the papers and to listen to war stories and learn how the Union soldiers act. I guess we're all revved for a good fight."

"That's true," T. G. said. "We'll see you men later. Looks like we're up next in our line to get papers."

The Reverend waved a hand toward Albert Henry and took his own place in the first line. Jim Stewart went in another direction. Each followed the procedure prescribed for mustering in—alphabetical order by last name.

܀

The Payne men and their friends and relatives in Calhoun County had signed up for just sixty days. Whether they stayed longer depended on how badly they were needed. A line in the sand was drawn when the South finally knew what it had to work with. Just eleven states not including the Border States, and Robert E. Lee, a colonel in the United States Army and Virginia had sided with the South, though Lee was caught in a strait between his own native Virginia and his commission in the United States Army. The Old Dominion, once steadfastly devoted to the Union and the Constitutional Convention, believed the inalienable right of self-government was violated when the President of the United States coerced the Sovereign States who wished to peacefully withdraw from the Union, and they willingly withdrew and took up arms to fight with the Confederacy. Lee had everything to lose by a decision to fly the Confederate Flag, but he could not fight against his own countrymen. Sad was the day when he wrote to his wife and told her to prepare to leave their beautiful and serene home in Arlington. He couldn't even tell her where to go, knowing that the Grim Reaper would, in time, drop his sickle over all parts of Virginia.

What may have had its origin in romance for young men, to begin with, had converted to reality. They left the warmth of a mother's arms to suck in the hot breath of hell. They exchanged a warm feather bed for a cold oilcloth and an army blanket. A comfortable cane bottomed chair for a roughhewn log. And a dipper of clean, fresh water from a cold cistern to that of a muddy, sometimes bloody, pond. And before it was over, they would give two lives to take a shot in the side of the head, to lose a leg, an arm, an eye, a hand. Anything to get them back to the warmth of that mother's arms, to the loving embrace of a wife, to the feather bed, to a drink of cold water from a deep well.

But they had dedicated themselves to follow the great generals through the bloody battles of war, praising God for victory, trusting him in defeat, knowing that he had bigger and better for the South, and a few million Yanks gnawing away at them would not take away their honor and dignity. It would be the Cause that set the country on the right course, with accountability to God alone. The Yanks didn't need God, for they had it all. Troops, money, food, wine, supplies, ammunition. Their factories and foundries pounded out steel and iron for weapons of war. The South just marched from one battle scene to the next, courage and devotion moving them toward the Greater Cause, liberty for their families, their homes, and their Confederate states.

*

The men received their papers, uniforms, and gear; and T. G. motioned for his sons to follow him to the hitching post where they could talk. He never said as much, but he was already feeling less of himself, missing his chestnut mare, and out of habit, he leaned against the hitching rail and addressed his sons.

"You'll have the urge to ask for tougher duty from the onset, anxious to battle the enemy. I'll tell you, boys, if you start out running, you're going to end up exhausted before the race is run. Try to pace yourselves. When they tell us to go to the rear, we go to the rear. It won't be an insult, and we won't be less a man for going. Remember, *to obey is better than sacrifice.* There's as much to do at the rear as on the front line. Opportunity will come all too soon.

"Don't embrace the dread that you might go home without wound or scars. If you get shot or take a saber slash across the face or get part of your head blown off by a Minié ball, it could mean you're done, or it may mean you continue to fight with a disadvantage. If we're too beat up to continue, what good are we?

"We've got to be vigilant, longsuffering, patient, steady, but aggressive. Sounds like a contradiction, but it isn't. Don't take unnecessary chances with your safety. A good soldier doesn't give up his life unnecessarily. Let every stone, every log, every fence, every tangible be your valued defense. Use them to protect yourself. Remember, we're fighting defensively, and we have a great deal to defend."

"Pa, we've heard stories that the Yanks are as timid as rabbits, soft, petty. If the South plays this right, we'll win this war. They say they retreat at the first sight of blood, and the least flesh wound. And you know, we always say, 'I've had worse than that on my eyeball.' The newspapermen say the regiments from Ohio and Maine are pansies. The only thing that could possibly keep us from watching them all tuck tail and run would be the fact that they outnumber us three to one. That's a bit alarming. But remember what they did at Manassas."

The three men laughed at Henry's recollection of the tale of Manassas.

"Truth or not, it makes for invigorating conversation for the wagon drivers to pass down to the soldiers who are energized by it. But don't get your hopes up about that. The Yanks have had seven months to learn what we already know—how to fight like men. We'll see all too soon.

"Boys, we're going to stay together. We'll draw strength from one another and from the Lord. The officers are with us now. Real close, but there'll come a time when they'll pull away. You'll see. And the bond will grow weak. We'll have each other. There's a sense of community now, but that too will fade with time. The romance of war will be gone and reality will set in. We're not conscripts, we're volunteers, patriots. Remember that. Duty called and we answered on our own, and we can expect to find ourselves tolerable lonely at some point in time. I heard stories first hand from my grandpappy. That's what happened in the Revolutionary War. Men got tired of fighting. They kept on, but they commenced to go their own way.

"Your feet are going to get sore and blistered. Throw some things out of your haversacks if you must, but whatever you do, leave in that little tin of bear lard I'm sure your mother sent along. And use it sparingly. It will work wonders on the sore feet. Soon the calluses will form and they won't hurt as bad."

Jonathan had been silent for a long time, taking everything in. It was different. He had been the protector of the home on behalf of his father. He had hovered over his mother and the boys. His position had been one foot propped against the roughhewn wall of their cabin, always watchful. Many things would change, but his philosophy would not. He knew what to do, and he would do it.

"Did they say where we're going first and how we'll get there?" Jonathan asked, breaking his silence.

"Talk is that we'll commence marching to the nearest railway station, they say in about a week. We have to elect officers and get acclimated to camp life and come to understand what it means to get reasonably comfortable in a situation only to be told we'll be packing up and leaving on short notice. It'll be a long hike, but just think about what we're doing. Enjoy the handsome new uniform, and carry your weapon proudly, even if it is your own. Think of your mother and the boys back home, Cassie, everything we hold dear, and the trip will be more tolerable."

"Pa, you need to know, I'll keep my rifle with me at all times, but likely as not I won't use it. I've got my knife and hatchet. That may be all I'll need."

"Son, I won't try to talk you out of that, but if at any time you want to reconsider, don't think it cowardly to change your mind. I've heard a lot of this war is fought from picket lines and from rifle fire distance, and all you can use is a firing weapon. You'll be good with any weapon you take up. I know you. Let's get on over to the campsite. It's getting dark, and I'm a mite tired. Some good food will strengthen and comfort us, and I could drink a whole pot of coffee. I sure hope the boys made it back home."

ও

The campfire was nothing new to the Mississippians, especially Jonathan. It would take no getting used to, for nothing could be as bad as what he had experienced in the Yalobusha wilderness just months before. At least, he couldn't imagine it, but since his father's dissertation, he was already reconsidering the use of a rifle or some kind of firing weapon, remembering how much easier it would have been for him to bring down the old black bear that night in the wilderness.

Grenada's citizens welcomed the Rebel soldiers with open arms, allowing more freedom than common, not wanting to dissuade their youthful exuberance. Freshly enlisted soldiers hung out all over town, young men not yet dry behind the ears left their mothers' skirts to fight this war. The sound of rifles cracking and shouts of *Southern Independence* rang through the cold night air like fireworks on Independence Day. Young manhood's inexperience yelled out the war cries in an aggressive dress rehearsal; for though they had anticipated it, they had never known war. T. G. and the boys sat close to their own campfire listening intently to the chatter of young men about to be heroes, telling war stories about their own heroes.

"With Confederate pickets on the Virginia side of the Potomac, from Alexandria to full view of Washington, there was a line of fortifications."

T. G. whispered, "Listen to this. It'll be good."

The boys grinned, anxious to hear what the young man had to say. He couldn't have been more than sixteen.

"We tested their grit, or lack thereof, at Big Bethel, and from what happened there, the Union best not take us for granted."

He bravely repeated what he had heard more than once.

"Yeah," said his friend, picking up his tale of Manassas. "Well, the Yankees called it Bull Run. I hear tell the Yanks name their battles after rivers mostly. We call ours by the name of the town. Well, anyway, our General Beauregard had been sent to Manassas Junction, a high place over a little stream called Bull Run River, where our soldiers were fortified fast against this elevation. Where General Jackson got his sobriquet, you know. *Stonewall*. The Battle at Manassas."

The young soldier proudly spun the story in terms that could not have been better described by one who was there. It was obvious he had told it time and again. He was talking so fast they could scarcely keep up.

"What's a *sobriquet*?"

This was complicated for some of the young volunteers, who knew little or nothing about what was going on, and they had never heard of a sobriquet.

"Why, it's a nickname."

"Well, go on. What did they nickname him?"

"I told you *Stonewall! Stonewall Jackson!*" the young soldier replied.

"Well, are you goin' to tell us the rest of the story? Why did they call him that?"

"Because, he just sat on that steed, a-ponderin' the battle, like a stone wall. And his defenses were like a …like a stone wall.

"Anyway, the world knows who he is and they saw for sure the bravery of our skinny Confederate sharpshooters. Why, they could hide behind a hickory stick and still not be seen. So they hid in the woods, picking off gunners at their batteries. Both sides put on a show, but the mistakes the Union made gave them excuse to forfeit that first real battle of the war to our side. Our men wore 'em down, repulsing 'em unmercifully. McDowell's army was reduced to what it was—worthless.

"Our General Joseph Johnston had been there all day, and I guess they thought he only had the army that was there when he arrived, but the rest of his men came in a little later a-thunderin' in on the lower fords, and the defeated Union Army took flight on foot. Can't you see it?"

The storyteller motioned high with his hand, waving the Union soldiers eastward in his vivid imagination.

"Yeah, they hightailed it to Washington, and the people in the city took care of 'em. They dried 'em out from the rain, fed 'em, patched up their wounds. I bet they was a sorry lot! They got all babied and pampered by the city folk."

In a singsong voice, the young southern soldier embellished the story, poking fun at the enemy.

"But what was really a hootin' laugh was that all the town folk followed them out to the battle. Have you ever heerd tell of sich a thing? They was a-thinkin' it would be a fine show by the Union and the war would be over. So here all them fancy women and senators and bands a-playin' came out to watch, and our boys sent 'em a-whoopin' and a-hollerin' toward Washington."

The men hovered around the blazing fire, breaking into roaring laughter at the descriptive narratives of war, but mainly from the theatrics of this young Rebel soldier.

☙

That battle, played down by the Union but gloriously touted by the Confederates, happened in mid-July, 1861, and came when fighting men from both sides attempted to prove their skill in battle. They were raw troops, most of them volunteers. But on this one, the North got an eye-opener, consciously recognizing just how strategic those southern gentlemen could be. For the South, it may have been a wild and wonderful force from within, sheer patriotic panic that led to the realization they could muster up a great fight from the depths of themselves. The South had the finest generals, and southern men had learned as boys how to hit their mark. They never missed. They knew how to take quick, accurate shots at small moving targets. Rabbit, squirrel, and quail on the wing. The Confederate sharpshooter could pick off a Union soldier before he could even raise a weapon.

After Manassas the Confederate States had hopes that the war would soon end victoriously for them. But the battle tested the resilience of both sides. The North realized that day they were fighting not only flesh and blood, but also fortitude and emotions of mammoth proportions in the southern men, who fought on principles, but above that— on their own soil. To that degree, the South had the advantage and they fought more fiercely to defend everything they held dear.

Confederate pickets lined the Potomac River on the Virginia side of Manassas Junction, on a plateau. Below it was the Bull Run stream. The story was pretty much as the young Rebel soldier spun it. The South was entrenched and fortified on the plateau, with the capital in view. General Beauregard did some brilliant maneuvering at that battle. He sent for General Joseph E. Johnston and reinforcements. Almost a half dozen commanders rallied with troops, among them Generals Longstreet and Jackson.

The North had reason to be embarrassed because of Big Bethel and some other incidents prior to the battle at Manassas. And, too, Sumter was not yet avenged. The Union, with their insatiable desire to see a correction made for southern rebellion and for the acts of secession they deemed unlawful, had the idea the war would end in this one grand battle, so much so that an elite group of citizens, dressed to the nines, followed the northern army out to watch the war end. Newspapermen, congressmen, and sightseers all turned out in their fine carriages or on foot to cheer the demise of the South.

But they were rudely awakened when men and boys came out of the woods, stealing closer yet to the array of guns and Union soldiers, and they began to pick them off one at a time like crickets on a cornstalk. The Confederate Cavalry charged, magically clanking saber and rattling the enemy. The South fired a volley into the Yanks that bewildered them, and as if this were not mortification enough, the Confederates rushed in and got the guns of the North. First one and then the other side stole the guns. The Union was worn down, totally confused and disorganized. McDowell's army went into full retreat, an exercise he had not ordered. But they were so whipped by the South they began to panic, so repulsed they went running like scared rabbits toward the safety of Washington. The Union soldiers soon learned fighting a war demanded focus and fortitude, for that day they proved they had neither.

∽

The stories went on for hours, enhanced by rifle shots and shouts from the Johnny Rebs, anxious to get to the defense of their side, never dreaming such bloody, dreadful scenes lay ahead of them.

T. G. and the boys spread their three oilcloths and one of the blankets full on the cold ground like a thousand others. By the warmth of their fire, they would sleep side by side, fully clothed in wool uniform, covered with the other two blankets, happy to be together. They would lie down to sleep—only when the noise abated.

"While we're waiting for these passionate young Rebel soldiers to settle down, let's see what your mother packed in our knapsacks. Socks, drawers, lots of soap pieces, baking soda for teeth cleaning, some paper and pencil, and a tin of bear lard, thanks to Jonathan. I told you she would remember the bear lard. And look here, she sent us some name cloths cleverly stitched, each with a pin. She was thinking ahead, wanting her men to be identified in case—well, just in case. Boys, you'll want to pin one of these inside your jacket when you go into battle. As a matter of fact, let's just go ahead and pin one on now. We may never change uniforms, since we only got one. Oh, and a dozen or so of Cassie's cookies. And here in the bottom is … let's see, what have we here? Why it's the Stars and the Bars, the Confederate Flag. It's beautiful."

T. G.'s eyes filled with tears, and at the mention of Cassie's cookies, Albert Henry stepped away from the fire until he could regain his composure. T. G. took out the paper and pencil and wrote his beloved wife of twenty-two years.

Camp Alcorn
Grenada, Mississippi
December 6, 1861

My dearest Rachel,
Muster went hastily for Jonathan, Henry and me. Guess they will be signing up men well into the night before they stop to sleep. At least two thousand converged on Grenada and I'm certain there will be thousands more in the coming days and weeks. Young boys scarcely big enough to leave their mamas' coattails are wearing the uniform.

For the present time the Confederacy's infantry regiments are arranged in ten-company units. The infantry regiment is the war's basic element. Of course, the boys and I are in the infantry. Our uniforms are wool. Thank God we're in the eastern theatre of war for this is what we will wear winter and summer or until they wear out. But for now, tonight, they afford much needed warmth.

The things you sent along will be treasured for as long as they last. When I think of your loving hands, my heart is warmed. That will sustain me for a long time.

We're camped on the outskirts of Grenada knowing not where we will go from here, likely Tennessee, to the nearest railway station where we will take the cars to somewhere in the mountains. And that will end comfort when moving. It will mean marching from then on, going where we're needed on foot. The extra socks will come in handy.

You will remember the governor of Tennessee took the state into the Confederacy back on April 16, and Virginia seceded on the seventeenth. That was great news for us, for it meant Robert E. Lee would fight with the South. General Joseph E. Johnston is in command of the Virginia defenses at the present time. We're Mississippi's Volunteer Army of Ten Thousand, and it is rumored we will make our way to Virginia at some future time.

We'll be heading into battle soon after some infantry training, possibly in Tennessee, until we can connect with the army in Virginia. The boys are filled with vigor and youthful desire. I've had a long talk with them concerning the pace they should allow. I believe they listened and will heed.

I'm glad Cassie is there with you and that we left Isaac to manage the homestead. I hope he will remain with you and not get any wild notions about joining the army. We need him at home at the present time and he's way too young to enlist. Some of the generals will not allow young'uns to come in if they're not at least seventeen. I know Isaac wanted to come along, but the need is just as great there at home. As a matter of fact, we have heard that Grant's men may revisit parts of our country because he has a warped passion as it regards the Mississippi River and a real dislike for our trusted generals.

Rachel, I don't want to scare you, but you need to be prepared for enemy aggression at home. There's been talk of thieving and raping out of the Yanks. Just keep a close watch and don't let the boys stray. Protect what we have there at home. Make sure Isaac is armed or that he can get to his rifle in an instant. You keep that old shotgun high over the mantle and keep it loaded.

I want you to have Isaac call on Jessie Jamison and the girls from time to time. Duncan was not able to get anyone to stay with them. Isaac will need to make sure she has firewood stacked and that the animals have feed sufficient. If not, have Isaac take from our supply and give to her.

I will write as often as possible. We can receive mail. It may take a while, but it will finally catch up with us, or you can send mail by some safe hand coming our way. For now, we have no needs. There will come a time when we'll ask you to make provision but not yet. We have oilcloth and blankets and we will sleep under the stars tonight, the first of many such nights, and sleep will come, for we are tired in body though not in spirit. Yes, we will sleep with the Confederate Flag blowing in the cold December wind right here beside us and made by your loving hands.

Rachel, I want you to pray for the boys and me for we will need it. Until we meet again, I remain thine forever, Thomas Goode Payne

Part Two
Mississippi Volunteer Army of Ten Thousand

Chapter 16
Gentlemen of the South

Seven days at Camp Alcorn in Grenada and thousands of soldiers prepared to leave on foot the following morning, but not before a night of excessive disorganization in the camp. They had elected officers, and that without incident, but preparing food for over two thousand soldiers for a three-day journey was no simple task. Besides, fighting a war, especially in one's own country, did not come with instructions. Everything taking place was new to the enlisted men. By the time they got to bed, they were weary, but some scarcely slept at all. The oilcloths and army blankets were a far cry from the feather bed, and it was taking time to work through the aches and pains that came with sleeping on the cold ground.

☙

Reveille blast came early, and the troops started the long trek across the balance of Mississippi into Tennessee toward Kentucky. Lieutenant Thomas Goode Payne knew little of military tactics, for he and his sons, like so many untold thousands, left the peaceful villages and towns of the Mississippi hill country, never having used their weapons except for hunting and participation with the militia. They had few arms and no artisans to make them much less factories to supply their needs. Whatever they had, the Gray-clad troops took with them. Squirrel rifles, carbines, shotguns, bowie knives, and hatchets.

Young patriotic men and boys shouted war cries as they prepared to march. Blacksmiths struck the anvils that rang out over the hills of Grenada to the valleys below and beyond like cymbals in a marching band, making their contribution to the war effort. Women and children, en bloc, crowded the streets of the hill town, shouting, crying, cheering their heroes as they began the long journey on foot, some saying goodbye for the last time.

Southern rifles cracked, men revved—freshly enlisted men from Mississippi were now ready to move up in defense of the Provisional Government of the Confederate States of America, joining those who were already on the battlefields in one of the three theatres of war.

"Fall in! F'd! M a a r c h!"

The sergeant bellowed orders for the first company of soldiers to march before the commissary and artillery wagons and for the second to bring up the rear. T. G. had told the boys they needn't try to figure out why some were at the rear. They had not seen action, yet, and someone had to follow up the troops and the wagons. Later, it would be those who were either wounded or were needed for something specific, something they could do better than anyone else. It wouldn't take the officers long to know who could be trusted with what duty. Thomas and the boys marched with their newly organized regiment, the Second Mississippi, all Calhoun County men. They were up front.

"We've got miles and miles of wilderness to cross before we get to the cars. A pretty good hike, huh, boys?"

"We'll be wishing for those horses soon," Albert Henry said.

"At least we'll stop for meals. Better enjoy now. Food is plentiful and will be for a while. I hope it'll last until the gardens start coming in and we can get some good farmer's family to share. Until then, it'll be interesting to see what's on the mess wagon."

By noon, the forces had reached the Yalobusha Wilderness, and they stopped. Lieutenant Payne and his two sons performed their duties no questions asked. Jonathan had connected with the cook and sought permission from his captain to get some fish for their noon meal. He slipped down to the river to the familiar spot where he had camped months before. Where he had grieved for his little brother who was dead. Where he mourned leaving his family behind. He thought about his mother and the little boys. Cassie. And about Isaac who longed to be with them. He kicked the burnt wood and his eyes followed the trail where he dragged the dead bear from the fire to the water's edge with the help of Jackson and Glory. Blood rushed to his head as he recalled the details.

Being here brought back that heaviness in his chest, but he must not linger in reminiscence. Duty had called him to another time and another place, and he could ill afford to live in the past.

In no time he had caught twelve large perch. He headed up the hill to the camp, took out his knife, and cleaned the fish. He left the smaller ones whole, cut the rest in filets, and handed them to the mess sergeant.

"Nice catch, Payne!" he said, surprised that Jonathan was back so soon and with a nice string of fish into the deal.

"Yes, sir. I figure this will feed about thirty men in the regiment up front, but there are well over a hundred men up there. Do you think the others will settle for bacon and beans?"

"Aw, there's s' many of 'em, they won't know the difference. Better luck for 'em on the next go-'round, don't you think?"

"Good way to look at it. I'll try to get a deer next time. My pa and Henry will help me dress him out in no time. You can make us a pot of Brunswick stew."

"Oh, man! I like that idea."

Cook took pan after pan of hot biscuits off the burning wood, and the coffee brewed hot over the fire. Just what T. G. wanted. He got a cup and sat on a log beside his sons.

"This is how it will be for sixty days. The war may be over long before then. But if not, this is how it will be. Only, there may be days when there'll be no food, at least not much. I just don't want it to take you by surprise. The lack of food, that is."

"Well, at this rate, if the food doesn't get scarce, we'll be as big as the side of a house," Henry said.

"I don't know if there'll be a chance of that. Looks like we're going to walk it off. I dare not think about how far it is to the rail cars in Tennessee."

The men sat on their logs, scraping the last from the tin plates, enjoying each other's company.

"Pa, does it trouble you that we'll be traveling through states with divided loyalty?" Henry asked.

"Well, since the war started back in the spring, I've thought a lot about it, and frankly I can understand about those in the Border States. Some of the people didn't have much of a choice. I'm just hoping those who favor the North will stay inside their homes until our army gets to Union City."

"Jethro Parker's brother is fighting in the Union Army. Jethro thinks it's evil. It hurts him, but he knows he's doing the right thing, fighting with the South. I wonder what'll happen when the war's over and they both go back home, if they both make it."

"What state, son?"

"Kentucky. He married a couple of years ago and moved up there. Kentucky's so divided. So's Tennessee. East Tennessee went with the North."

"Yes, I heard that. We may not get a very nice reception when we come to that part of Tennessee. And, you know, somehow I feel worse for Jethro's pa than for him and his brother."

Thomas poured himself another cup, sat down on the ground and leaned back on his log, thinking how blessed he was to have two faithful sons sitting right beside him. Otherwise, this war would be in vain. All in vain.

☙

Men of the Mississippi Volunteer Army of Ten Thousand marched for days before they reached Jackson, Tennessee, getting a real sense of the war in a house divided. Youngsters stood to the sides of the dirt roads shouting anti-southern slang, some throwing mud balls at the men in Gray, but the orders were to look straight ahead and keep marching. Their battle was not with the children. Poor judgment on the part of a mother or father or guardian who failed to discipline their young offspring would issue in difficulty enough as they grew to be men themselves. The South must fight by the rules of war with no regrets when it came to a close.

Or—until there came a time when all the rules were laid aside and the human conscience was so seared and warped that the prototype began to change and men were forced to employ animal instincts out of humiliation, hunger and hatred. But for now, they were gentlemen of the South, and they would conduct themselves accordingly.

Chapter 17
Off to Paducah

It was cold. The rain beat brutally on the weary soldiers, but they had no orders to halt, not even for shelter. Tramping ten miles through ankle deep slush, they reached the State Line Station, their new gray wool uniforms heavy with mud and dripping wet. The Payne men made a futile attempt to scrape the mud off their boots and the ankles of their pants.

With so many other exhausted and rain-soaked soldiers, Jonathan, Henry and their father boarded the cars of the New Orleans and Ohio Railroad. They took a seat on the floor and huddled together, so weary they could scarcely hold up their heads. They leaned against the wall of the car, each longing to be home, dry, full, and cozy under a pile of Rachel's quilts, but they dared not verbalize their thoughts. For now, they embraced contentment to be out of the rain and mud and off their blistered feet.

It was dark in the car except for a crack in the slide where they could get a breath of fresh, though cold, air. They were pleased to be in an enclosed car, for some of the men were less fortunate, riding in the open air. The rain stopped for the moment, revealing a moon covered in part by clouds, casting enough light so they could see each other. They hung their wet blankets on the rusted nails on the walls, secured them, and opened the slide a little wider so the night air would flap them about, hoping they would dry out before the train stopped.

There were at least forty men in the car—their friends, fellow soldiers, some of them neighbors from Calhoun County—Rev. Eli Davis, Jim Stewart, Doc Whitaker, Captain Savage, Andrew McAllister, Duncan Jamison, and Jethro Parker, whose brother was somewhere fighting with the Union. A kindred spirit pervaded the place, a strong measure of comfort surrounding them in spite of the pitiful state of affairs. A soldier began to sing, and soon the whole car joined in. *Amazing grace, how sweet the sound that saved a wretch like me; I once was lost, but now am found; was blind, but now I see.* Duncan Jamison moved to the corner where the Payne men sat. T. G. reached out and shook his trembling hand.

And sleep came—sweet, peaceful, longed-for sleep, in clothing that was still soaking wet. Tomorrow would be another day, a chance for a good washing in an icy stream and a blazing fire where they could attempt to dry out their uniforms and blankets.

By morning of the next day, they arrived at Camp Beauregard in Grayson County, Kentucky, discovering far greater trials than wet and muddy uniforms. Army camp life had its unthinkable hardships. The South fought the enemy, but equally as dreadful were the hazards of disease and epidemic—pneumonia, measles, dysentery, and the fever. Soldiers were dying before they could get into battle, some from the diseases, but some from no apparent cause, better described as homesickness. And it was impossible for some of them to escape a deep, dark fear of the unknown.

Thomas sat on the campstool writing to Rachel, the harsh December wind blowing about his cold body. The fire blazed, yet the wind pierced him like a blade of ice. Jonathan was on guard duty and Albert Henry was off and about the camp socializing and learning all he could about events taking place in other parts of the now war-torn South.

Camp Beauregard
Paducah, Kentucky
December 30, 1861

… the boys are always at their posts and never complain of performing any duty that is required of them. We have about twenty-five hundred men in this place, all from Mississippi, and I think that we will be very hard to whip if we encounter a fight while here. Our time is very near out and you may look for me home when that time comes …

Camp Beauregard near Paducah was an infantry training camp for Confederate soldiers from six states but at the present time they were all Mississippians. T. G. and the boys, though they voluntarily enlisted for sixty days, would likely come to the end of that time before they could reach a field of battle. But they would soon learn that duty would usurp, and the desire to muster out and go home when those days were spent may be possible, but only to re-enlist, and more than likely with another company.

But for now, word about the camp was that this war would be quickly fought and won and they would be on their way back home to Mississippi.

Thomas hesitated to get Rachel's hopes up, but at the same time, he wanted her to have as much good news as possible, so he wrote from hearsay passed down as they sat by the evening fires.

Camp Beauregard, Kentucky
January 19, 1862

Dear Rachel,
From what we're hearing—and your knowledge may be more precise than ours—there is talk of a speedy end to this war, that we've had enormous success repulsing the enemy in recent weeks, and that there is renewed hope victory will soon be ours.

I know this sounds far-fetched to you, since we left in early December, 1861, having enlisted for a mere sixty days. We are nearing the end of that time, but who could have known or thought this war would have continued even this long.

The boys are getting on very well, infinitely proud to be serving in the Confederate Army. They will make good soldiers when we finally reach the battlefield. Until we meet again, I remain forever thine, Thomas Goode Payne

Snow lay deep on the hills surrounding Camp Beauregard. Wind out of the north blew cold, as cold a night as Jonathan had endured since they arrived. He tugged at the collar of his uniform, pulling it up around his ears, wrapped his warm woolen scarf twice around his neck, and silently thanked his mother for the wonderful gift she made for him last Christmas. It was gray, thank God. Now a permanent part of his winter uniform.

He shivered at his post and struggled to stay on his feet. His fever raged. He couldn't recollect when he had ever felt like this. Men were dying every day from the fever and pneumonia, and it came on him without warning, not unlike so many others in camp who suffered the same. It was taking two to three weeks for the men to recover, if indeed they recovered. He had to get a grip on this, for they would be leaving in a few days, joining the rest of the Mississippi Volunteer Army of Ten Thousand—somewhere. He didn't want to be left behind and he didn't want to delay his father and Henry.

Guarding training camp was as serious as securing any bivouac area. Enemy soldiers tramped the grounds outside the camp's perimeter. The Confederate cavalry rider was always out there ready to spread the word if the enemy were spotted, for nothing would please the Union generals more than destroying a Confederate training camp. Grant had already dug in on Kentucky and truth be known, Camp Beauregard was in enemy territory.

But the cavalry couldn't be all places at once, and hundreds of Confederate recruits were left vulnerable to attack at all times, especially those who stood guard on the perimeter.

Jonathan did everything in his power to stay alert. He didn't want any slip-ups on his watch. He had to pump himself, and the best way to do that was to recollect the victories that belonged to the South thus far in the war. Up until now, the Federals had enjoyed a few small successes, but in June of 1861, the South put an intense embarrassment on Union General Butler's army. He had audaciously attempted an advance on Big Bethel Church, west of Yorktown, and right behind that, on a hot and muggy Sunday in July, Confederate General Pierre Gustave Toutant Beauregard, that handsome Creole military genius from New Orleans—who directed the bombardment of Fort Sumter that started this war—and his army, by means of a bit of female espionage out of Washington, brilliantly outwitted Union General Irvin McDowell in the Shenandoah Valley. The Battle of Bull Run, Manassas. It was recollection of this battle that had caused the young rebel recruits in Grenada to howl with laughter that night they mustered in. Though his fever raged, Jonathan managed a slight grin as he recalled how the young recruits had revved that first night in Grenada. Now he was doing the same thing, just trying to stay alive to finish his watch.

He held his thoughts for the moment, sensing something, someone, was close. It was not his relief. Not time. He figured he had about half an hour left. Besides, it was on the enemy side of their perimeter. He walked up on the ridge. A horse whinnied and Jonathan took cover in snow-covered bushes behind a tree. He touched his long knife with freezing hands and positioned himself to take care of a Yankee nightrider.

"God, give me strength," Jonathan groaned, knowing he must be alert, but fearful he would pass out at any moment from the fever.

The trees and underbrush were covered with snow. In another time and another place, he would have reveled in its beauty, for he had never seen this much of the white stuff at one time. When he moved, it crunched beneath his feet, revealing his location. Good.

As quick as a flash the Blue-coated rider came within a foot of Jonathan. Forgetting the raging fever and aching body, he reached out and with one arm, pulled the Union soldier from his horse, and with the skill of a Mississippi wilderness boy, he wrangled him to the ground. Jonathan could tell the boy was as scared as a rabbit, but he would take no chances. He pulled his bowie knife from its scabbard on his side. When he did, the Yank tried to overcome him. Jonathan caught him by the arm, whirled him over, put the knife to his neck, and nicked him just enough to draw blood. He was not going to kill him, but he didn't want the Yank to know that. He wanted no conversation with him, either, so he bound and gagged his prisoner and tied him to the tree until his relief could arrive, then led the boy's horse a little deeper inside the perimeter and tied him. There could be more Union soldiers out there, but by this time, Jonathan was ready to collapse from the fever. At long last his relief came.

"Great day, Payne! What's this you got here?" McAllister said.

"Oh, I had a little company while I was waiting for you to arrive. I'll take him to the guardhouse. You be careful tonight. There may be more of his kind out there. I'll get Captain Savage to send you some assistance."

Jonathan knew Andrew McAllister was tough as shoe leather and could take care of himself, but he was compelled to send help back. Some of these Yankee nightriders were big and McAllister was a bit scrawny.

By the time Jonathan got his prisoner to the guardhouse and handed over the horse and weapons he took from the Federal soldier, he was ready to collapse. He staggered, fell, then half-walked, half-crawled to his tent.

"My Lord, son! What's wrong?"

With Henry's help, Thomas picked his son up and carried him inside their tent.

"I'm terribly sick, Pa." he said. "Sore throat, aches, pains—all over. I'm hurting bad. I'm sorry, Pa."

"Son, you don't have to be sorry because you're sick. You just have to get well. Your clothes are damp."

"Not too bad. Mostly snow. Better snow than rain, I'll say. I thought I couldn't make it until my watch was over, but I managed to. I'm freezing."

"Well, strip down and wrap up in this blanket. I'll find you some dry underclothes and a couple of long john shirts, and you must go sit by the fire until I can fix your bed. I'll get you some hot coffee and something from Doc Whitaker. Pull up close to that fire. Henry'll lay your clothes out to dry."

"Yes, sir."

"As soon as you warm yourself real good I want you in that tent under all our blankets. What's this blood on your hands?"

"Don't worry. I didn't kill him. That Yankee buck got too close for comfort and I met him on the ridge with a little surprise. I cut him just a little. Took him to the guardhouse. He had a pretty fine horse. Got that, too. Pa, they're out there, stealing closer to our camp. But the cavalry should be back through here clanking saber pretty soon. Until then, you and Henry need to keep your eyes open and listen for they're a sneaky lot. Henry, you need to get over to Captain Savage's tent and get some help for Andrew McAllister. He doesn't need to be on guard alone tonight. Now, I'm about to die."

Thomas brought hot coals and placed them at the foot of Jonathan's bedding and he and Henry stayed up all night in shifts in case Jonathan took a turn for the worse.

"Henry, there're men all over this great country of ours suffering like Jonathan is tonight. The weather is so bad. We're losing a lot of men to the fever and pneumonia. When I think of what my sons are going through, it grieves me. And Benjamin—why, sometimes I think it's best he went on when he did. He didn't have to ever know about this fight we're in. Thank God."

"Jonathan's going to get well, isn't he?"

Henry didn't like the way his pa was talking.

"I'm going to do all I can to see to it. But, look! He's lying on the cold damp ground. There's no other choice. At least we have three oil cloths beneath his blanket."

In the long, cold nights, Jonathan was delirious with fever, thrashing about, sweat pouring. First hot, then cold, and when he was cold, his body trembled. His father could only mop his brow and keep him as warm as possible. But Doc Whitaker gave him up to the harsh reality of statistics. They had lost many men and boys to this same illness. In this camp. He said Jonathan was bound to die and that T. G. would have to care for him as best he could; all other duty must be suspended until he died or recovered. But as far as T. G. Payne was concerned, death was not an option for Jonathan. He would see to it his son lived to fight this war.

"Pa! Henry! Don't leave me!" Jonathan cried out in his sleep.

"We're right here, son."

In scarcely audible tones, Jonathan muttered, "Mother! Where are you, Mother? Cassie!"

"Pa, he's calling for Ma and Cassie."

"He's delirious, son. Lie down close to your brother. He needs the warmth."

Henry pressed his gray-clad body against his brother's. T. G. stepped outside and stoked the fire in their tent door, piling on more logs. He brought the embers inside the tent and laid them on the dirt at Jonathan's feet then sat down beside him in the small hours before dawn. He laid hands on Jonathan and prayed for his healing and for the long and sleepless night to be over.

In spite of all they could do, Jonathan lay on his blanket for days. Lifeless.

Thirteen days passed, Jonathan only having taken water and broth when his father could find it. And one day, out of the clear blue, he miraculously began to rally.

"It is a strong constitution you've got, son."

Thomas, though he had prayed believing God would heal his son, couldn't help himself and gave in to tears.

"Aw, Pa, don't cry. I think I'm going to make it. I know that's thanks to you and Henry. I couldn't let you down. Have I missed a lot of infantry training? I don't even know what day it is."

"No, there's really not been too much we could do what with all this snow and bitter cold weather. You just concentrate on getting your strength back. Biscuits! You need biscuits and gravy. Lots of them. You know how to use a gun, and you proved yourself heroic the night you took that Yank down. You can take care of yourself. You'll be just fine. Our company had to move up, but don't worry, we'll catch up. We'll travel just as soon as you're able. A lot of new recruits have come in since you fell sick. And Jonathan, so many of our men have died from the fever. None of our close friends, but it's always sad to learn that we've lost another one. The Lord spared your life, and I'm grateful."

"Me, too, Pa. I thank him for that. Do you think you could find me a biscuit now?"

✧

The movement of their own Confederate armies was mysterious to the foot soldier. They only knew what they saw, what was around them, and what they could hear passed down by the wagon masters. The Payne men were fighting a war in the eastern theatre and scarcely knew what was going on in the West. Without their wagon master, Jed McGrew, they would know little.

"Boys, the enemy is getting too close to our home for comfort," T. G. said. "It seems to me we're trying to fight this war in all theatres without enough men. I fear for Rachel and Cassie and the boys. Find out what you can, Henry."

"Yes, sir. Did you talk to Jed McGrew tonight?"

"No. What's he saying?"

"Not enough men. We don't have enough fighting men. He says Albert Sidney Johnston is having a terrible time holding the territory from the Cumberland Gap to the Mississippi River because of it. Says Ulysses S. Grant is ambitious. Aims to gain control of our rivers at all hazards."

Night fell on the camp, and Thomas sat by the fire writing to Rachel when Henry returned with word passed down to Jed by the quartermaster.

"Grant's got control of the lower Tennessee River. Happened on February 6, and now he's headed for Ft. Donnellson on the Cumberland."

"That man's got a one-track mind. Like a boy playing with matches, only he's obsessed with controlling our water. Where's Jonathan?"

"Trying to find out what he can."

T. G. trekked through the maze of tents to the main campfire and filled his tin cup with black coffee. "Just a little sugar, Jed," he said. "I need dessert tonight."

"Come on back up here when your cup's empty, Lieutenant. I'll be sure to have some more for you."

"Much obliged, Jed. You know I will. By the way, is there a reason you didn't move up with the other men in our regiment?"

"Why, as a matter of fact, there is. I'm to wait for you and the boys, and there's another wagon of recovering men that will travel with us to catch up with our company."

"Excellent!" T. G. said, happy they would not have to travel by foot, at least not all the way.

He walked back to the tent where Jonathan sat talking to Henry in whispers.

"Pa, thirteen thousand of our soldiers surrendered. Donnellson is collapsed. That leaves Tennessee, Alabama and Mississippi wide open to attack."

T. G. dropped his head to his knees and wept. "Dear Lord! What are we going to do about Rachel and the children?"

"Now, Pa, don't you worry about Mother. Why, she can handle that old shotgun like a man. And Isaac knows how to use that squirrel rifle," said Albert Henry.

"But they only have those two guns. If they had a couple more, she could teach Joab and Cassie how to shoot. I wish now we had left ours at home. We could've gotten issue weapons."

"She'll think it through, Pa. Don't be worrying. When it comes to protecting her own, she's as cunning and skillful as any woman I've ever known," Jonathan said.

"You're right about that. We've got to stay focused on these Yanks up here, but that's not going to keep me from worrying about them."

"Pa, Captain Savage says Grant has pushed General Johnston back to Corinth. There's no telling what he's planning."

"Just keep your ears open and let me know what's going on, Henry."

❧

The weather broke, Jonathan was fully recovered, and the Payne men were moving up.

Chapter 18
Unsullied Courage

Education hung on by a thread in the South because of the war. Most of the men were on a battlefield, their sons by their sides. Male teachers were scarce as hens' teeth; colleges were temporarily closed and used for hospitals. It was times like these that Rachel was thankful for her own education, for she was able to teach Joab and Isaac with no interruption. Life went on despite the war stories and the constant threat of brutality toward women and children by the Federal soldiers who milled in and out of Calhoun and neighboring counties.

Southern men put everything of ownership on hold while they were away. Farms went to wrack and ruin for lack of masculine effort. They lost their jobs, unable to return in the time allotted, and there was no more pay until they could get back home and take up work again. Harvests were cut to the bone, for there was no money for seed and no feed for the livestock. For the time being everything was sacrificed in exchange for service to the Confederacy.

Sooner or later Rachel and the children would be affected by the threats, but for now, they were holding steady. There was still food in the cellar and meat in the smoke house.

The Payne men had done as much as they possibly could before they left that cold December morning in 1861, and in a letter to Rachel, Thomas had told her without mincing words to protect herself, the children, and their food supply from the Yankees at all hazards.

I want you to try to take care of yourself as much as possible. If the Yankees come into our country, don't let them take what belongs to you. Do what you have to, but protect yourself and the children. They're ruthless and you need to be prepared to take care of yourself the best you can.

War raged with intensity, and news traveled fast that the northern soldiers were not as gentlemanly as those of the South. His words rang in Rachel's ears. Isaac reached for the rifle that rested securely over the mantle board. Then the shotgun. He checked the chamber. Both barrels were loaded.

"Joab, get Sam up to the attic and tell Cassie not to move, and don't come down until I come for you. All of you sit on the bear rug, and be as quiet as possible."

"Yes, Mother."

Rachel could see the fear in her son's eyes.

"Don't be afraid, Joab. Everything's going to be fine. Just do exactly as I said. You'll be helping me."

"Yes, ma'am," he said, lugging Sam to the ladder.

"Up the steps, brother! Hurry! I'm right behind you. You're not falling. I've got you."

Rachel quickly laced her shoes and whispered to Isaac, motioning to her left. "Take the shotgun and go. I'll go the other way. Don't fire unless you absolutely have to."

Rachel and Isaac had seen the men on the ridge and thought it best to try and catch them unawares. As she slipped around the front of the house toward the cellar, she could hear muffled sounds of young men talking and laughing under their breath.

The cabin rested hard against a low hill and the cellar beneath it housed all of their canned fruits and vegetables—their food supply for the winter. The cellar door was propped open with a stone, and three horses were tied to the tree. Just as she thought. Federal soldiers. She could see the insignias on their saddlebags. Behind those, all the meat from the smokehouse. They were thieves. Rachel had heard horror stories of how they raped and pillaged, even hanged one young girl in Panola County. Her heart raced and she was hot with anger. Not because they were stealing food, but because they were violating the rights for which her men were fighting. She paused to collect her wits and to gather all the courage she would need to handle this ordeal and to avoid potential disaster.

By the time she got to the cellar, Isaac had already arrived, having taken the short cut over the hill to reach the entrance. He stood on the bank above the open door. Rachel heard him engage the shotgun, and so did the three Union soldiers. Isaac could take one of them down, but in so doing buckshot would scatter, possibly killing them all and wrecking the cellar. She needed to avoid that at all hazards. Be calm, she told herself ... and God help us.

The Yanks turned swiftly, both arms loaded with loot from the cellar. Isaac stood with gun raised, waiting for his mother's instructions.

"Gently lay the jars on the floor," she said to the Yankee soldiers.

They did as she said, but only to reach for their weapons, and smiling through curled lips, they broke into laughter, scorning the two supposedly illiterate southerners.

"Hold it right there or you'll regret it," Rachel said calmly.

"Spirited little thing, aren't you?"

The soldier mocked Rachel's southern drawl and continued.

"Maybe you haven't heard, but the South is losing this war. We're Federal soldiers and pretty much in control. This stuff will sooner or later belong to us anyway, so we'll just take it on with us now, and there's not a thing you can do about it."

Stirred by his tart mouth and her own southern rebellion, and employing the Union soldier's sarcasm, Rachel lifted the rifle a little higher. Looking down on them, she said without raising her voice, "Maybe you haven't heard, but we're Confederates, and this land belongs to us—this and everything in it, and you'll not leave here today with one thing that belongs to my family. Now drop your guns on the floor."

"You're crazy, woman."

"You'll see who's crazy."

Rachel remained calm.

One of the men turned toward Isaac and Rachel brazenly said, "Raise a gun to my son and consider yourself dead."

"How's that?" The boy laughed.

"It appears that you don't know much about a shotgun. My son doesn't miss, and if he shoots, he's going to get you and your comrades. That's what buckshot does. Don't make me have to clean up this cellar and haul out your remains."

The tall one with the heavy northern accent curled his lip and slowly raised his gun to Isaac's head. Rachel made a swift decision—some poor woman's son in exchange for her own, and he couldn't say she didn't warn him.

"Isaac, get down!" she screamed, as the soldier fired on him.

Isaac obeyed. He fell flat to his stomach, still holding the shotgun on the Federal soldiers, narrowly escaping the shot meant for him, and in the same split second, Rachel skillfully fired into the arm of the trigger-happy Yank, knocking the gun from his hand and shattering jars on the shelf. Squash and peas flew everywhere, stunning the shifty Yanks. Not sure what had just taken place, the other two soldiers dropped their rifles and lifted their hands. They were stunned by the audacity of this southern woman, and were taking no chances that the boy would fire that shotgun into the hole, making mincemeat out of all of them.

Isaac stood to his feet, towering from the hill above the door, still holding the shotgun on the men—the less than honorable soldiers—for they were caught in the act of stealing food from the enemies' women and children while their men were at war, to say nothing of firing on a young boy, not even of conscript age. Surely Lincoln and Grant didn't condone such actions when the rules of war applied to both sides.

"Get out of the cellar," Rachel said. "Quick! Get your wounded friend and get out of there."

The Union soldiers looked silly in sharp Blues covered with peas and squash. It was all Rachel could do to keep from laughing, a little frivolity into the seriousness of the moment. The one who fired the shot was bleeding profusely. She pulled a flour sack from her apron pocket and tossed it to him to tie around his arm, secretly desiring to clean him up, pour in the healing oil, and bind his wound. But he would be fine. The flour sack would suffice for now.

Isaac brought the weapons out of the cellar and laid them down.

"Before you mount, lay the meat on the ground and don't touch your guns. Toss over your ammunition."

"Lady, we'll be back."

"No, you won't be back," Rachel said, with blind faith and raw courage. "You're going to ride out of here and back to your regiment empty handed, and you're going to tell all manner of lies about what you did and what happened to your thieving friend, for this day you've proven the kind of people you are. But what you don't know is, I would have given you food and water if you were hungry. We're generous people, but we're not cowards. Your friend fired on my son, and that didn't pass muster with me. Now, get on out of here, and don't look back. When you think you want to do this again, think about what just took place. Next time—we'll oblige you with buckshot instead of squirrel."

And then Rachel went into lecture mode. Mothering was in order, she thought. She needed to get through to them. Bring them to their knees.

"It's not enough you're killing our men and boys. You've got to prey on the South's women and children. Why, you're children yourself, still wet behind the ears, scarcely big enough to fill up a blue uniform. Shame on you for so many reasons, boys. Now ride and think long and hard about what you've done. We're aware of your reputation for thievery, your lies, and your murderous acts against our women and children. The raping and hanging of young girls. But we don't let it go unnoticed and unpunished.

"And one more thing, when our soldiers ride into your towns, or southern towns for that matter, it is with the understanding from their commanding generals that private property and non-combatants are in no way to be harmed. Our soldiers are commanded not to disturb the home or insult the women, unlike you and your commanders, who march through our towns ravaging, despoiling, and burning. Our men are heroic, dedicated to the cause, and willing to give up their lives for the principles we live by. I know, you look at us and think we have nothing of which to boast, but we do. We have dignity and restraint. That is, until you push us to protect our own. Think on these things, boys. This is war. Now hurry on back to camp. You're going to need to find yourselves some weapons and take care of your wounded friend."

The boys tucked tail and rode hard. Rachel owned they would have trouble sleeping in their camp tonight, but she also knew they would never ride down the Payne road again. They would be too embarrassed.

"Mother, you were amazing!" Isaac said. "I didn't know what to do or say, but there was no need. You did it all. You know, I would rather take a bullet to the head than get that tongue lashing you gave those Yanks. I wish Pa and the boys had been looking on."

"Son, their spirit of patriotism and duty was giving me strength and courage to do what I had to do. Your Pa told me to protect what's ours, and I was just trying to do that. When that boy raised his rifle to your head, I had no choice."

"Well, you did it, Ma! You did it!" Isaac said, picking up the three rifles and the ammunition belt.

"You're going to need to put up some more racks over the mantle board. We're getting quite a collection. However, I hope that's it for a while. But before you do that, would you please start cleaning up the cellar? I'll be back to help you as soon as I check on Cassie and reassure Joab. And Isaac, do something with those sabers. Take them to Cassie's room and hang them high on the wall."

"Yes ma'am," he said. "Mother, did you see the squash and peas all over those boys?"

They both broke into laughter that could be heard clear to the attic.

"What on earth is happening, Joab?"

Cassie was relieved to hear merriment. Her worst fears were Rachel and Isaac in confrontation with the soldiers, visions of something dreadful happening—the two of them dead—she would have to take Joab and Samuel and go live with her parents.

"I don't know, Cassie, but I'm sure glad to hear Mama and Isaac laughing. Especially after that rifle shot we heard."

Rachel went to the steps leading to the attic and called to Cassie. "All is well. Stay there. We'll be up in a few minutes."

When the ordeal was past and the cellar was clean except for a few bloodstains, Rachel bolted all the doors. She and Isaac climbed the steps to the attic.

"Cassie," she said, without giving her details of what just happened—not in front of Joab. "You've got to be sensitive to future possibilities of confrontation with the Union soldiers. This could happen again. I certainly hope not, and if those three Federals take the word back to camp, I don't think it will, but we can't be too careful."

"Oh, Rachel, I'll be more watchful than ever."

"It won't always be this way, children, but we have to protect ourselves as best we can. Your father and brothers are off at war to defend our part of the country, and we would be less than patriots ourselves if we let the Yankees take over what we've worked so hard for. It won't happen as long as I'm breathing."

"You were so brave," Isaac said, the adrenalin still rushing from the experience.

"Isaac, don't let what happened today give you ideas to leave and go to war," she begged. "You can see how much I need you right here at home."

But Isaac was motivated. Stirred to go and fight alongside his father, Jonathan and Henry. He secretly desired to join the cavalry. He could ride and groom a horse as well as any man in the county, and now he even had access to a saber. He would keep his thoughts to himself for the present time.

Rachel took her Confederate flag down from the wall.

"Isaac, come go with me."

"Yes, Ma," he said, grabbing the end of the massive flag.

"Climb up on the cellar hill and hold this end against the wall as high as you can get it. I'll rig something to get the other end up."

The two of them draped the flag across the end of the cabin and nailed it down. It faced the Payne road where all who ventured close could see.

"There," she said. "How better can we say it?"

Cassie, Joab and Samuel applauded.

"Rachel, there's just one thing—what were you and Isaac laughing about?"

"Peas and squash, Cassie. Peas and squash—all over those tart-mouthed Yankees! Nice touch to the uniform!"

Joab howled. They all laughed.

"Now. Let's have a party. We'll celebrate victory at the Payne house."

"Yes ma'am!"

"Oh, and Isaac, tomorrow I want you to take the buckboard and go check on Jessie and the girls. Your father promised Duncan before they left Grenada. I'll send a cake and some other food. I worry that she has no man like you to help while Duncan is gone. Be sure to take some corn for her hogs and chickens. You'll need to spend a couple of hours helping her with chores. Chop plenty of wood and stack it for her. Take Joab if you need him."

"Gladly, Mother. Should I warn her to watch out for those old Yanks?"

"By all means," Rachel said, shivering from the thought. "And stress to her the importance of keeping all those girls close. It would be awful if something happened to one of them. Jessie couldn't bear it.

"I think tomorrow will be a good day to teach Cassie and Joab how to shoot. Before this is over we may need another hand or two, though I hope not."

"Soon as we come back from Mrs. Jamison's," said Isaac.

☙

In time, news of Rachel and Isaac's confrontation with enemy soldiers traveled from the low hills of Mississippi to the campfires of Kentucky, to the ears of the Payne men in the hills of Virginia, but not to Rachel's knowing. In the light of a bivouac fire, Thomas wrote to her, lauding her glorious womanhood, her bravery for protecting all they had there at home. And she was to tell Isaac how proud he was of him for remaining with the family and helping Rachel stay the enemy. They were keeping the home place safe while Thomas and the boys occupied some lonely hill, cheered only by the campfire, defensively waiting for the enemy to make a move.

There was no room to doubt the spirit of patriotism and support of the South and its favorite sons, not from the Payne house, at least. They made merry until sundown, rejoicing in their strong effort to relieve the oppression that had been heaped upon them by the Union soldiers.

Before long, the Flag of the Confederacy was flying over every home in the valley and in the towns and villages from the Yalobusha Wilderness to the county seats. Southerners were no longer joined to a hateful Union, and a cry went up across the Southland that urged the women and children to protect themselves from the dreaded enemy.

☙

Isaac, still romanticizing war, pictured Richmond the day Virginia announced allegiance to the South. His mother had let him read the account in the newspaper. History unfolded before the eyes of its citizens, every event embellished in circus-like ambiance. Oh, how he would love to have been there. The streets were filled with laughter and shouting, as all day and well into the night the crowds celebrated. Reminiscent of Grenada the day he said good-bye to his father and brothers. Blockades were set up as far as the eye could see, torches lighting the path of devotion. Fireworks burst in the night sky and music played. Children, old men, and every Confederate woman in Richmond waved their flags. Another state had joined the Confederacy. That all-important state. High hopes for the South rang from the lips of the people of the Commonwealth, their cheers wooing southern soldiers toward Baltimore. Toward Washington. Thank God, the Old Dominion was in!

He mulled over the things his mother had taught him about the flourishing city of Richmond before the bombardment of Ft. Sumter and the start of the war. They had an abundance of food. Her people were intellectual and refined. They enjoyed the rich life a majority of the South could only hope for. Like his grandparents in Natchez. That is, before the war. Likely those beautiful and serene city streets would be turned into a battery for artillery, infantrymen poised behind manmade breastworks to defend the streets and the river, just like all the other major southern cities. In time, that is.

The incident with the Union soldiers had jarred every fighting bone in Isaac's body. He knew that day it happened he would not be able to wait until he was seventeen to join the Confederate Army. His mind was wandering, racing, planning, plotting, conniving, moving toward Richmond. How could he do this and maintain a right relationship with his mother who needed him and his father who depended on him? His best judgment was that the army needed him more.

When he sat with the old men in the square and listened to talk of General Stonewall Jackson's exploits, he was revved to the point of no return.

He was going to war.

Isaac would fight with the Confederate States of America.

Chapter 19
Cause to Celebrate

Cassie lay across her bed in the beloved attic room, pining for Albert Henry and thinking about their short-lived marriage before he left to fight a war she knew little about. Tears rolled down her cheeks as she stroked her stomach. She had to tell Rachel. The baby was growing inside her, and before long it would be impossible to hide. She had fought nausea for three months, eating little, and now she was very thin. It would be hard to hide a pregnancy on such a small frame. She missed Henry. She missed his gentleness, his loving spirit, his strong arms about her, his warmth in the night. Now her bed was cold, and she literally ached for his presence. He should be at home to share this part of their lives, but as it was, he didn't even know about the baby. She could only hope her loneliness for Henry would be quelled by the attention she would give her baby when it arrived.

Rachel knew a lot about the war, about the politics of it, and the Cause—even the Greater Cause, and she had helped Cassie understand some of the reasoning behind the sacrifice. Cassie could trust her. She was painfully honest. And when Rachel ran out of the house toward the Secret Grove, Cassie knew she was at her wit's end. But what strength the woman had in prevailing prayer!

ဢ

She would not ask, but Rachel knew Cassie would reveal her pent-up secret when she was ready. It had been four months since the men left, and if Cassie were going to have a baby, she would soon be showing.

Rachel taught her how to shoot after the Union soldier episode. How to best handle a gun to take care of herself. Cassie learned quickly. She told her about the young girl who was raped and hanged by some Union soldiers over in Panola County, not wanting to frighten her, but Rachel was determined her family would not be caught off guard. Cassie especially needed to be watchful, for she was young and beautiful. They had all ridden to Sarepta in the wagon, more times than once, and it was common knowledge that all the Payne men were at war except Isaac. Rachel could not express too strongly the need for all of them to stay alert to the possibilities of danger. There were Union soldiers all over the place.

"Rachel, I have something to tell you."

"What's on your mind, Cassie?"

"I was sure you would have suspected by now, but I guess I've done a good job of hiding it."

"And just what are you hiding?"

Rachel would allow her the privilege of announcing her own news.

"I'm going to have a baby. I've known since right before Albert Henry left. I'm over four months along."

"Oh, Cassie, that's wonderful. Does Henry know? Have you told him in a letter?"

"No. I didn't know whether to or not. I was dying to. Before he left even. But I wasn't yet sure, and I didn't want him to worry, leaving to fight, and all. But I know I have to tell him sooner or later. I should have already done it. How can I tell him, Rachel?"

"Well, I suppose it will have to be done in a letter since that's the only means of communication with the soldiers."

"I was thinking about taking the train to Virginia and telling him in person. Is that insane?"

"Oh, Cassie, I don't know—"

"I know what you're going to say. Traveling that far in my condition. I'd have to go by carriage to the nearest train station."

"But most of the southern passenger trains have been turned into transports for soldiers, and you know how determined Grant is to destroy our tracks and our bridges. I would worry so. And Henry is on the battlefield. Why, they could get orders to move up before you arrived. And what would you do if you encountered fighting on the way? I just don't know if it's going to be safe enough for you to travel to Virginia."

"I've thought about the danger, and you're probably right. I don't need to get stuck somewhere unable to get back."

"Why don't we write a letter to Thomas? He might be able to get Henry some leave time when the baby comes. Or maybe even before. The men should have been home by now; their time is up, you know. But that doesn't necessarily mean they will come home."

"Yes, a dreadful thought."

"The South fights this war with so few men. I fear they will keep the ones they have and grant no mustering out privileges. The Army of the South has a vested ownership in our men now. Just give it some more thought, and you'll come to a decision. Whatever you decide, I'll abide and give you my blessings. In the meantime, let's celebrate with afternoon tea. I'll bake some cookies. We're going to have a baby!"

"Oh, thank you, Rachel. I knew you would understand."

"Well, this is going to be my first grandchild, and I'm happy beyond words."

"I want to go to Houston in the next few days and tell my parents face to face. I need to see them anyway. It's been months."

"Of course. Isaac can take you on the buckboard, or you can ride Glory—she's gentler—and Isaac can ride Jackson. Whatever you would like."

"Since it's only about twenty miles from Calhoun City, I think we should take the buckboard. If we go on Saturday, Isaac can stay overnight, go to church with us on Sunday, and bring the buckboard home in the afternoon. I'll have my brother bring me home in a few days. You'll be alone Rachel. Can you manage without Isaac until he returns?"

"Of course. Joab can ride to Sarepta if we have an emergency. How about this coming Saturday when Isaac gets home from the mill?"

"Yes, I'll be ready."

"I'll talk to Isaac," Rachel said. "He'll be glad to do something different. Maybe it will get his mind off this war."

Chapter 20
The Hornets' Nest

Albert Henry and his father settled down around a small campfire away from the crowd of soldiers in their brigade. Not that they didn't want their company, but they liked to be alone at night. They had things to talk about. Jonathan would be back eventually, and he would sit with them. He didn't talk a lot, but when they probed, he opened up, sharing radical information, some of it unknown even to the generals. His perception of the war and his interpretation of events that were taking place and those that had already occurred were uncanny. What they didn't know was that he was a battle hardened soldier of life's idiosyncratic wars fought long and hard before he left home on December 6 last year. Those experiences had brought him face to face with reality and with danger—enough to radically change him.

The nights were cold and still, though winter had ended. The spring rains swelled the streams, affording a place to bathe and wash clothes in water not so icy cold. The gray Confederate uniforms issued in December, worn day after endless day, had frayed and started to ravel. It hurt to walk, for shoe leather had worn to a thin layer. Blistering, bleeding, oozing sores finally healed over and formed calluses, but it was still difficult to walk. Rachel had sent extra woolen socks that helped, but constant marching through the briars and brambles, over rugged mountain terrain, and through the elements had taken a toll not only on their shoes and clothing, but on their psyche. Snow, sleet, and slush had worn the men to a frazzle, and they were glad winter was over and gone for another season.

Paper was scarce in the camp, and the Payne men wrote on whatever scraps they could find. Letters back to some of the soldiers came in envelopes made of old wallpaper pulled in pieces and turned inside out—a red rose, a bouquet of violets. Quite romantic in retrospect. The love of young wives and family members waxed warm and free, unlike the fetters of war that bound their young soldiers. And to suggest that these fair-haired men of the South joined the army for wealth and fame was preposterous. Their draw consisted of eleven dollars a month to begin. Those of low officer rank reached sixteen dollars, scarcely enough to purchase clothes and shoes after they sent the first fruits to their wives and families.

༄

T. G. reached for his tin cup and poured it full of strong coffee. He and the boys had learned to live on the black liquid and biscuits and a piece of side meat occasionally. By mid-summer the corn would be ripe on the stalks, and food would be plentiful, but for now the blackberries and raspberries grew wild along the roadsides. A tin plate of berries sprinkled with sugar and some hot coffee effectively took the place of cobbler.

April 10, 1862

My dearest Rachel,
'Twas a beautiful blackberry winter's day, the fruit luscious and satisfying. The dogwoods and redbuds bloom in full color, and cherry and plum trees droop, laden with pink blossoms. It's cold yet, and the extra pair of woolen socks you sent give padding and warmth to the feet.
We walk endless miles each day, though moving from place to place is slow. We have to stay with our company, ready to boost the commissary wagons from valley to hill, and it will get more difficult as we get deeper into the mountains.
The country is beautiful, untouched by human hand, at least in the distance. Take the hills of home and magnify them a hundred times over and get a vision of the foothills of the Shenandoah. I wish these were different times and circumstances and that you were with me to enjoy the wonders the Lord has wrought in this great land. I'm so thankful to have been born in the South and proud to be seeing parts I've never seen before.
We have a fair amount of food for the time being—mostly what can be made from flour, meal, lard, sugar and salt. We have side meat and coffee. There's nothing better in the wilderness than the smell of fresh coffee brewing over an open fire.
Soldiers sit around the campfires, smoking their pipes and eking out the tiniest measure of contentment. Stories told, songs sung. Soon taps will sound and we'll take our oilcloth and blankets, find a comfortable place, and the three of us will sleep side by side. Sweet, blessed rest.

Rachel, as you know, we should have been out of the army and home by now, but it looks like that's not going to happen. In time, we will likely organize another company. I'll let you know when a decision has been made, but we must honor our commitment, and somehow I know you understand.

Give my love to the boys and Cassie, and know that you, my dear wife, are loved beyond measure. Yours until death, Thomas Goode Payne

"Pa, I was talking to Jed McGrew today, and he said one of the night riders brought word that General Lee has been made commander over the entire Army of Northern Virginia. General Joseph Johnston was wounded at Seven Pines. I saw him today, sitting on that steed."

"You saw Joseph Johnston?"

"No, Pa. General Lee. On the hill. Talking to Longstreet."

"You did, son? What'd he look like?"

"Oh, he was big compared to me."

"Well, Henry, that's not saying much."

"A graying beard covered his face. His eyes were shining, but when he rode down the hill, I could see he had that far-off look about him. I wonder if he was thinking about his own sons. I heard two of them, George and William, are in his army somewhere. They may be close by. I don't know. Or maybe he was thinking about his wife. She's sick. Did you know she was Martha Washington's great granddaughter? Her name's Mary."

"No, I didn't know any of that."

War had deprived his sons. Robbed Henry of golden moments with Cassie. His devotion had changed, circumstances influencing him. Resentment began building as his son continued talking about the great general, and with voice shaking, trying to avoid crying aloud, he said, "Henry, I never wanted you to be here like this. Your mama needs you back home. She's got the boys to raise by herself. What if I don't make it back? And there's Cassie. She's young and she needs you."

Thomas had let his emotions get the best of him, and he had let down his guard concerning Henry. He had prayed that Henry would harden so he wouldn't miss his wife. For the first time, he realized his son was fine, committed to the Confederacy, but he was not so sure about himself. The conversation continued.

"Don't talk like that, now, Pa. Sometimes I wonder why we're fighting this war myself. But I have to tell you, when I see General Lee, I know I'll be fighting until the last Union soldier lies face down in the mud, or until my blood runs to the Potomac. I love that man and what he's done for the Confederacy."

"So do I, son. He understands the Greater Cause better than all of us, for Virginia is ravaged. And those Union soldiers don't have a notion what it's like, for it's not their soil we're fighting on and their land getting raped and pillaged. If not to protect what's ours, I would have never left your mother and the boys or the hills of home. I know we're not there yet, but our tired bodies are moving toward Washington any way you look at it, and that's a far cry from the real South."

"I know, Pa."

Albert Henry respectfully responded to his father, not conscious of the pain that had suddenly laid hold on him, heart and soul, and he continued.

"When I get back home, Cassie and I are going to have a son. His name will be Lee. Robert E. Lee Payne. And I'm going to teach my boy to be just like him—to sit up straight and tall in the saddle and ride like he's going to battle, all the time praying he'll never have to go. I want him to be calm and peaceful in spite of everything that's going on around him just like the General."

And Thomas continued down his own candid path.

"Son, listen here. Before this war started, I used to go to the square in Sarepta and talk to the men. We talked about a lot of things, but when this war started to brew, I knew I didn't want to leave your mother. I didn't want to fight and I sure didn't want you boys to fight. Don't believe in killing folks. You know that. Even if they are the enemy. Why, time was they weren't the enemy. We were all one big country. Our grandpappies fought the Revolutionary War together so we could have our freedoms. Now we have to fight for our second independence. Doesn't make sense to me. Sometimes I think it will never end—this fight for freedom."

"Did you know the General's Pa's name was Light-Horse Harry? He fought in the Revolutionary War. He was a cavalry commander."

"How'd you know that, Henry?"

"I listen to every word about him."

As the conversation continued, Thomas regained his composure and the anger abated. He knew some things about the general, and he would share them now.

"What I do know is that he had to make up his own mind to leave the Union and fight with his kin. He had a good commission in the United States Army and he resigned it, hoping he'd never have to take his sword from its sheath, but that's not the way it happened."

What they could not have known was how the war was affecting General Lee's family. By December of 1861, when the Payne men were just getting into the war, the Federals had desecrated Lee's Virginia home. In a letter to his wife, Mary, he wrote that he feared it was by now uninhabitable. The enemy had likely taken it over entirely. He expressed fear that the Mount Vernon relics were gone; but her gracious southern gentle husband told her they could never take away the sacred memories of the place.

He had a desire to purchase Stratford where he was born, and concerning it, he had said ... *it is a poor place, but we could make enough cornbread and bacon for our support, and the girls could weave us clothes. You must not build your hopes on peace on account of the United States going to war with England. The rulers are not entirely mad, and if they find England is in earnest, and that war or a restitution of the captives must be the consequences, they will adopt the latter. We must make up our minds to fight our battles and win our independence alone. No one will help us.*

And he wrote to his daughter on Christmas Day of that same year ... *your old home, if not destroyed by our enemies, has been so desecrated that I cannot bear to think of it. I should have preferred it to have been wiped from the face of the earth, its beautiful hill sunk, and its sacred trees buried, rather than to have been degraded by the presence of those who revved in the ill they do for their own selfish purposes. You see what a poor sinner I am, and how unworthy to possess what was given me; for that reason it has been taken away. I pray for a better spirit, and that the hearts of our enemies may be changed.*

☙

"Henry, do you know where Jonathan is? I can't keep up with that boy. He slips away at the first chance. Barksdale's got him scouting somewhere out there. I think he's the only one in our regiment that scouts on foot. He won't use a gun unless he's on picket, but thank God he carries it. That boy fights like an Indian. I think he played with those boys on the Choctaw Nation too much when he was growing up, something for which I'll forever be grateful. I'll tell you one thing, those Yanks don't want to face off with him and that bowie knife. He can brandish the blade before they'd have time to draw a gun."

"I haven't seen him for a few hours. You're not worrying over him, are you?"

"I always worry about both of you. It's just in me, I guess. I've got to make sure you get back to the hills of home somehow. But for now, we have to spend a few nights here in these Virginia hills until we can get on up to Richmond or wherever it is we're headed. I'm going to get a little shuteye before this fire goes down. You watch, Henry, but stay close. I love you, son."

"And I love you, Papa."

With those sentiments expressed, T. G.'s emotions were stirred again. He was gripped by homesickness to an indescribable degree. He turned his back on his son and went inside the tent.

His father had said stay close, Henry mused. There was nothing more comforting than a faithful father who wanted his sons to stay close. Henry added some logs to the fire, stoked it good to keep his father warm, and paced back and forth in front of their tent, mainly to stay awake until Jonathan returned. It was not long before he saw him making his way through the rows of tents and around the campfires that burned for warmth and light, and as Jonathan approached, Albert Henry could tell from the look on his face the news was not good.

"Henry, Shiloh fell on April 6."

"No, God no! That's too close to home!"

"I know. Pa's going to have a fit."

"What happened? Did you get the story?"

Jonathan told it as he heard it, talking low and fast.

"Earlier this month, the Yanks were near the Mississippi border. General Albert Sidney Johnston's army had strengthened forces to counterattack, and then, the way I understand it, the hot breath of hell blew unforgettably on both sides. Jed described it as one of the fiercest battles fought so far. Henry, a hundred thousand men fought at Shiloh. That's hard for me to imagine. Grant lost over thirteen thousand men and Johnston, over ten thousand. And listen, Henry, General Johnston took a bullet and bled to death right on the battlefield."

"My Lord, my Lord!" Henry said, shaking his head in disbelief. "What a loss for the Rebs!"

☙

The country would soon realize that while the South claimed victory for one battle and the North another, there were no winners in this war. Both sides were losing good men in every skirmish, every battle, and somewhere out there, whether in Mississippi or Massachusetts, a mother was mourning the death of her young son; some wife, a husband; some son, a father. And by this time, there was no end in sight.

The *Hornets' Nest* was stirred at Shiloh and the blood filled the pond that day. It was not long before the North had control of Missouri and northern Arkansas. And Grant was still after the South's waterways. New Orleans was seized, closing the Mississippi River to southern commerce, Grant's best hopes becoming reality. The Confederacy was slowly deprived of manufacturing capacity—and men. They scrapped for food, clothing, and ammunition. Slowly but surely, they became the ragtags.

Chapter 21
I Shall Wish for the Same

Jonathan joined his father in the tent. He would not wake him tonight with the horrendous news of Shiloh. Clearly he needed the sleep. He lay on his back, and Jonathan could see where tears had dried on his face. He looked old. Jonathan couldn't stand to see his father this way, and the news about Shiloh would only make matters worse. He pulled the blanket over his weary father and lay down beside him.

Henry sat on a campstool close to the fire.

April 12, 1862

Dear Cassie,

I hold fast the lonely moments at the end of each day to write you. The three of us are fine. Pa and Jonathan are asleep in the tent, and I remain outside with my thoughts of you. The nights are still cold but not bitter as in the past. Flowers bloom, assuring us spring is in store, and it gives us pleasure to look forward to fresh food from the gardens when the time comes, for southern farmers' wives will share. Oh, mind you, the biscuits and bacon are plenty sufficient, but they tend to make a man heavy. If it were not for the marching, especially across these mountains, I fear I would be extremely large.

Cassie, I dream of you at night and long for you in my waking hours. One day this war will be over and I will come home. It is then that we will have a son and he will be named Robert E. Lee Payne. I trust that will suit you as well as it does me.

I close with the last thoughts of the day being only of you and with my best love I remain ever thine, Albert Henry Payne

Cassie clutched the letter from Henry close to her heart. He had said he wanted a baby. A son. As soon as she arrived at her parents, she would sit down and write him. He must know about this baby. Now, she hoped it was a boy. Robert E. Lee Payne.

On Saturday, she kissed Rachel goodbye. Isaac padded the wooden seat with extra Indian blankets for her comfort in riding the near thirty miles, and she climbed onto the buckboard with his help. Her young brother-in-law put her baggage and his own knapsack in the back directly under the seat.

"Take good care of Cassie, and stop often for her to rest and walk around a bit. Watch carefully, for Union soldiers are out there. Did you get yourself and Cassie a rifle? I can't stress enough the importance of vigilance since the Federals took Shiloh. They're everywhere now. Please promise you will be careful."

"Yes, Mother, I'll watch, and I've got two of those old Yank rifles."

"We will look for you to return tomorrow afternoon, Isaac. Please come before dark."

He simply waved a hand at his mother, and they made their way slowly down the Payne road to the main dirt road where they picked up speed.

The two young people arrived with no incidents at the home of Cassie's parents in Houston. She greeted them with the good news that she and Henry would soon have a baby. Their first grandchild. Happy over the announcement and even more so to see their daughter, the Walkers prepared a fine supper for the family and Cassie retired early, exhausted from the travel and excitement of seeing her family again.

༄

It was the same as the day she left, the gauzy white curtains blowing slightly in the gentle breeze of an April evening. The old wood plank walls mudded and sanded were covered with wallpaper years before—wallpaper with roses. She remembered counting the roses with her sisters by the light of a low lantern on nights too warm to sleep. Familiarity brought a tear. Her youth had been grace-filled, God's providence granting her godly parents she revered, sisters she adored, and a brother who was the coup de grâce. Icing on the cake.

She sat at her writing table in the old room she had shared with them in times past and wrote to her husband.

The Mississippi Boys

Houston, Mississippi
April 20, 1862

Dear Albert Henry,

Your letter came quickly by safe hand, and I treasure every word. My dear husband, we may not be able to wait until this war is over to have that baby boy or girl, whichever, it matters not with me, but since you so want this to be a son, then I shall wish for the same. Our baby should arrive sometime in early fall. I am exceedingly happy, and I have a feeling you are the same.

I traveled to Houston today to spend some time with my parents and to tell them our joyous news. Isaac brought me on the buckboard, and I am none the worse for travel, though a bit tired as I write. Isaac will take the buckboard back to Sarepta in the morning. I'll stay a few days and Jesse will take me home on my father's wagon.

My dear husband, I wanted to tell you this in person, and I pondered taking the cars to where you are, but my better judgment and that of Rachel intervened. The mail will surely suffice.

My days are full but lonely for you. I miss your tender voice and sweet embrace. My bed is cold and empty at night without you beside me, and I weep at the thought that you may be deprived of the barest necessity. I know you are strong. You are brave, truly a magnificent Confederate Soldier, and my love is stronger still than the day we said our vows together. Do not find cause to worry about me. The morning sickness is past, and I am wonderfully healthy. I remain encouraged and happy that we can each spend our lonely moments thinking about the baby and how utterly splendid it will be when he arrives.

Give my regards to Jonathan and your father, and know that I am forever your loving wife, Cassie Walker Payne.

Chapter 22
Stand in the Gap

The buckboard held fast Isaac's secret. The night before he had filled his own saddlebags with the necessities of travel and secured his saddle and bedroll under the seat on the buckboard, covering it with an Indian blanket to conceal his intentions from Rachel; and Cassie was so preoccupied with thoughts of Henry and their baby that she was numb to all else, including Isaac and his scheme. It had been months since his father and brothers joined the Confederate Army, and he would be fifteen in a few days. Others had gone at that age. He was going. And he wasn't going to let anything keep him from it.

Sometimes the best-laid plan is tremendously flawed, and Isaac's was no exception. He had not completely thought it through, but at this point, he would not allow himself to think that it might not fulfill his desires. He rose early, long before there was a stir in the Walker household, and dressed. He laid the note he had written Cassie the night before on the hall table and quietly slipped out to the buckboard. He pulled the gear from beneath the seat and in the darkness saddled Glory. Returning to the buckboard, he grabbed the saddlebags and flung them over his shoulder then reached for his rifle and the saber he had hidden under the seat. He slipped the saber into its sheath and mounted. Leaving the wagon behind, he rode alone in the darkest hour before dawn.

He felt gallant—gallant, but guilty, though compelled to follow through with his intentions, and he needed the distraction of this trip with Cassie to front his plan. His friends awaited him on the outskirts of Sarepta, and together they would ride toward Tennessee. The journalists had done a decent job of charting the route of General Joseph Johnston and the campaigns of the Virginia forces, and he had pieced together a map of sorts from the newspapers. He had a pretty good idea where his father and brothers were from their letters to his mother, and he would find them if he could get past Shiloh and Pittsburg Landing.

☙

Cassie awoke to bacon frying and the aroma of warm sorghum molasses wafting through the house. She was hungry and the smell of coffee brewing did nothing to curb her appetite. Pulling her robe around her cotton nightgown, she made her way to the kitchen of the house where she grew up. Her mother stood over the stove. A splendid sight.

"Mother," she said, "I have longed to be here, and I've missed you terribly."

"And, oh, I've missed you, Cassie. I'm so glad you're finally here."

Cassie was close with her family. Always. It was a great loss to them when she made the decision to go and live with the Paynes and to stay when Henry left. Her father, a successful blacksmith in Houston, had met with a terrible accident that mangled his right leg just five years earlier. A piece of steel flew from the anvil and penetrated his leg, shattering bone and tearing muscle. When it healed, he was left with a limp and unable to get with a company of the Confederate Army that would have him. He had to stay behind when all of his friends, one by one, left to fight in the war. But the army needed his services as a civilian blacksmith. He provided for his family while enabling the Confederate soldiers.

"I thought you would return when Albert Henry left, Cassie."

"Mother, I just couldn't leave Rachel. She has those little boys, and she needs me. You're blessed with all the girls to help here at home, and for the time being, I need to stay with Rachel."

"I know, dear, and I don't blame you, but promise to visit often, especially after the baby arrives. We must know our grandchild."

"You know I will. If our baby's a boy, it looks like he'll have Papa's name, though quite frankly, only because his name is "Robert." Henry says he must be named after the greatest general of all time."

"I know exactly who you're talking about, Cassie, and I think that will be just fine—to be expected, but I have a feeling there'll be plenty of those little namesakes toddling around before this war is over. He's a fine gentleman, that Robert E. Lee."

"Mother, where did Isaac sleep? He's usually up by now. I should call him."

"Oh … I thought you knew. He's gone. I heard him leave out real early this morning, long before daybreak. But he didn't take the buckboard. Rode out on his horse. Must've had a saddle on that wagon."

"Why, I didn't know that was his plan. I told him Jesse would bring me home in a few days. I was expecting him to take the buckboard back, but not until later today."

"Then I don't know. Seems strange to me."

"Me, too. I'll have to think this through. What if Rachel needs the buckboard before I go back? He just shouldn't have left without telling me. I don't understand his intentions. There's something suspicious about this."

Cassie's three younger sisters, Mandy, Priscilla, and Camille joined them in the kitchen, and laughter filled the family's gathering room. Jesse came in through the front porch after stacking the wood he brought up for his mother.

"What's all the girl noise?" he said, flinging his arms around his older sister. He smelled of balsam wood, a fragrance Cassie loved.

"Some things never change, Jess. We were just catching up on all the gossip of Houston."

"Well, here's s'more, I s'pose," he said, handing Cassie the note from Isaac. "And excuse me for a few more minutes. I have to get that other load of wood to the back porch for Mother."

"What's this?"

"Danged if I know. I saw it sittin' on the hall table when I came downstairs this mornin', plain as day with your name on it, Cassie. I stuffed it in my pocket when I went out to get the wood, afraid I'd forget to tell you and that you might not see it."

"Excuse me," Cassie said to her family, and she went to the back porch to read the note Isaac had left.

My dear Cassie,

By the time you read this, I will be far and away, so there will be no need for you to hasten home to tell Ma I'm gone. Yes, I'm gone. Gone to find Pa and my brothers somewhere in the mountains of Virginia. I know this sounds far-fetched and in a sense, without thought or care for my mother and the little boys. But I'm a man, now, and men go to war. My mother has proven she is gloriously brave and quite capable of caring for things at home without me. I know there will be some hardship for her, but Joab is eleven years old now, quite clever, and he will take my place at the homestead, and he can continue stacking lumber at the mill for a few dollars pay.

> *I'm leaving with you the last of the money I earned, save a few dollars I will need for food for myself until I arrive at camp with my father. Please give it to Mother when you return home.*
>
> *I beg you to stand in the gap on my behalf. Soften the blow for my mother. It is selfish of me to ask that you take care of her in my absence, but I have moved beyond consideration of how anyone thinks or feels about me.*
>
> *I know not how or if I will be accepted in the camp, but I have determined to give what little I have to offer in service to the Confederacy. I have every intention of joining the cavalry at some future time. I've longed to do so. I am skilled and ready, having taught myself all that is necessary. I know my age is a consideration; however, the powers that be need never know my true age. That is to say, I will own that I am near seventeen for I look every day that age. God forgive me for the lie I will have to tell in this regard.*
>
> *Cassie, I will not be traveling alone. Three of my friends from Sarepta will be with me. We will look out for one another, so no one is to worry. I'm sure my pa will write home to let Mother know when I arrive.*
>
> *I have no rights to ask, but consider that I need your prayers for safe arrival to a Confederate camp. I remain respectfully your brother by marriage, Isaac Beauford Payne*

Cassie folded the letter and walked back inside the kitchen where the family had gathered around the table.

"You're whiter'n a ghost," her father said. "What is it, girl?"

"Isaac Payne has run away from home. He's gone, Papa. Gone to find Thomas and Jonathan and Albert Henry. Why, they're in the mountains of Virginia. The child has taken leave of his senses, but if you will, Papa, read this letter. He sounds like a man of forty. He's been determined to get into this war ever since it started. His pa's going to have a fit, him leaving Rachel and me and the little boys. He was to stay home at all hazards and take care of things there. I'm going to have to get back to Rachel as soon as possible. Jesse, when can you take me?"

Jesse glanced toward his father for an answer, and Cassie spoke again.

"Mother, I'm so sorry for such a short visit, but I'll come back before long."

"Don't you worry about that. The only thing is, I hate to see you set out so soon after you just got here. You're going to tire yourself out. It won't be good for you, I fear."

"I'll be fine, Mother. I've got to get to Rachel before the grapevine gossip gets back to her. She's had far too many trials over the past few months, losing Benjamin, then the men went off to war, and now Isaac. What on earth is he thinking? I'm thinking I'd like to get my hands on him right about now. He's always been so considerate and obedient, and now this."

"Law, child," Mrs. Walker said. "He could be in all sorts of danger. Why, he'll be traveling straight through a Border State, and there are Union soldiers all over the place."

"I know."

"This war is doing strange things to our people. Keeps me on pins and needles all the time." Mrs. Walker nervously arranged breakfast on the table and seated her family.

Cassie was exasperated, her trip home spoiled by Isaac's selfishness. The family ate breakfast without saying much and she began making preparations to return home.

"Jesse, can you hitch your horse to the buckboard and drive it? You can spend the night and start back home in the morning. We didn't encounter any problems on the way over."

Jesse was patiently waiting for instructions and his father was still pondering the situation.

"Papa, do you think it will be safe for Jesse to go?"

"I'm allowin' we better hitch two horses, and I'll go with him," said Robert Walker. "Those shifty Yanks make me awfully nervous. You never know when they're going to ride out of the woods."

"That would be even better," said Cassie. "We can visit some more on the way."

Cassie said goodbye to her mother and sisters, promising to return soon, certainly before the baby was born. Jesse helped her onto the buckboard, still laden with Indian blankets Isaac had arranged for her comfort. Isaac! My soul, Isaac! What had possessed him?

"Wait a minute, Pa," said Jesse. "I'll help you."

"I can make it son. It might take a little longer, but I can make it. Hand me those rifles."

He kept one beside him and when Jesse boarded, he handed the other one to him. Cassie's lay at her feet. They were well armed. Jesse picked up the reins and started the horses down the trail to the main dirt road.

"Rachel taught me how to shoot, Papa."

Chapter 23
On Forbidden Ground

Isaac was living in a dream world, still romanticizing the war. He rode high and gracefully in the saddle and could hit target all day, the finest of sharpshooters, but to up and leave all the comforts of home, to shirk his duty to his mother and little brothers, to disobey his father—he was treading on forbidden ground.

∽

    Cassie, her father, and Jesse chatted as the horses clopped their way over the hard packed dirt road to Calhoun County. They had plenty of time to make it before dark, even stopping for Cassie to rest. Robert Walker skimmed the road from side to side, determined to notice anything that appeared uncommon. He had not been away from Houston since the war started except for an occasional trip into Aberdeen for supplies. With four women to protect, and Jesse his only son, he had a lot at stake just by making this reasonably short trip.
    The closer they got to Calhoun County, the more preoccupied Cassie became with thoughts of her baby, with Albert Henry, and now with Isaac. If he didn't change his mind and come back home, she would blame herself. Life was getting more complicated day by day.
    Jesse turned the buckboard down the Payne road, and Cassie burst into tears.
    "There's no sign of anyone."
    "Rachel's here, Cassie. Where else would she be with those little boys?"
    "I know, Papa, but the place looks callously lonesome. Benjamin is dead. Thomas, Jonathan and Henry are gone, and now Isaac has disappeared into

the countryside with three of his friends, in search of his father and brothers. Everything is changing, and I don't understand. Every day it's something else. I don't know how much more Rachel can bear."

Cassie had been away for just one night, but she was inexplicably glad to be home under this sad state of affairs. Poor Rachel would need to be comforted once she knew about Isaac.

Jesse tied the horses to the hitching post, reached for his father's walking cane, and assisted his father to the ground. He would unhitch the buckboard soon and take the horses to the barn, for dusk was upon them. Cassie jumped down from the buckboard before Jesse could reach for her.

"Dang, Cassie! I was going to help you down."

"Sorry, Jesse, I've got to get to Rachel."

With skirts pulled to her knees, she dashed up the steps to the porch and pounded on the door. Rachel appeared holding Samuel. His face was swollen from crying. An earache. Joab sat alone at the table, agonizing over schoolwork his mother required. Bible. It was Sunday and they had no way to go to the meetinghouse. Besides, Samuel's ear ached. Joab bounded to the door expecting to see Isaac. To be freed from the schoolwork and Samuel's pitiful crying.

"Oh, Cassie, thank God you're back. What happened? No matter, I'm just glad you're here. We've been lonely without you and Isaac, and I've had this eerie feeling like something bizarre was going on."

Before Cassie could reply, her father and Jesse entered the room.

"Why, hello, Mr. Walker. And Jesse, my goodness you've grown into a fine young man. It's so nice you could come with Cassie and Isaac. Isaac! Where is Isaac, Cassie? Oh, no, has something happened to my son? Where is he? Cassie, where is Isaac?"

"Rachel, be calm. Isaac is fine, but I have a bit of distressing information for you."

"What on earth … ?"

"He slipped out early this morning leaving me this note. He's gone to find his father and the boys. He left before daylight long before any of us got up. My mother roused when she heard hoof beats and thought it was Isaac. She went to check the room where he slept and he was gone. She assumed I knew he was leaving, but I didn't. Oh, Rachel, this is my fault! If I had just awakened, I would have heard him, and I could have sent Jesse to stop him. However, I don't think anyone could have stopped him. You'll see when you read the letter."

Rachel handed Samuel to Joab and took the letter from Cassie, silently reading words she was bound to read sooner or later. My God in Heaven! This war was driving her insane. Had she not given enough?

Samuel cried and pulled at his ear. Cassie took him from Joab. She laid a warm cloth over it and held him close.

"This is preposterous," Rachel said as she finished the letter.

"Isaac knows they'll not accept him when they find out he's way below the age limit, and they'll find out. They have their ways of knowing. He's just a boy. And now I must worry, not only that he may be going to war, but that he has to get there somehow. How does he know the way? Looking for Thomas and the boys will be like looking for a needle in a haystack. Why, they hardly know where they are themselves. Why? Why on earth did he do this? He's heading straight through Union occupied territory."

Tears streamed down her cheeks. Another one of her boys was gone, and like a mother hen whose chicks had been hopelessly scattered, she no longer had the wherewithal to gather them under her wings. She stood limp as a dishrag, holding the letter from Isaac in her fingers.

Joab put his arms around his mother in an attempt to comfort her. She willingly accepted.

Chapter 24
In My Lonely Hour

Rachel read the letter from Thomas and groaned. Isaac could have picked no worse time to try and get into the army, and she had not yet told his father. She didn't have the courage. But she must, for word would soon get to his camp. The grapevine, which had its merits, also had its downside. She didn't want him getting the news from some nosey informant.

The South was losing men by the hundreds; they were hungry, shoeless, without sufficient clothing, dirty and ragged. Isaac would see that what he romanticized was nothing short of chaos, and he would return home. That was Rachel's only hope for him. Jonathan and Henry both had written letters home begging Isaac to stay put, for he would not be able to withstand camp life. True enough, he was raised in the wilderness, but he was also softened by a loving mother and encouraged by a godly father to stay by the family.

May 1862

My dearest Rachel,

We fight men, hunger, lack of clothing, holes in our shoes. Little pay, no glory, no fame. But we've learned how to be hungry and find food. How to be cold and find a warm fire. How to be thirsty and find a deep well. How to be soaked to the bone and sit by a fire drying out our clothes. And though we fight the scorn of the enemy, in our hearts, we win for time and eternity for the love of the South, our homesteads, and our loved ones.

Rachel, I hope I'm not complaining, for I have much for which to thank Almighty God, and I know that war has touched every part of the South and that men on the battlefield are not the only ones hurting. You're hurting at home just as much, if not more.

> *I pray without ceasing that God will protect you, that Isaac will be strong in your regard, and that the enemy will not return to the doorstep of the Payne homestead. Word reached us on the battlefield of your encounter with the Yanks and of your bravery. I bow my knee to you, Rachel, for you are a glorious woman of the South with unsullied courage. Every day I hear a man sobbing because today his house burned or was ransacked, his daughters raped, his mother beaten and left for dead. I could not bear knowing that you've suffered such atrocities. Heartache is all around us, but duty called and we answered. Now, pray to God that this will end soon and that we can come home. Until then or that glorious day when we meet in heaven, I remain forever thine, Thomas Goode Payne*

Although his letters were getting bleaker, Rachel knew he was omitting the real state of affairs. She had horrid visions of the carnage. Fire belching from Union artillery, pelting the poorly clad, shoeless, hungry soldiers of the South. Men bleeding from every pore, begging for death, the only end to the dreadfulness of war.

She clutched her breast and cried aloud, "Cassie, please watch the boys for me. I'll be back in an hour."

"Of course, Rachel."

Cassie gazed out the window in wonder and respect as Rachel ran frantically to the first tree line, skirts pulled to her knees. Cassie had seen her make this trek up the hill many times, but never with more deliberation. She stumbled, fell to the ground, and lay there, clutching the letter. Cassie gasped, her eyes filling with tears. And after a long moment, Rachel was on her feet, running again. She disappeared in the clump of trees to the grove—the Secret Grove, his voice ringing in her ears.

> *…Do not forget me and the boys when you go to the Secret Grove for you may affect much in that way. Tell the children to be good children and teach them to love God. Oh, you don't know how bad I want to see my little ones and hear them talk. Kiss them for me and tell Sam to kiss you for me. And remember that I think of you and them often in my lonely hour and after I retire for the night. So farewell for the present. But I hope not forever. Put your whole trust in God. I remain your husband until death.*

"I hope not forever … not forever … in my lonely hour … until death … I remain yours until death … "

Rachel bowed low, passing under the hanging grapevines hard-twined around the oak trees. Ivy lay thick on the ground, weaving a path of green from one end of the grove to the other. She could scarcely see the sun's rays, typical of how she felt in this moment. The dark storm clouds of war had swallowed up all hope of the brighter day. But the rays were there. Somewhere. Hovering over the tops of the trees, giving her a fragment of hope.

She could be alone here. Alone with God. Otherwise, she would be angry, near losing her mind. Even angry with God. She swallowed hard, fighting the oppression and knowing that relief was an exercise in futility without God's help. He awaited her, and she could tell him what she needed. He knew anyway. He knew where Thomas was at this moment. He knew the soreness of his feet, legs and knees. He knew the condition of her boys. If they were hungry, cold, tired, lonely.

She sat down on the stump of the tree Thomas had cut for that purpose years ago. This was holy ground—a place where God had met with the two of them for over twenty years. She had made frequent trips to the Grove since her men left on that cold December morning in 1861.

Lord, it would be presumptuous to try and tell you what's going on in the Shenandoah Valley. You know every bullet that whistles across the hills, every strong volley that comes the way of my boys, for war rages. Dreadful, despicable war. They stand endless hours on the picket, their lives always in danger. Day after day, night after night, they bow under the burden of need. Shoes for their tired feet. Socks for comfort. Balm for healing. The little amenities we take for granted become priceless possessions when they are absent. O, Balm in Gilead, soothe the aching feet. Pour in your healing oil. Let it be sufficiently their portion. The blistering, burning—replace with comforting thoughts of home and our love. Fill their empty stomachs with nourishment of a far more splendid sort. May it effectively be manna from above.

Lord, I can't bear the thought of losing Thomas and the boys. Protect them from the enemy's bullet, from the saber's slash, from the Minié balls, the horrifying volley they may be receiving at this moment. Turn the enemy in another direction. And, God, where is my Isaac? Where is he? Is he lying face down in a pool of blood, or did your grace and mercy see him safely to his father's side? Please, God! Help me in this regard!

Rachel moved from the stump to the ground, face down on the blanket of ivy. She lay there, pouring out supplication until relief came. That same relief she embraced the day Ben died and the day her men left for war. She didn't know what it meant, but she gratefully received it. And when she knew she had affected much, as Thomas had said, she rose to her feet, wiped her eyes with her apron, and made her way back to the grove's entrance, where the sun greeted her with warmth and hope.

Chapter 25
Restless One

The warm spring sun inched downward in the western sky behind Isaac and his three friends, Cliff, Abe, and Billy. It was their best compass. They turned and faced it, dismounted and basked in its pastel light until the last vestiges were gone, enjoying a measure of warmth, for they would soon sleep on the cold ground. They were hungry, and the four of them pooled the small amount of food they had left. Abe doled out a portion to each of them and put the rest in his saddlebag. For two weeks they traveled through the wilderness and in the edge of the woods by the side of the dirt roads, through small towns in Union-occupied territory, avoiding contact with human life, making fairly good progress as they figured it. But Isaac was having second thoughts that he might not be ready for what he was getting himself into. So far, they had not encountered Federal soldiers, but he wondered how long that would last, especially as they moved closer to the eastern theatre of war. He didn't want to discourage his friends who were as bent on joining up as he, but he couldn't help wondering if they felt the same way he did. Maybe he had over-encouraged them, and maybe they had not come clean with him concerning their own feelings, not wanting to appear less than ready to fight like men.

They made camp beside a stream somewhere in the mountains of Tennessee.

"According to our drawing, we're approaching this area right here."

Isaac pointed to the Cumberland River on the map.

"I don't know how we'll cross this river when we come to it. Doesn't look possible to me. Furthermore, I don't know how we're going to cross these mountains. Take a look in the distance. These are the tallest hills I've ever seen. I had no idea."

Billy scanned the horizon, and as far as he could see was the impossible. They could in no way scale those mountains. And what if there were bears or panthers?

"What are we going to do Isaac?" he said, scared as a rabbit.

"Well, we were going to take the route on this drawing, but it appears we may have taken on something we can't accomplish without help. I don't know if there's a better way to travel. If we try to hop a pontoon or hitch a ride on a boat across the Cumberland River, we may risk getting sent home. Shall we rest for the night and keep going in the morning? We can go through one of these little towns and ask if there's a better way to reach the Shenandoah, but we may come face to face with the enemy. And if they know we're trying to find a certain Confederate camp, there's no telling what they'll do."

Abe, reluctant at first, earnestly spoke his feelings.

"Uh … I don't know. I'm … uh … awfully tired and sore from all this ridin'. As a matter of fact, you don't know what I'd give just to be back home with Mama and the girls. I didn't want to say so, but after the first week, I've been wishin' we'd never left."

"What about you, Cliff?"

"I kinda go along with Abe. I … I didn't think this thing through, and if war is any worse than the wilderness, I … I'm not ready for it. I'd like to go back m'self. But I'll stick with it if you think there's any way on earth we can ever make it."

"Billy, what do you have to say?"

"I'm s' tired I could cry, quite frankly, and I just might at any minute."

As the words issued from his lips, the youngest of the four boys burst into tears, trembling from head to foot, unable to finish the little speech he had prepared for such an occasion as this. Sick of himself for appearing to be less than a man, he cursed under his breath then apologized to his friends.

Isaac sat high on a fallen tree trunk, his long legs extended and his feet propped on another felled log. He dropped his head and carefully thought through all he had just heard from his friends. He didn't blame them. They were all too young to be in the wilderness alone, without the consent of their folks, including him. They were tired, hungry, and dirty, and the nights were cold. They didn't have sufficient clothing and they were chafed from riding.

He sat straight up on the log and put his feet flat on the ground, took a deep breath and slumped, resting his elbows on his knees. He thought about what he wanted to say, lifted his eyes, and began to confess.

"I don't blame any of you, because I feel the same way. I'm as unhappy as I can be. I thought I couldn't wait to get to the battlefield, and I still want to get to Pa and Jonathan and Albert Henry. I miss them so much I can't stand it, but I'm supposed to be at home with my mother and my brothers. I just up and left them without so much as a goodbye. I cowardly left a note with Cassie, because I didn't want to write my mother. I knew if I did, I would back out. I should never have done this, and I should never have encouraged you in my mischief. My apologies, boys. We'll start for home in the morning if that's what you want to do. If this war lingers, we'll join up next year when we're older. We'll be ready then."

The boys breathed a sigh of relief. The conversation had taken place and they were going home. Out of wilderness experience, and as they had for the past two weeks, they kindled a fire and sat around it, eating the last of their food. They must scavenge in the morning or do without, but for now, they would sleep and dream of home.

Shortly before daybreak, Isaac awoke.

"Boys, wake up! Let's ride! We're going home today!"

At those words, Cliff, Abe, and Billy were on their feet. With blankets rolled and fire extinguished, they saddled and mounted their horses. They sauntered out of the woods in the direction of home. Doubtless, it would take another two weeks to get there.

"Make sure your rifles are loaded," Isaac warned. "We're heading right back through possible Yankee camps. You know, if we encounter the enemy we have to fight like soldiers, so be ready. Remember your training."

For some reason, that didn't bother the boys, no more than it did Isaac, for they had long since prepared themselves to defend the Confederacy. Every boy ten years to conscription age was trained. By an older brother or friend. Their fathers had insisted, for after the war got underway and appeared to be endless, they feared their boys would come of age before the war was over. Isaac had made sure his three friends were trained properly.

༄

Rachel Payne labored at the stove, canning beans and tomatoes from her garden.

"How can I best help you, Rachel?" Cassie asked.

"To be perfectly honest, you've done a great deal of work picking beans and tomatoes, but now that they're all gathered for the time being, the best help would be to keep Samuel out of this hot kitchen. I'm afraid he's going to get burned."

"I'll take him upstairs and play with him on the bear rug until he falls asleep."

"And I'll join you as soon as Joab and I have filled the last of these jars."

Rachel lined the canning tub, thinking about Isaac. If she could just hear some word from him it would momentarily relieve the anxiety, but she would not rest until he returned home. It had been three weeks, and none of the boys' mothers had heard anything. Quite possibly the Yankees had captured them, for they all had rifles and would be posing as militia or Confederate soldiers, she supposed. Rachel shuddered and tried to dismiss the thought from her mind. Isaac was a wilderness boy, tough as shoe leather, and he could take care of himself. If something had happened, surely word would have gotten back to her or to Thomas. Confederate soldiers were all over the place, too, and word was getting to the field. The grapevine had worked sufficiently for urgent messages since the war started.

Rachel and Joab removed the last of the jars from the tub on the stove and sealed the lids. When they cooled, the two of them would take the jars to the cellar.

"Joab, I don't know what I'd do without you. I'm so glad you're here with me. You're the oldest son left at home, now, and I guess you know you're the man of the house. How does that make you feel?"

"Splendid!" he said. "I thought I'd never get to this place. There were so many ahead of me."

Rachel laughed and put her arms around him.

"Well, you've arrived, son. And promise me you'll stay with me a long, long time. At least until you marry the girl of your dreams."

"Aw, Mama, I ain't gonna get married. I'm gonna always stay with you."

"Oh, you'll change your mind."

"Only if I meet a girl like you or Cassie."

"Well, until then, let's get these jars to the cellar, and we'll go upstairs and join Cassie and Samuel. They're up there having fun without us. Listen."

Samuel's laughter rang through the house. Joy unspeakable!

༄

The four southern boys rode at their fastest speed, trying to make it home in less time than it had taken to get to the Cumberland River. Isaac held his hand up to stop his little posse.

"We'll cut across the river at Shiloh. I figure we're about a hundred miles from there. We can cross the Mississippi line just north of Corinth and go down through Harrisburg to stay on a beaten trail, then we'll angle off through Pontotoc County and you'll be in Sarepta before you know it. I'll go on home by myself. I've got music to face, and so do you, but at least we're going home. Besides, I'm tired of roasted rabbit and dewberries."

"He'ah!" they shouted, slapping their mares for speed.

Two days later, as night fell on the young Mississippians, they made camp by the river on the north side of Shiloh. Isaac shivered at the thought of what happened here just two months earlier.

"We'd best keep quiet tonight," he said. "The Yanks think they own this part of the country, now. Boys, it was a dreadful thing that happened here, and I've wondered at times what Pa, Jonathan, and Henry thought when they found out about the bloody battle at Shiloh."

"What *did* happen, Isaac?"

"Well, Abe, I heard that Grant was ordered to move down the Tennessee River with his forty-some thousand men to Pittsburg Landing. That's where we're sitting tonight to the best of my knowing. The battle took place on April 6 and 7 on the Shiloh Church grounds. Can you beat that? Those Yankees desecrated the Shiloh Church grounds. I think they're all heathens. Generals Albert Sidney Johnston and Pierre Beauregard decided they had to attack, and with their forty thousand men, they almost squashed Grant's troops, but Johnston was killed in the heat of battle. They said the little pond on the church grounds turned red with the blood from both sides, men trying to cool their wounds and wash off the blood. The next day, Grant got reinforcements of about twenty thousand men, and pushed our army back to Corinth. Grant botched this battle, and we heard a lot of Yankees wanted him replaced, but Lincoln wouldn't hear of getting rid of his "fighting" man. Said he couldn't spare him. They're still fighting up in here, trying to get control of the Mississippi River clear over to Memphis. So, I'm telling you, we've got to stay low tonight. They're all over this place and in our country, too."

"Well, Isaac," said Cliff, "I'm sure glad you're with us, 'cause you've had experience shootin' them Yanks."

"That was my Ma that shot the Yank. She's the bravest woman I know. He aimed and would have shot me in the head, but she downed him. Just a bloody flesh wound. He had more peas and squash on him than blood. Sleep with your guns tonight, boys."

Isaac put the fire out and rolled over on his side, his eyes wide open. Truth be known, he was scared stiff, but mostly of the unknown. If Yankees came near his little camp, he knew what to do, and he lay there vowing to himself that he would do it. There was no way he was going to sleep tonight, but at least he could lie still and rest his saddle sores. Poor Glory must be tired, for she had never taken him this far before and he feared he had ridden her too hard.

Isaac could tell by the placement of the moon and the stars it was about midnight, and he was still wide-eyed. He was scared but more than that, anxious to get home at all hazards. They had camped near the road in the trees, and the way he figured it, no human being knew where they were. But suddenly, he heard hoof beats. A single rider. He sure hoped so. Glory and the other horses, still saddled, moved about, whinnying softly. Isaac got up and raised his gun. He shook Abe.

"Wake up," he whispered! "Something's happening. Rouse the boys."

"What is it, Isaac?"

"I don't know yet," he said.

"Stay put. And be quiet. Don't say a word."

Isaac crawled to the biggest tree in the thicket and crouched behind it. He looked in all directions, motioning for the boys to stay down. He inched low to the ground until he reached Glory and pulled the saber out of its sheath. The boys lay still with their rifles cocked. In a split second, the blue-coated Yankee nightrider veered off the road and raced through their camp as though he were taking a short cut somewhere. Isaac mounted Glory with saber in hand and rode hard behind the Union soldier. He couldn't afford to let him get away for fear he would alert more of the enemy and their lives wouldn't be worth the powder it would take to blow them up, for he had seen Isaac. The boys mounted and followed behind him. The Yankee drew his saber and turned around on Isaac. This was all new to him. He had never used a saber, but he had seen it done. In some swift and energetic exercise, the Yankee began to wield his sword. Isaac, in a sort of masterful pretense—that he knew what he was doing—lifted the sword and began to fend off his enemy. Before he knew it, the Yank was on the ground begging for life. Isaac's three Confederate accomplices surrounded the nightrider with squirrel rifles cocked. The boys had done it. Four against one, but they had done it. They disarmed the Union soldier, bound and gagged him, tied him onto his horse, and began their journey toward Mississippi. When they arrived at Pittsburg Landing, they quietly tied their prisoner's horse to a tree and abandoned him. Isaac had already affixed the soldier's saber and rifle to his own saddle, cunningly adding to his arsenal of Union weapons. The Yank's comrades, who were more than likely all over the countryside, would find him. And Isaac's little band rode swiftly away toward Corinth, away from the water—Grant's obsession, an insatiable desire to control the South's waterways

It was not long before Isaac and the boys reached Corinth. They tied their horses to the hitching post in front of the hotel and started inside to beg for food.

"Isaac? Isaac Payne?"

Isaac turned around to see what familiar voice was calling his name. He was elated to see the sweet, stocky frame of one of his favorite ladies.

"Mrs. Whitaker! What are you doing in Corinth? Am I glad to see someone I know!"

"Well, since Doc Whitaker joined up with the Confederate Army, I have to take care of his patients in Corinth. I come here once a week, or as often as I can to help out. Isaac, your mother is worried sick over you. I sure hope you're headed home."

"Yes ma'am. That's exactly where we're going. We got as far as the Cumberland River in Tennessee and turned around. I know we did the wrong thing, but we just wanted to do our part. I wanted to find Pa and Jonathan and Albert Henry. We've been on the road for over three weeks, and we're about starved. We were going inside to beg for food."

"Well, son, you know Doc owns this hotel and dining hall. You and the boys go right on in. I'll see to it you get fed, and then you promise to be off to your home in Calhoun County. I'm going on in and make arrangements for you. As a matter of fact, why don't you just take a room here tonight and rest yourselves? That'll be on Doc Whitaker. I'll telegraph Calhoun City and get Howard to ride out and let your mother know you're coming home. I can certainly do that for the war effort. You were just trying to help. I hope everybody will see it that way."

"Yes ma'am. Thank you ma'am."

"Take your horses over to the livery stable. Those saddles need to come off after all that riding. I'll take care of that, too."

"Much obliged, Mrs. Whitaker. You're much too generous," said Isaac.

She winked at him and went her way.

The boys stood in front of the hotel with their mouths open.

"What just happened, Isaac?"

"Why, Almighty God just gave us some food before we starve to death and a place to sleep without fear of being shot before dawn. Now let's get on in here so we can laugh our heads off at pretending to know what we were doing when we captured that Union soldier. Why, I've never used a saber in my entire life!"

"You couldn't prove it by me. I believe you've been practicing," said Billy.

"Yes, that was a splendid display of chivalry, Isaac," said Cliff, chuckling at his own choice of words.

"Or ... that ole Yank was just like us. He didn't know what the heck he was doin'." Abe threw his head back and laughed so loud the whole town could hear.

Part Three
The Bravest of Men

Chapter 26
Fighting on the "Southern Side" of the Potomac

In the spring of 1862, General McClellan arrived on the Virginia Peninsula with over a hundred thousand men, occupying Yorktown and pressing forward on the York River. By late May, he was within six miles of Richmond. General Joseph E. Johnston attacked McClellan on May 31. Johnston was wounded, and Jeff Davis appointed Robert E. Lee to replace him. Between May 4 and June 9, Stonewall Jackson launched the Shenandoah Valley Campaign, defeating several Union forces, driving them to the Potomac River. In the meantime, Lee was strategizing as the new Commander of the Army of Northern Virginia, and Jeb Stuart led his cavalry around the Union army three times and only lost one man. His chivalrous exercise conjured up tactical information for Lee, sending southern morale soaring. And then Lee fell on McClellan in the Seven Days Battle. From Mechanicsville to Malvern Hill McClellan ran, and by July 1, he had retreated to the James River. The Payne men and what was left of their company re-enlisted with the Mississippi Forty-Second and were fighting in Lee's Army of Northern Virginia. Isaac had gone back home, and T. G. was none the worse for that saga, since he never knew about it until it was over. Rachel could not bring herself to lay that burden on him while he fought a war. Not until she had word that Isaac was dead or until he came home.

☙

Low campfires flickered in the darkness. Fog, a mist of rain—the dreaded rain. It meant mud up to the knees on the morning march to heaven knew where. But in the middle of the night, the thundering hoof beats of a cavalryman brought the news.

"Break camp! Pack it up! Take what you can. Kill the fires. We're moving up."

Captain Payne yelled orders to his men: "Let every tree, every ditch, every mound of dirt be your shelter. Only fools neglect the most insignificant cover. Keep your weapons dry at all hazards. Now, let's move."

Those familiar words initiated the great adventure. Once again, the soldiers ran in the pouring rain. Commissary and weapons wagons mired in the mud. Cannons roared behind them, followed by a heavy volley. There were endless skirmishes, all leading into the great battles where thousands of soldiers converged, picketed, fought from a distance, cannon to cannon; and up close, hand-to-hand, saber-to-saber. Captain Payne taught his men to lie down in ditches and reload while bullets zinged over their heads, some men falling. Faces were covered with the hideous gray colors of battle, dust, dirt, grime and gunpowder settling on them in sheets with nothing revealed except the whites of their eyes and lips licked clean by parched tongues. The death angel hovered.

"Fall back! My God in heaven, protect us," T. G. cried. "There are so many of them."

Finally, the aggravating enemy tired and turned in another direction. Confederate soldiers lay still on the ground until they no longer heard the trifling sound of the Union soldiers. It was near impossible to fight in the darkness.

༄

The South fought battle after battle, their greatest enemy the outrageous number of Union troops and the taunting night exercises. There was no peaceful scene in the middle of it all. Not one spot, in the world as they knew it, where they could lie down and rest, if only for a moment, without fear of the dreaded enemy.

And then they found it. A hillside camp with tents erected, campfires dancing on the landscape, coffee brewing, and meat frying in the skillet. In beautiful four-part harmony, they sang hymns and prayed. Soldiers sat about the borrowed campfires with thoughts of home, unspeakable loneliness taking some to the depths of despondency.

Thomas thanked God for the extraordinary companionship of his two sons. They would fight together until the war ended or until they lay dead on a Virginia hillside. He was too old when he volunteered for duty, and it was not mandatory for a man over forty-one to leave his family and go to war;

nevertheless, he did it to stay by his sons. Rachel knew, and she admired him for it. He was torn between his two older sons and the younger family who also needed him, but when he looked at Jonathan and Henry, his strength was renewed. He would stay beside them.

But this was not their camp. A bite to eat, a night's rest, and they must move on, even before daybreak.

"Fall in! Fall in!"

The soldiers were weary, their stomachs still achingly empty. Some slept as they walked, lagging behind like disobedient children unable to keep the loathsome pace.

"Close up the ranks, men!"

The shouts of the officers tightening up the lines jolted them awake, and they rushed to catch up, feet blistering, tears rolling. Moving, moving, always moving and running.

The rush continued until exhaustion miraculously turned to momentum, renewing their energy. At last, the soldiers were ordered to lie down in a piney wood to rest. The shelled corn in their pockets alone was sustaining them until they made camp again, which could be days. Then they must forage for food. Theirs was gone.

"Hey, Jon! I may not want corn kernels again—ever! They're killing my teeth and gums. I don't know what hurts more, my teeth or my feet."

"I agree, little brother, but I guess it beats starvation and gives us something to work on while we're marching, or running, I should say. But I'm like you, I'm afraid it's going to break our teeth. Be careful, Henry. It's not worth it. If we can stop long enough, I'll get some food for us."

"No doubt about that," Henry said.

"Where's Pa? I hope he's not trying to crack that stuff. His teeth are a lot older than ours. I couldn't stand it if he was hurting. Course, we'll never know if he is or not."

"I know. He never complains about anything. I see him. Back there with Eli Davis. Probably getting spiritual advice."

"Or giving it," said Jonathan.

"True. He knows the Bible, all right, and lives it. Everybody knows that. Have you noticed he never goes ahead of you and me? Always got his eye on us, when it should be the other way around. But, hey! He's the captain, right?"

"Yes, little brother, and he's our father," Jonathan said.

"Looks like we're nearing our destination," said Henry. "The riders are prancing about, and tents are set up. Sure hope there're cots in those tents."

"Me, too. I've not been this tired since the night I killed that bear in the Yalobusha."

"Halt! Open camp!" the rider called.

"Blessed words," Albert Henry said. "I don't think I could have run another step. I wonder where we are."

"I don't know, but Pa will soon know and he'll tell us what's going on. And Henry, I have something for all three of us when Pa gets here."

"Oh, a surprise! And out here on the battlefield! You are amazing, brother!"

"I know. But remember I promised to tell you all about that old black bear some day on a battlefield in Virginia? Well, it's time for the tale."

And Jonathan, without embellishing a word, told his brother about the day he downed the old monster. He didn't need to exaggerate, for the story was as gruesome as any day they had seen in battle. When he finished, Henry was in awe of his brother, though he needed no story to put him there. Jonathan was his hero, plain and simple.

"You went through all that just to get Cassie and me a bear rug?"

Jonathan rolled his brother over on the ground and with his fist, scrubbed Henry's head. They both laughed so hard they disturbed the entire camp.

"Jonathan, you're messing up my hair," Henry said, almost losing his breath with laughter.

"Henry, did you lose your mirror? For your hair has been messed up for nigh onto two years!"

"Here comes Pa, now," said Albert Henry. "Let's get on with the surprise so you can stop being jealous at how handsome I look."

"Hey, boys, what's all the commotion?" Thomas said, anxious to partake of something more exciting than sore feet and an aching back.

He sat down on a campstool and the boys sat at his feet not six inches apart.

"Oh, I was just telling Henry how I killed that old black bear last year. And I have something for us."

Jonathan opened his haversack and dug to the bottom to get the fur pieces he had cut and cured months before.

"These go in your boots, but put the fur sides to your feet, then put your socks over the fur to hold them in place. This should help a lot, just like having a new pair of leather boots, and they'll keep your feet warm, too. I don't guarantee the smell will be all that great when you start sweating, but never mind that. We haven't smelt fresh for a long time, anyway."

They all three howled, understanding from experience that marching feet smelled less than fragrant in any regiment.

"Jonathan, this is like Christmas in July. It's really the best thing we've had since your ma sent new socks she knitted. Thanks, son! Much obliged!"

"Well, it seemed like a good time to make the presentation, since our feet are killing us, but you might want to wait a couple of months until it turns cold again to wear them."

"I'm wearing mine right now," Henry said, taking off his boots and socks and inserting the fur pieces against his war weary ankles.

"This is splendid, brother." He tied his shoelaces twice around his ankles and seriously asked, "Pa do you know where we are?"

"We're at camp Mott near Richmond, and we may be here awhile," he said. "I'll tell you some things I heard from the quartermaster."

"It's being told Lincoln wants to destroy Jackson and defuse the Shenandoah. Course, there's nothing new about that. But in just under fifty days, Jackson's foot soldiers have trudged over six hundred miles, engaging the enemy in several formal actions and five pitched battles, outnumbered three to one, but he won victory in almost all situations."

"Amazing! We can relate to his foot soldiers. If their shoe leather is as thin as ours, they're hurting for sure," said Albert Henry.

"I'll say, but he's bringing high hopes of winning the war. We need every good word we can hear to prop these young men up, for our next worst enemy is homesickness. It's deadly. Robs men of their focus and senses. I know it does me. If not for you two … well never mind that, for I'm blessed to have you."

৩

Rachel opened the letter from Thomas. His handwriting was exquisite, and she hung on every word as usual. He had written often, sending his letters by carrier, or sometimes by kin who were in the camp. She read the letter once, twice, and put it in her pocket. When Isaac and Joab came home from the mill, she gathered the boys and Cassie about the kitchen table and pulled the letter from her pocket.

Camp Mott, near Richmond
July 1862

My dear Rachel,

We worked for food today. Cut a cord of wood, pulled endless bushels of corn, squash and tomatoes. We were tired when we headed back to camp with our arms loaded with bounty. The fresh roasting ears laid on the fire in the husks slathered with butter from the farmer's wife were good beyond mention, a far cry better than the hard kernels we've been trying to crack and eat. Now our food wagon is replenished, and we're happy soldiers.

Some things that give us pleasure are those we took for granted at home. The skillet— oh, how we love the black iron skillet with fresh hog meat frying. And sugar in a cup of coffee. I never used to love sugar in a cup, but now … well, it's like a slice of sugar pie.

The oilcloth. I've come to depend on that old oilcloth, taking pleasure in rolling it up of a morning. When we travel it goes with us, the blanket rolled inside. The knapsack is our pillow at night. The blanket feels good even on a summer evening, for it is always cold in the mountains after dark.

Oh, these are good things.

Early call and sun on the horizon, God's big landscape touched gently by the dew of the morning, fresh air free from smoke and the smell of bombs bursting and buckshot shattering, moss on the back side of the trees. And sleep. Sweet rest, side by side, Jon, Henry and me, silently thinking of home and you and the boys and Cassie. Coffee boiling on the fire, a brook at the bottom of the hill, soap, towel, comb from the haversack, safely hoarded away; a good head wash and body scrub in that cool spring of water. The metal plate and tin cup, a campstool.

Mail. When it arrives our hearts leap to our throats. Is there one for me? But some of the news is not so good thanks to the scavenging Yanks. Most parts of the South are affected, the letters say. But many nights after reading our mail over and again, I look around and see on other faces what I feel on my own—happiness, for I've heard from home. It doesn't take fine things to make a southern soldier happy.

Until we meet again, or in that Home beyond the River, accept my best love for you and our boys and Cassie, Thomas Goode Payne

Wives and children waiting with faces pressed to the window of their cabins or stately mansions; from their sawmills, storefronts, gristmills, blacksmith shops; from some lonely cotton or cornfield, gazing long and hard down the dirt road to see if their Johnny would come marching home again—that was their courage. The longer they fought, the more audacious they became, the more ragged their clothing, the more callused their hands, knees and feet, and the thinner their shoe leather, courage sustained by remembrance of their grandfathers who fought the Revolutionary War for the same reasons. When would it end? Perhaps never. As long as there was a freedom cry, it would not end, and they would continue to pay for sacred privilege in southern red blood.

August 29-30, 1862

Second Bull Run Manassas, almost a duplication of the first battle, brought yet another victory for Jackson joined by Lee and Longstreet. The South regained almost all of Virginia, and a whipped northern army traipsed back to Washington in the pouring rain, repeating history, only this time no dignitaries showed up to applaud them, for First Manassas was embarrassment enough for the Union.

And Maryland cried, longing to be with the South. Feeling dejected in part. They lay just over the border from Virginia, forty-five miles from the pickets of Fredericksburg. Too much of the North was in certain men, though. It would never work for Maryland. But Lee needed a victory in Union country to gain foreign recognition for the Confederacy. It just might work for him.

On September 11, Jonathan Payne wrote his mother from a Confederate camp near Richmond prior to their march to Maryland.

> *I take the present time to write you a few lines to let you know that I am well and would be glad to know that you are the same. At this time our army is in Maryland and we are going on through. There has been some hard fighting, but we run them every time. They cannot stand here, and I am glad that they cannot, for if they would stand, they would kill a great many of our men. I think there soon will be peace made. We are whipping them so bad that they are bound to give up the ghost. They know that there is no use for them to fight our men for we are like dogs to fight.*

Rachel read his letter wiping tears. Jonathan was so much a man, but still her boy. He had sent her his ambrotype, and said,

> *... There are so many that would make fun of it. I want you to keep it yourself. Mother, I have been to preaching and I heard a fine sermon. I would like to be there to go to meeting and see how the old meetinghouse looks, to see if it looks like it once did and to see how many are missing—*

Tears poured as she wiped the fingerprints from the glass and leaned it against the wall on her bureau. A photograph of her son developed in a glass plate. She was so proud of it. She had seen them before. A photographer had been to Calhoun City once, and she had heard about how they were photographing the war in Virginia and other places. She wasn't sure she could bear to see any images of carnage. But she was happy to get the ambrotype of Jonathan. She hoped Thomas and Henry would do the same.

She read his letter again and pondered ... *to see how many are missing—* All their men were missing. Meetinghouse was half empty. No boys, no men. Just women, old men, and little children. Rachel looked at her ambrotype of Jonathan and cried some more. Oh, how she missed all three of them!

❧

The Army of Northern Virginia was not just hungry, but famished—and barefoot. The general wanted to recruit in Maryland, but that was highly improbable. One look at the men in rags left little or no desire for Maryland to join forces with the South. When the impoverished southern soldiers marched through the streets of Baltimore gazing on its women and children, gaily strolling the streets of home, they longed to be in their own homes. It would be difficult enough for Lee's army to go back to the treacherous hills and valleys of Virginia, to the muddy banks of the Potomac or to Bull Run River or even as far back as Shiloh's Bloody Pond. To ask Maryland's men to join them in such a humiliating exercise would be asking too much.

Southern gallantry was threatened by grim reality. But good, brave men, ragged and weary, passed through the streets of Baltimore, some riding double, most walking, with full understanding from their Commander-in-Chief that private property and non-combatants were in no way to be offended or harmed. The orders had not changed. They were not to disturb the home or insult their women. Unlike Sherman who burned everything in his path, the Confederate generals rode through Maryland's towns, disturbing nothing.

While Lee's dirty, bearded, struggling, shoeless army was not much to look upon physically, their faith never once diminished. It was God's grace that moved them forward—*through many dangers, toils and snares, I have already come; 'tis grace hath brought me safe thus far, and grace will lead me home.* Nothing else could have. They were outnumbered ten to one now, though in almost every battle the North had lost more men than the South, but then—they had far more states from which to recruit. Their example was not only the fervor of their forefathers who fought in the American Revolution, but of their courageous leaders, Robert E. Lee and Stonewall Jackson, men of faith and strong belief in God. And southern fighting men, with undying faith in the Confederacy, stayed the enemy time and again.

Lee, with about fifty thousand men invaded the North in September, sending Jackson and twenty-five thousand men by way of Harpers Ferry. Something immensely unfortunate happened on September 13. A Union soldier found Lee's orders at an abandoned Confederate campsite, dropped by a runner to Lee's officers. Strange as it seems, McClellan didn't attack until the seventeenth, giving Lee time to regroup with Jackson's men after his success at Harpers Ferry. Union troops pounded the Confederate lines almost to the breaking point until A. P. Hill's corps arrived. Rebel forces could see him coming and noisily cheered the gallant southern general as he thundered in.

By now, General William Barksdale's brigade consisted of fragments of several regiments whose generals had fallen in battle, the Mississippi Seventeenth was among them—the *Magnolia Guards* from Calhoun County. He had led the Thirteenth Mississippi into the First Battle of Bull Run in the summer of 1861. In the spring of 1862, Barksdale took his regiment into the Virginia Peninsula Campaign and the Seven Days Battle and that summer into the bloody Battle of Malvern Hill. These fighting men were now *Barksdale's Mississippi Brigade*, and by August of 1862, he was Brigadier General William Barksdale. The old southern gentleman, the silver-haired fire-eater, rode high-booted in the saddle and fought fearlessly for the Confederacy. Most of his corps was detached for duty up in Suffolk.

And so ... the war raged on the summer of 1862, and the Payne men fought side by side from one skirmish to another. Up in Suffolk, and on toward Fredericksburg, they marched, still burning with high purpose.

☙

The Union called it Antietam; the South, Sharpsburg. The world would come to call it one of the most foreboding battles of all times, one that would leave indelible memories. On September 16, 1862, General George McClellan led his army to the eastern banks of the Antietam. General Lee and the men in Gray awaited him on the opposite slopes near the quaint little village of Sharpsburg. No breastworks, no bulwarks of any kind protected either army.

The green grass of late summer moved in the slightest breeze, and fields of corn, their tassels blowing gently over countless yellow ears of a bumper crop, innocently separated the North and the South, creating a battlefield of unmatched splendor, a beautiful sight under different circumstances, had there been no meeting of the armies to do battle, had there been no conflict, no carnage, no death.

Each side flaunted the flags of their country, an intimidation one toward the other, reminiscent of Goliath taunting David. Behind the Union Goliath was the wide road to Washington that must be protected at all hazards. Behind the Southern Shepherd Boy, the Potomac, too deep to cross. Lee ordered Stonewall Jackson from Harpers Ferry to meet McClellan on the eastern slopes and the battle opened with the Union batteries first to desecrate so magnificent a scene.

Belching smoke rolled up, followed by shells exploding, smashing the Rebel lines but by no means breaking the spirit, for Lee was there, and with piercing shouts, the Rebel army railed on the Union line, pushing them back and recovering the ground they lost. The battle raged for hours and came to an abrupt halt, both sides completely exhausted, and Lee seized the moment to ride from one end of his line to the other, his very presence giving them courage, inciting them to do battle as never before.

The Union moved with bayonets sparkling in Antietam's September sun, no guns, no ammunition, just sabers, four lines to the one line of Confederate soldiers, and just as Lee expected, drove toward the center of his line into General John B. Gordon's army, but that splendid Georgian general had taken a brief moment to contemplate every possible recourse and his decision was made. He ordered all horses to the rear and his soldiers to lie down in the grass on their stomachs with rifles in firing position. The Union soldiers charged, the Rebels waiting for the order to fire. When it came, they opened up on the enemy in a stunning display of firepower, downing the first line and sending the Blue into retreat with three lines left. General Gordon lost not one man. The Union regrouped and sent up the second line, again repulsed by Gordon's men. Four times the unrelenting Union commander led his army into General Gordon's men, and on the fourth, the Union took up arms. Gordon knew they would, but unfortunately it had to be part of his plan. He was wounded, his men down by the scores, either dead or wounded, but not before Gordon had wreaked havoc on the Union's first three lines. Brilliant and heroic!

Over eleven thousand Yankees fell that day and nine thousand from the South. Antietam was a draw, they said. But the Confederates inflicted enormous disaster on General Burnside's forces of the North. Forces that held fast to the bridge over the Antietam River. As usual, the North claimed victory, but proof was in the reality they never followed up on that battle. The South whipped them down. The ragtags again fearlessly fought for what bit of ground they could take. General McClellan feigned victory only to find his troops repulsed and pushed into the stream of the Potomac by A. P. Hill's forces, and so lofty position was lost for McClellan over this botched battle.

> *It is beyond all wonder such men as the Rebel troops can fight as they do. That those ragged wretches, sick, hungry, and in all ways miserable, should prove such heroes in fight, is past explanation. Men never fought better. There was one regiment that stood up before the fire of one of our*

long-range batteries and of two regiments of infantry, and though the air around them was vocal with the whistle of bullets and the scream of shells, there they stood, and delivered their fire in perfect orders.

From a Federal Officer's Journal

Maryland reached out with despairing hands and broken hearts. They reached out, but to no avail, for they were chained to the Union. And after fighting the greatest pitched battle of the war at Sharpsburg, the great General moved back across the Potomac from Maryland into Virginia. Home. A space of quietude where only could be heard the prancing and dashing about of the cavalrymen. Jeb Stuart, sitting high in the saddle with boots polished and saber clanking and spurs jingling, confirmed the South was still there, and though its infantry and artillery men were all the worse from battle, its men on horseback were still sharp and chivalrous, pompously keeping the fires of war burning while Lee and his marching men took but a moment of respite.

☙

And so … there was a lull in the war in Virginia. Lee had proven one thing. His army could make its way in and out of Maryland and Pennsylvania, and his men were as gallant as their commander.

Virginia bore the brunt of the war, the biggest loss of once beautiful hillsides trampled mercilessly and ravaged by foot soldiers and mounted riders from both sides. Destruction cleared a path beside the Potomac through the now wasted Shenandoah Valley and across the mountains. Both sides were not just fighting. They were foraging for food and shelter from once fertile soil. They aimed to get it at any cost, for now they had no choice. Everywhere a foot could march or a horse could run was ruin. Virginia gave and gave, and there was yet more they must give. But for now, there was a lull in movement in the Old Dominion. Calm before the storm.

My dearest Rachel,

I embrace this opportunity to write after a full day. We rushed an enemy camp at dusk. Those little cowards tucked tail and ran leaving all manner of wonderful food the likes we've not had since we left home, maybe ever. How sumptuously the enemy dines customarily. But not tonight. And it was a far cry from cornbread and a piece of salt meat for us.

In times less comforting than today, we have hardtack. Crackers, so called by the Union. It's poor eating, but Cook has learned to soak them in water and fry them in bacon grease. That softens them. Pour over some sorghum and they're not so bad. We make do.

I fear the boys are tiring of this war, and I know that I am. We scarcely know what's going on outside our camp, and it's unnerving. There's a big picture out there somewhere and we hear about other skirmishes and hard battles, but we cannot see them, therefore, we don't understand them.

It seems Longstreet and A. P. Hill always arrive at just the right time to give reinforcements when needed. Thank God! We got word the Battle of Boonesboro Gap looked dismal and doomed, and Longstreet came, bringing renewed strength to a tired army. Young General Garland was struck through the breast with a musket ball. He fell dead on the field. Our soldiers have seen so much. We can't afford to lose our good generals, for we are blessed with them far beyond what was afforded the North.

General Jackson captured Harpers Ferry on September 14, deeply repulsing and humiliating the Union Army. We heard it was a sight to see the Yankee soldiers decked in Blue drawn in a line, stacking their arms in surrender to the southern commanders.

Though we're in Maryland with Lee's army, we were spared what we heard was horrifying at Sharpsburg. General Gordon took several Minié balls to different parts of his body, but is still alive.

General Lee needs time to draw aside and gather his forces to make ready for what he knows is ahead. The enemy didn't start out so, but they have become refined, trained, disciplined, and they far outnumber us.

We wonder how Lee could accomplish victory at some of those battles. He is an amazing commander, but as Jonathan says, fighting the South is like fighting a dog. We're hard to beat down.

Soon we will enjoy Lee's respite in Virginia, resting our weary bones. Accept the best love of your husband until death, Thomas Goode Payne.

Chapter 27
The Name is "Lee"

Summer came and went in Calhoun County, Mississippi, and things were decidedly better upon Isaac's return home. All Rachel's anger had turned to fear and anxiety before Mrs. Whitaker's runner brought the news that day, but when she knew he was safe and on his way home, she rejoiced like the father of the prodigal and the Payne household once again found something for which to make merry—a welcome home for the restless son. Isaac hung yet a fourth saber on the wall in Cassie and Albert Henry's room and another Yankee rifle over the mantle. For the time being, he would mention war no more, but he was only biding time. He needed to age. He needed to be seventeen. Or this war would end before he could do his part.

⁓

Cassie was still quite small, but she was not used to the awkwardness of carrying a baby, and the loft was not the most convenient place for her right now.

"Rachel, please come stand by while I climb into the loft. I keep getting my feet caught on my skirts, and my stomach is getting way too big. I'm afraid I'll lose my balance and fall."

"I wish you would let me make a place for you down with me. There's plenty of room," Rachel said, following her up the steps.

"I know I'm being stubborn about this, but you know how much I love the loft. It reminds me of Henry and I feel close to him when I'm up here."

Cassie was out of breath. She fell across her bed, and Rachel sat down beside her.

"Well, it's September and almost time for the baby to arrive. You'll have to come down when it turns cold."

"Yes, I know I will. But maybe we'll have a few weeks before autumn ends and winter begins. Oh, how I miss Henry, especially at Christmastime."

Rachel didn't want to say much about Henry right now for fear of making matters worse for Cassie. She missed him, too, but Cassie was agonizing over the fact that he was gone and she was about to have a baby. She needed him.

"Well," Rachel said, "when you decide, we'll work it out. Samuel is ready to go to the bunkroom with his brothers, and you can have the cradle, of course. We'll need to keep it by the fire and you can bundle up on the sofa at night. I think it will be quite cozy and much easier to take care of the baby down there."

"Oh, I can't wait for the baby to get here, and I so hope it's a boy. It's going to be 'Lee' either way, you know."

Rachel laughed. "Albert Henry is going to be so proud. And look at the odds in favor of a boy!"

༄

By the end of September, Rachel sent Isaac to alert Doc Malone that Cassie's baby would be coming any day. She knew what to do, but having him there to deliver would be far better. In fact, just having the old doctor in the house a couple of days would be a real treat.

Two days later as dusk fell on the Payne cabin, Rachel heard the clopping of hoofs in the distance. Doc Malone. She was relieved. She met him at the door and took his medical case and overnight bag.

"Thought I'd best come on over tonight. I got all my rounds done and left word with Mrs. Doc Whitaker to take care of things for me until I can get back. She's eager to help now that Whitaker is off fighting with the boys. How's Cassie doing?"

"Anxious, but otherwise fine," Rachel said. "She's still in the loft, Doc."

He rolled his eyes and said, "You're kidding, of course."

"No. And, Doc— "

"Yes, Rachel."

"I'm so glad you're here."

Rachel sighed and dropped her shoulders in relief. She hugged the old doctor and led the way up the ladder, Doc groaning with each step.

A soft glimmer of light danced on the windowpanes across the backside of the room. Warmth from the fireplace below had taken the chill off. He took a look at Cassie and felt her stomach, timing the irregular contractions.

When he was done, Rachel pulled the quilt over Cassie and she and Doc Malone descended the steps to the cabin below. Isaac stayed with Cassie.

The old family doctor was at home in the Payne house. He sat in the chair close to the hearth and smoked his pipe, rocking to the irregular beat of the crackling fire.

"Brought you a cup of tea and some apple strudel."

"Somehow I knew this was coming and I was looking forward to it. Rachel, you've done a splendid job without T. G. and the boys. It amazes me, but I always knew you were a strong woman. He would be immensely proud of you."

"I've a lot of help." She sat at the doctor's feet sipping her tea. He was such a comfort.

The flicker of a good fire dispelled the autumn chill, and when he got still and warm Doc Malone began to nod. Rachel insisted that he go to the sofa. She had padded it with quilts and laid a light blanket out for him. He gladly submitted.

She climbed to the top of the steps to check on Cassie. Isaac was asleep on the bear rug. All was well for the evening.

Rachel was up long before daybreak. She shook her young son who slept peacefully in his bunk.

"Joab. Wake up. Time to get ready to go. When you've dressed, come on out to the kitchen and eat breakfast with Doc Malone and Isaac."

"Her pains are increasingly harder and closer together," Rachel said. "Should I give her breakfast, Doc?"

"No, no. Just a little hot tea with a touch of honey. Nothing more," he said.

Rachel sent Isaac up with the tea, and when he returned, the four of them sat down to a breakfast of hot biscuits and sausage. Isaac poured coffee from the pot on the grate as Rachel buttered the biscuits. Joab opened the jar of blackberry jam and scooped some to his plate.

It was early yet. Rachel closed the door to the bunkroom so Samuel could sleep on. If she knew anything about birthing, it would be a hectic day, and he would be up and about all too soon, requiring her attention.

"Joab," she said, "off you go. Isaac has your horse saddled. Hope you won't be lonely riding by yourself this morning, but I need your brother here today. Remind Grandpa Church Cassie's about to have her baby and you must leave the mill in time to get home well before dark. Take your rifle, and be cautious. Do not shoot unless absolutely necessary. Understand?"

"Yes, ma'am," he said, eager to get moving on his journey alone, an adventure upon which he had never embarked. It gave him that grown-up feeling.

Rachel walked back into the house musing about all the changes that were taking place in her family. She didn't like the idea of sending her young son off alone, especially armed with a rifle for protection. One among many reasons she would be on pins and needles today. All these changes helped keep her mind off what might be going on in Virginia, or Maryland, or wherever the men were fighting—things that were not so good, in fact, miserably horrid things. This birthing would give them a welcomed reprieve from the war. At least Rachel hoped for that. After the baby came and a measure of normalcy returned, they could resume schooling in the evenings when Joab and Isaac were home from the mill.

"This may be tricky, but we're bringing Cassie downstairs. It will be better for all concerned. It's far too dangerous for her to be up there, even after the baby arrives. Besides, we're going to need lots of boiling water and other things that will be easier to come by down here. Rachel, you know the routine. Don't you agree with me?"

"Why, yes, Doc, but Cassie—"

"Never mind Cassie. We're bringing her down. Isaac, are you ready to help me?"

"Yes, sir."

The three of them started up the steps, wondering what kind of resistance they would get from Cassie. But Rachel loved Doc's assertiveness. It meant she didn't have to make the decision herself.

Cassie groaned, but submissively accepted the instructions from the old doctor. After all, it was not fair for him to have to go up and down the ladder. Nor would it be easy for Rachel and Isaac. And the way she felt in this moment, she didn't care what they did to or with her.

"We're going to do this right now, before we get some serious labor pains going and the water breaks. She's going to have this baby in your bed, Rachel. Now, Isaac, pick her up and bring her to the loft steps," said Doc Malone. "She doesn't weigh a hundred and ten pounds anyway."

"I know," said Isaac. "This will not be the hard part."

Isaac wrapped Cassie in a flannel blanket and lifted her in his arms. Rachel descended the steps to help below.

"Now stand here by Doc Malone," Isaac said. "I'll start down. Just turn around backward and I'll be right behind you to take you on down."

"Oh, Isaac, you're so chivalrous and quite strong," Cassie said, "—and I'm having the worst pain of my life right now."

"No—not yet!" Isaac said, terrified of what might happen before he could get her downstairs. "Hold on Cassie. No pains allowed, yet."

When they reached the bottom step, he picked her up and carried her to his mother's room. To the bed where he and all his brothers were born.

"Cassie, when you think about it, Henry was born right here just over eighteen years ago. Makes this a special place for Lee to be born," he said.

"Ohhh!"

Cassie tried hard to smile, but grimaced from the pain that had gripped her in the moment. She clung to Isaac's hand. When it subsided, she said, "Then I'm glad we're down here. The special place is best for all of us. Thank you, Isaac. You're doing a wonderful job of taking Henry's place, and all."

"Why, you're welcome, Cassie. I would have done as much for Glory," he said.

Her eyes were filling with tears, but they both laughed as he gently put her down on the feather bed Rachel had prepared for the splendid occasion. In that moment, Isaac didn't know what to do or say. Doc intervened.

"Now Isaac, make sure there's plenty of water boiling. I'll let you know when I need a basin."

"Yes, sir, Doc. I remember some things from Samuel and Joab's birthing, but I get scared every time. Looks like I'd be used to it by now."

"Nothing to worry about, Isaac. A couple more and you'll be good as me."

"No, sir, Doc. I could never do what you do—well, if it was a colt or a calf, I'd be okay."

"Same thing," Doc said.

"Isaac, you help Doc until time to deliver the baby. Samuel is up and I have to feed him. Come get me if need be."

"Yes, Mother," he said nervously. "What time is it?"

"About ten o'clock," she said. "I can't believe he slept this long, but it's been a great help to all of us."

Doc sent Isaac out of the room and examined Cassie, covered her, and called for Isaac to come back in.

"It won't be long, son. Hold her hands and talk to her. I've got work to do."

"Yes, sir."

Cassie began to thrash about feverishly, the pains getting more severe. Isaac took both of her hands and held them tight, talking incessantly to her about everything, anything.

"Just think about Henry and how proud he's going to be when he sees this baby," he said.

"Try to relax between pains, Cassie. You're doing just fine. Isaac, go and get some more hot water and some of your mother's white cloths. Hurry up, now."

"Isaac, don't leave me," she begged, holding fast to his hand.

"He'll be right back, Cassie. I'm here. I'm right here."

"Ma, I think you need to get in there. I'll take care of Sam."

"I believe you're right."

She took the water and cloths and headed for the birthing room. Cassie was in the middle of a hard pain, and Rachel was momentarily living in the past. She had done this six times, and she knew the excruciating pangs of birth. She set the boiling hot water down for Doc Malone and took Cassie's hands. She mopped her brow and the tears with one of the warm cloths. The pain subsided and Cassie drifted off to sleep.

"We'll just let her rest a bit. The pains will wake her, but she may have a ways to go yet," said Doc Malone. "You can go on back to Sam. I'll give a yell, or more than likely, Cassie will."

Rachel waited a good ten minutes then peeked into the room. Doc had nodded off to sleep in the chair. She caught his reading glasses just before they hit the floor and laid them on the dresser. Cassie appeared to be out cold. Rest was the best thing for her right now—for both of them, for soon she would wake up to pains coming with a vengeance.

An hour later Cassie screamed, waking Doc from his nap. For a moment he forgot where he was. What he was doing. He needed to collect his wits, refocus.

"Ah, yes," he muttered, "Cassie is having a baby. How could I forget that?"

He called for Isaac to come quickly.

"Yes, sir."

"It looks like Cassie is ready to commence having some serious pains. Be ready to help me. Now, what did I do with my glasses?"

"Ma!" he yelled. And Rachel quickly joined them in the bedroom.

"Go ahead, Isaac. I think she feels like you are with her for Albert Henry. Just hold her. You're doing a great job."

"Yes, Ma," he said, wiping sweat from his own face.

"Cassie, you're doing quite nicely," Doc said.

"Just another push or two and you'll be there, and I can return to my nap. But wait until I say so."

"Ohhhh," Cassie moaned. "It hurts!" And the tears rolled down her cheeks.

"Now, Cassie, just take a deep breath and squeeze my hands," said Isaac. "Stay with me, now. Stay with me, Cassie."

"I ... I ... where on earth do you think I'd be going?" she snapped.

Doc chuckled, and she cried out again with insufferable pain. "Oh, Doc, you're killing me! I do want out of here! I'll go anywhere to get away from you!"

"Cassie, I think it's Lee that's causing the pain. Not me! He must be a big boy! And just where did you want to go?"

Cassie laughed at the doctor between pains.

"You're so funny! Ohhh!"

"Okay, this is it. Give me a good strong push."

Isaac held her hands and buried his face in her hair, not wanting to experience childbirth from any viewing angle, and in that moment Cassie felt the whole world was against her, pushing hard in opposition to her youthful body, and in one hurtful, hideous instant of agony, it was over. The baby came. The pain subsided. A young Confederate soldier's son arrived, undeniably doing the Rebel yell.

"Splendid!" said the old doctor. "Really quite splendid! It's four o'clock in the afternoon, and we have a fine specimen of a boy baby. Guess that's what you wanted, huh? And I've already been informed his name is Robert Edward Lee Payne. My, my, you Payne women do have the boys."

He cut the cord and tied it down, wrapped the baby in some of Rachel's cloths, and handed him to his mother. Tears plopped from her eyes as she caressed her baby boy, and then she cried aloud, "Oh, Albert Henry! How I need you and wish you were here! And Doc Malone, I'm so sorry I was mean to you."

"Dear Cassie, every woman who has ever delivered has hated me at some point during the ordeal. And after all is said and done, they love me more than ever."

Rachel and Isaac, with tears falling, hovered over Cassie for a few minutes, reassuring her that everything was fine and that Henry would be home soon. Cassie drifted off into a well-earned deep sleep. Rachel took the baby and she, Isaac, and Doc Malone went to the warm kitchen to clean him up and dress him.

At six o'clock, Joab came bounding in the door, and seeing the baby in his mother's arms, he could hardly believe his eyes.

"Aw, me!" he yelled. "That baby arrived and I missed all the commotion."

He put his hat and coat on the hook and said, "Well, what is he? A boy or a girl?"

They all roared with laughter.

"A boy!" Doc Malone said. "What else do we get at the Payne house? The name is 'Lee'."

"Splendid! Exactly what I ordered."

When the long day ended and the family, including Cassie, was satisfied with a delicious supper of hot homemade soup, Doc Malone took his seat in the rocking chair by the fire and the family gathered around him, Rachel holding her new grandson all snug in the blue flannel blanket she had made. Oh, what she would give if Thomas could see his grandson and Henry could see his baby boy.

Doc took the old worn leather Bible from his medical case, put his reading glasses on his nose, and opened to Isaiah 61, for God had once again given a garment of praise for the spirit of heaviness—something wonderful out of incredible pain.

> *The Spirit of the Lord God is upon me; because the Lord hath anointed me to preach good tidings unto the meek; he hath sent me to bind up the brokenhearted, to proclaim liberty to the captives, and the opening of the prison to them that are bound; To proclaim the acceptable year of the Lord, and the day of vengeance of our God; to comfort all that mourn: To appoint unto them that mourn in Zion, to give unto them beauty for ashes, the oil of joy for mourning, the garment of praise for the spirit of heaviness; that they might be called trees of righteousness, the planting of the Lord, that he might be glorified.*

Chapter 28
Life is Uncertain, Death is Sure

It had been almost seven months since Isaac returned to Calhoun County, and he had been silent far too long. He had done everything asked of him, and now he must speak to his mother again. This time he would do it right, though he feared the reactions would be the same. Cassie had fully recovered from childbirth and was already pulling her share of the load, but Isaac knew it would mean hardship for his mother, for now there was yet another little boy to care for.

> *… Thomas, Isaac has not been happy since you and the boys left. I know he tried it once and came back. I fear he will die on a battlefield, but who am I to hold him back when he feels so strongly about fighting. He has the heart of a soldier, and it is bursting within him.*

He read Rachel's letter with fear and trembling. Even the boys had said Isaac would never be able to endure camp life. The discipline, deprivation, homesickness, and physical illness would get the best of him, they were sure. But these were strange times. Boys became men far too early, and once they got the hankering for war, it would not go away. What Thomas did not need at this time in his life was conflict over Isaac. At the same time, he didn't want Rachel to be strapped with the decision. He would make it himself.

> *Goldsboro, North Carolina*
> *January 30, 1863*
>
> *If you find that Isaac will not stay at home with you, send him to me. I concur. He will never be happy until he's in this war. There are some boys*

younger than sixteen. I don't know how they enlisted unless they lied about their age. Don't let him try to enlist or join the cavalry, for I can best take care of that when he gets here. I've drawn a map to the best of my knowing. He needs to come to Goldsboro, North Carolina, where the road forks, one going to Wilmington and the other to Raleigh. Our camp is near Goldsboro. I allow he will travel with Abe, Cliff and Billy as before, provided their parents give consent. I cannot be responsible for their well being. Jonathan and Henry are acclimated to war. I will worry over Isaac as long as he is on a battlefield, but I will do my best by him with God's help.

I cannot stress enough how dangerous it is to travel. He will need to try and take the cars when he can, especially where there are rivers to cross, otherwise, he will never get here. The railroad will transport the horses. Send ample food with him, at least enough to last for ten days. And send this letter along with him to ensure free passage. Your faithful husband, father of Isaac Beauford Payne, Captain T. G. Payne, Mississippi 42nd.

Isaac and the boys arrived at the camp near Goldsboro on February 13, 1863, just as T. G.'s company was moving up to Virginia.

Dearest Rachel,

Isaac was sick with the fever when we left Goldsboro and I left Henry with him. He's well now, and we're all together here in Black Water, which is about seventy-five miles southeast of Richmond. Don't worry about him. I will ensure his safety to the best of my knowing. But if times get really bad, I will send him home in some safe direction. He must abide by my decisions whether he thinks they are right or wrong. Try not to worry yourself over the situation.

I will write more when I can, but now I must return to the picket line. Accept the best love of your husband, Thomas Goode Payne.

Isaac Payne was living out his dream. His brothers had sold him far short. He snugly fit into army life with them, doing as he was told as a civilian servant, wishing he could muster in. But for the time being, he would cut wood, forage for food, stand picket on the Black Water River. He pompously carried the rifle and saber he had taken from the Yankee nightrider at Shiloh months before. He would make his father and brothers proud.

T. G. managed to get another oilcloth and blanket, and their tent now housed four Payne men instead of three. Billy, Cliff, and Abe were dispersed into the company. T. G.'s colonel was glad to get the help, though none of them were allowed to enlist in the army. They could, however, keep their horses in the camp with them, for sooner or later they would be going home.

The days were cool, the nights cold on the Black Water. In late March of 1863, Thomas and his son sat alone at the campfire. Time for the conversation Isaac had internally resisted since he arrived on the Virginia battlefield, he guessed. He was compelled by the dignity his father deserved to listen carefully to his decision. He had promised to in no way resist. He would make good that promise, but Isaac was surprised at his father's words.

"Isaac, I'm going to let you stay with me for a while longer," he said, "but you must understand that I could order you to go home any day and without notice. If I say go, you must go. With no questions asked. Do you understand?"

"Yes, Pa. I never wanted to be a burden to you, but I'm as good at picket duty as most of the soldiers."

"Better than most. I have never questioned your courage and fortitude, son. It's your age, and I don't have to tell you that. You've been fighting the fact of your youth for almost two years, now. Since before this war started. Just be ready for what comes your way."

"Yes, sir," he said.

He would do as his father commanded at the appropriate time. If he went home, this time it would be to stay. At least until he was seventeen.

༄

March came and went, the men still doing picket on the Black Water.

Day had ended and the camp chores were done. Isaac sat somewhere around a campfire with his friends, a favorite pastime for the young boys before retiring for the night. Thomas called Jonathan and Henry aside.

"Boys, you don't know how bad I want to be heading in the other direction. I respect Lee and Longstreet, Heth and A. P. Hill—but for some reason I have the feeling we're heading straight into another Shiloh."

"What makes you say that, Pa?" Henry asked.

"It's just a hunch," he said. "I feel compelled to get Isaac out of here. He has seen enough action on the picket lines of Black Water and Fredericksburg, and now before it gets any worse, I'm going to send him and the boys home."

Jonathan sat with his head in his hands as his father spoke. He wished Isaac had never come. Oh, he was happy to see his brother, all right, but now their days may be numbered. Obviously, his father thought so, and the Rebel army had become exceedingly poor. Their uniforms were in rags, and they were hungry most of the time. The romance was gone. Long gone. Reality had set in with a vengeance.

"You're doing the right thing, Pa," Jonathan said.

"I agree," said Henry. "We'll back you, Pa. Isaac will understand. We thought when we came into the army this war would be over before sixty days had passed. I don't know how much longer it will last, but Isaac may have his opportunity to really get in when he turns seventeen. But if you think he needs to get out of here, I certainly agree with you. Anyway, I know Mother and Cassie need him, especially now that Lee ... "

Albert Henry stopped short of breaking. He had not even seen his baby boy, and Isaac had so willingly and bravely helped with the delivery. He should be back there helping Cassie with Lee until the war was over and Henry could get back home.

In an attempt to get Henry's mind off Cassie and the baby, his father continued. "I'm going to have to get A. P. Hill's ear to map out a way home for them so they travel away from the enemy. When I think of him riding back through Shiloh and Corinth like before, I get sick. Grant's boys are still all over the place, and I don't know if there is a good way for them to travel. I'm going to see if I can get them on the cars at least as far as Tennessee. They can ride their horses on from there."

"When are you going to tell him, Pa?" Jonathan asked.

"As soon as I can get a few minutes with General Hill."

Isaac brought wood up to start a fire. When it was blazing, he skillfully pulled a couple of burning logs over and started a pot of coffee for his father. Thomas watched his young son, wishing more than anything this war would end—even before he had to send him home.

༄

Suffolk had little significance in the war, but the Payne men had been ordered there to picket with soldiers from Heth's Division. The place was heavily fortified by General John J. Peck, commander of the Union forces there. In April, General Longstreet began a siege on Suffolk, his attempts failing. He constructed earthworks with intentions of bombarding the place, but was abruptly stopped by gunboats on the Nansemont River and heavy artillery in the enemy's works.

In May, Heth was summoned to assist Lee at Chancellorsville and withdrew some of his men from Suffolk. In the heat of battle on May 2, at 9:15 in the evening, Stonewall Jackson was accidentally shot by one of his own pickets. One of the shots severed an artery in his left arm. It would have to be amputated. In light of the misfortune, Lee sent for Jeb Stuart to lead

Jackson's troops in the final charge at Chancellorsville. Stuart assailed Hooker from the west, and as he draped on the mantle of one of the greatest generals of all time, he burst forth in song, pulling one of his favorite melodies from his repertoire and singing loud and clear his own contrived words: "Now, Joe Hooker, won't you *Come out of the Wilderness?*" —And Lee attacked from the south. The army Hooker deemed *the finest on the planet* retreated across the Rappahannock, leaving the South with a brilliant win at Chancellorsville, but an enormous loss in the finest of southern generals.

Stonewall Jackson was dead.
The South mourned.
The whole world mourned.

&

In May of 1863, Thomas wrote disturbing words to Rachel. Disturbing even to himself.

> *I want you to take special care of yourself and the children. When I think of the distance that we are apart, I feel that I would much rather be there with you. I want you to recollect that life is uncertain and death sure, and if I should never be permitted to see you again, it is my wish that you should train our children up in the way that will be pleasing in the sight of the Lord that their last days may be their best days.*

Rachel put the letter in her apron pocket and walked out onto the porch. That smothering mood engulfed her, the desperate, powerless sensation that had taken her to the nadir time and again since the day Thomas and the boys left. What did he know that he was not telling her? Or was it purely a gut feeling with him that may or may not be reliable?

The oak and ash trees at the end of the house had budded and fully leafed out and the weather was warm and mild, a beautiful time of year in the South. As far as the eye could see, their little corner of the world was untouched by this cruel war.

"Jesus, take away the despondency," she whispered. "Defeat the Enemy that takes me to this dreadful place of selfishness and despair. Protect my men. Cover them with your hand of mercy. *It is of the Lord's mercies that we are not consumed, because his compassions fail not. They are new every morning: great is thy faithfulness.*"

Chapter 29
Fredericksburg

Remembrance

It was early. The darkest hour before daybreak on December 11, 1862. Union engineers laid three pontoon bridges at Fredericksburg and three more a couple of miles down the river. Covered by artillery from Union soldiers, the engineers got the job done without too much trouble. But high on the tops of buildings and in rifle pits in the little town of Fredericksburg a brigade of Mississippians began to fire, picking off the engineers and Union soldiers as the sun began to rise over the little town in the Old Dominion. *My Mississippians*! The great generals had called them. For they were fearless, brave Soldiers of the South.

A. P. Hill's corps was there. The Magnolia Guards, Mississippi's Seventeenth, were there. The Payne men were there, soldiers of the Mississippi Forty-Second. The Battle of Fredericksburg in December 1862 was one of the greatest victories of the war for the South, one of the heaviest defeats for the Union. It was there that General Lee said, "It is well that war is so terrible—we should grow too fond of it!" Seated upon his faithful steed, he looked out over his victory and felt new vigor. The memories of the victories at Fredericksburg surely brought him swelling confidence, new energy to continue the fight for southern freedom and to press toward enemy country once again. But in the meantime, the pickets remained at Fredericksburg on both sides of the river.

And now in June 1863, A. P. Hill's Corps was once again at Fredericksburg, "across the river from the Yankee camp, expecting a fight any day," Jonathan had written his mother.

> *We're encamped in the entrenchments in full view of the enemy, with positive orders not to shoot unless attacked. We have no communication and we're forced to wait until the enemy's move develops. We can't tell exactly what is going on, but we know the Union soldiers are trying to cross the river. The Magnolia Guards left Fredericksburg and went up the river toward Culpepper. We worry about the Magnolia Guards when we can't hear from them.*

The Payne men stood picket day after endless day. And when they were not on picket, they were guarding prisoners. Fredericksburg was important strategically—gateway to the South. To the Old Dominion. It was ravaged as were all other parts of the Shenandoah, but for the time being, Fredericksburg belonged to the South, and there was no question they would not desecrate December's victory by leaving it unprotected.

The Mississippians had marched thousands of miles since the day they left Grenada in early December 1861. They cooled many a blister with the bear lard Rachel packed in their knapsacks. Now it was gone, but not before the calluses became permanent. It was hardly worth the effort to keep what little shoe leather they had left tied to their feet. Besides, they could walk without shoes now, sometimes without feeling but, more often, with pain.

Driven by the glorious victories at Fredericksburg and Chancellorsville—and with public opinion in the South insisting that the army move toward invading the North—Lee made his preparations.

The Confederate army was in dire need of supplies. Hope for help from Europe was diminishing, and Lee needed to strike a fatal blow to the enemy. His army had already proven they were unrelenting, but the fact that the army of the enemy kept growing instead of diminishing was increasingly demoralizing for the troubled Rebel commanders. The North still had men they could draft. The South had long since run out of men to replace those who were dying in battle or from disease.

June 1863

My dearest Rachel,

> *If not for the love and closeness of the four of us, life would be unbearable. The men have seen fit to go their separate ways. Oh, we still fight together, of course, but the sense of community is gone for all practical purposes. It's every man for himself—for food, drink, shelter, and that is the way it must be. Pity the man who has no kin fighting alongside him, for lonely is that man, indeed.*

But Jonathan, Albert Henry and I have always been our own outfit. Three heads and three hearts are better than one. And now, for a brief time, our dear Isaac has been a joy. Sometimes I feel like Abraham, offering my sons on the altar of sacrifice for our country, but it is our duty, and we press on, hoping it will soon end.

Don't worry about us. Our wagon has staples—flour, sugar, meal, coffee, and salt—but it seems never all at one time, and we have few green vegetables. But our company is blessed with a good cook. One of life's most enjoyable moments these days is the smell of coffee and watching those brown-topped biscuits come off the fire. Biscuits and gravy—the staff of life. I've watched the boys in the light of the evening campfire, their empty stomachs crying 'thank you' as they sop down the gravy with an extra biscuit from the skillet, the three of them laughing and talking together just like old times at home. Rachel, you would be so proud of your sons. They are real soldiers of the South.

Give my best love to Mother and Pap and regards to all the Calhoun County connection. Until we meet again, I remain faithfully yours, Thomas Goode Payne

Part Four
Gettysburg

Chapter 30
Isaac, Go Home!

Mid-June

If not for the war, it would have been the most beautiful place on earth as far as Thomas was concerned. The days were warm, almost hot, and the nights were cool and comfortable. The laurel and rhododendron spread pink and white blossoms beneath the lush foliage on the mountainsides, and soft summer fragrances filled the air until replaced by the hideous stench of artillery in the distance. The bluebirds sang splendidly and flitted about gathering nectar and dew from the wildflowers on the hills.

❦

Thomas rose early, about four o'clock on the morning of June 14, 1863. He made his way through the camp to Jed McGrew's blazing fire and took the tin cup the wagon master handed him.

"Sugar this morning, Captain?"

"No, thanks, Jed. I think I'll drink it black."

"A beautiful morning, eh?"

"Splendid."

Quite frankly, it was not. In fact, it may well be one of the worst days of his life. But he didn't want Jed or anybody else to know how he felt about this particular day.

He slogged back to his campsite. Now was the time. He picked up speed as he pondered the need to get Isaac out of here. He paced back and forth in front of their tent until five o'clock, not wanting to get him up too early. He lifted the flap and stood in the door of the tent where his three boys lay side by side, fully clothed, guns between them. Loaded. He thought of Joab, Samuel, even Benjamin, remembering when his three older boys were their age. How he desired to recall those years. My God in heaven, he thought! How did all this happen? Suddenly, he was nauseously homesick.

He touched Isaac and he jumped awake.

"Son, run up to Jed's and get you a cup of coffee and come right back. Get Billy and Abe and Cliff. Tell them to ride their horses."

"Yes, sir."

Isaac didn't say another word. He knew what was happening. He would tell the boys to bring their rifles and saddlebags.

"Jonathan, Henry. Come on and get up. It's five o'clock. Jonathan, wash your face and saddle Glory for Isaac. Henry, run up to Jed's and tell him to get you a sack of biscuits from Cook, at least eight, and some side meat. Tell him I'll explain later."

Thomas knew no other way to get this done. He had to be straightforward with Isaac. Within minutes, the four boys were making their way around the outer perimeter of the camp so as not to disturb those still sleeping, for reveille had not yet sounded.

"Wait here for me," Isaac said to Billy, Abe, and Cliff.

He respectfully approached his father. This was going to hurt.

"Son, it's time. You've got to go home. I've put this off as long as I can. I want you on your horse and out of here immediately. I've got maps for you from General Hill. He knows how you should go. Pay close attention to the directions, for you will take the cars out of Virginia and into Tennessee. It's all right here," he said, pointing to the map. "Now, get the boys and ride out of here. Believe me son, this is the best thing for you.

"And, Isaac—remember how much I love you. I will always love you, and I will sorely miss you."

With tears streaming down his cheeks, Isaac clung to his father, then his brothers. He took the sack of provisions from Henry and mounted Glory. He pulled tight on the reins until the horse reared on his back legs and snorted, reminiscent of Grenada. He hard saluted his father, motioned for his friends, and they rode off in the dawn's earliest light. The warrior child was going home.

Thomas cried aloud, gasped for breath, and fell to his knees when Isaac was out of sight. The boys draped themselves across their father like the cross bars on the Confederate Flag—their souls knit together as David and Jonathan of old—hoping to somehow ease their father's pain, but Thomas would not be comforted. Not in this dreadful moment.

Would the heartache never end?

Duty-bound by a series of events that began on June 3, Lee pressed onward toward Washington. On the ninth, Jeb Stuart led a valiant victory over the Union army at Brandy Station, and on June 14, the day Isaac left, Rebel forces took possession of Martinsburg, led by General Rhodes. Simultaneously, General Ewell took Winchester, and between June 24 and 30, Lee was successful in taking the Army of Northern Virginia into Maryland and Pennsylvania. Lincoln, consulting no man, replaced General Hooker with General George Meade.

Aghast at the sound of southern horses and foot soldiers trampling across Union country, Lincoln called for a hundred thousand more troops. And then the Union pulled out all the stops. The North had seen the fall of their best generals to the Rebel armies. They would put an end to the grimy, dirty, shoeless wretches once and for all.

Chapter 31
The Bloody Trough

Irony shrouded the events at Gettysburg. Both armies arrived near dawn on July 1. General Meade and his army had moved northward in the same direction as Lee, both traveling on differing paths toward Gettysburg with no plan of fighting there, with no thought even that they were both heading in the same direction. Many towns and villages had gone up in ruin without notice during this war, all a part of the conundrum, men falling like flies on molasses, scarcely honored for their bravery except by loved ones at home who got the word, wailed and mourned all night, trying desperately to remember the last moments at home. The grief was unspeakable. And here in full view was another contest that had no apparent rhyme or reason.

Gettysburg was progression, regression. The Confederacy was way past its best, fighting with far fewer men than the North, for the enemy still had men they could recruit. There were varying phases of the war up until this Gettysburg fiasco—first victory, then defeat, victory unexplainable, glorious victory in battle—and then the storm clouds erupted and the great struggle came. Lee crossed the Potomac in 1862. He crossed it again in 1863. What he hoped to accomplish on Union soil we know in part. His army would never know the full reasons for his decisions, for they would only issue when they rested *on the other side of the river*. And then it wouldn't matter any more.

༄

The Payne men stood on the picket lines at Black Water and Fredericksburg. They suffered deprivation and starvation, and they marched over unforgiving terrain, the calluses having formed months ago. Sixty days turned into well over nineteen months for these soldiers of the Mississippi

Volunteer Army of Ten Thousand, and they longed to be home. Henry hadn't seen his son, and he was almost a year old. The war had stolen time, splendid moments, that could not be retrieved or replaced in this lifetime.

The march into Pennsylvania was abhorrent for a multitude of reasons. It was hot. Their leather was in shreds, their toes and parts of their feet exposed. Some were barefoot. It was time for the army to put boots on their fighting men, and General Heth led some of his troops into Gettysburg for that purpose. At dawn he clashed with Buford's Union cavalry in town, and intended renewal turned into three days of all-out chaos, the likes not seen before or since.

A host of errors in battle plagued both North and South more times than not. Lee experienced major bestirring obstacles at Gettysburg, including his strategy. Stonewall Jackson was gone. Lee needed him. Errors in judgment, generals with their own ideas, fatigue and illness, and too few men. All this and more led the South to the fatal blow.

T. G. and Albert Henry were with General Heth, among those who met head on with the Union forces on July 1. Jonathan remained on the field with A. P. Hill's Corps, one of the few times he had been away from his father and Henry since they joined the Confederate Army. Had he known what was about to take place, he would never have left their side. But how could he have known? How could anyone have known?

༄

Jonathan and Andrew McAllister waited expectantly for T. G., Albert Henry, and the others. It was hot and humid, almost ninety degrees, though the July sun was just coming up over the hills. Jonathan wiped the sweat from his eyes and scanned the horizon in the direction of Gettysburg.

The wheat, heavy with grain, waved in the hot July wind and cast a golden glow that reflected off the rocks on Cemetery Ridge when touched by the first sun of the day. Roosters crowed and women headed for their barns to milk the cows and then retreated, horrified that the commanders had brought the war to their peaceful little town. Men in carriages making their way to work up Emmitsburg Road struck their mares for speed, for generals from both North and South plotted for position in plain view on the ridges. Thousands of them. Blue. Gray.

"Where are they?" Jonathan was frantic. "The sun's up, and they've been gone a long time. I've got a strange feeling, Andrew."

"Jonathan, I see them both. They're coming across the pike with General Davis and the others."

"Thank God!" Jonathan shouted.

He could see his father and Henry running. His father fell. He struggled to get on his feet, and was running again hard for the earthworks. Jonathan broke down and cried at the sight of his father stumbling and falling. He was too old for this. It shouldn't be happening.

"But wait—what's going on down there?" Andrew shouted. "It doesn't look good. That's no breastwork. It's something else."

"Stay down, Andrew. It's a railroad cut, and looks like Pa and Henry are stuck in there with the rest of Joe Davis' men except you and me and some of the others up here. Great God in heaven! What has the man done? They're getting blown to bits down there. Oh ... Oh, my soul!"

Jonathan and Andrew ran like rabbits as close to the ground as possible, to the trench. And in that moment, Thomas Payne took a shot to the chest. Blood gushed straightforward from his wound.

"Oh, Pa, no!" Jonathan screamed. "Andrew, help me! Help me get him out!"

"Get down, boys!"

Thomas struggled to speak.

"Find cover for yourselves. Don't worry about me ... I'm going home."

"Yes, Captain, yes, you'll be going home soon," said Duncan Jamison, who saw the fiasco in the railroad cut and ran to help Jonathan and Andrew.

"No, I'll never make it back ... not to Mississippi."

"You've got to hold on, Pa. Doc Whitaker's in the cut. He's coming. He's going to help."

Andrew looked at Jonathan and dropped his head. Doc lay face down in the railroad cut in his own blood.

"I've done all I can do. I'm going to the *land that is fairer than day*. I've seen it by faith. And ... I'm almost there. Ben's waiting for me ... and I think Henry beat me there. Jonathan ... Jonathan ... "

"Yes, Pa, I'm right here."

Jonathan choked. Hot tears were falling like water. He wrapped himself around his dying father to receive last instructions.

"Finish this fight, and ... go ... go back home, son. Your ma ... she needs you. Promise me ... take care of the farm and the mill ... raise Henry's boy. Promise, son. Do what I can't do, now."

"Pa! Oh, Pa!" Jonathan held his father, crying, begging, "Papa, don't die. Henry's gone. Don't you leave me! I love you so much!"

Blood gushed from T. G.'s mouth and nose; he gasped for breath, and with his last ounce of strength, reached for the bloody flag and pulled it close. He relaxed his legs on the crushed wheat.

"Oh, Rachel ... my Rachel. I wanted ... to see you again ... that glorious place ... we'll meet there ... my best love ... to you and the children."

"No, Papa! You're going to Calhoun with me."

And with his face lifted, last words gently spilled from T. G.'s bleeding lips, "Why, Henry, there you are, and Ben ... Henry, you've got Ben with you. Rachel ... "

T. G. drew the flag to his lips and rested his weary body in the arms of his son, then slept the silent, peaceful sleep of a child of God. His remaining soldiers hovered about him. But he was already there, in the warm and gentle embrace of a loving Lord and his sons, Albert Henry and Benjamin.

Jonathan was alone on the wheat field—surrounded by Confederate soldiers—but so alone.

A lull in the battle gave brave men from both sides a moment to bury their dead. They took shovels from the supply wagons and began to dig shallow graves.

Jonathan, covered in his father's blood, searched the battleground around the peach orchard for Henry's body. As far as the eye could see there was carnage.

"He's over here, Jon," shouted Duncan.

Henry lay dead at the base of a peach tree clutching his squirrel rifle. Jonathan sat down beside his body. He rolled him over and held him in his arms. He looked so small.

"I don't know how he got out of the cut. Here, Jon, let me help you."

"No, Duncan. I'll carry him."

He pulled his brother's bloody body next to his own and rocked him back and forth for a few minutes, wailing and moaning, then picked him up and walked the distance to the wheat field. He gently laid Albert Henry beside his father, covered them both with the bloody Confederate Flag his mother had made, and began digging a single grave.

With every shovel of earth, the scroll of Jonathan's life rolled, revealing his passing days—the boy who went to war, the man who fought it side by side with his father and brother; his mother's face pressed to the window of the cabin, Benjamin's grave on the hill under the old oak tree, and Isaac, his restless brother, who couldn't stay home and who was now riding Glory hard for the hills of Mississippi. Now Henry, his beloved blood brother and brother in battle and his father, whom he loved beyond belief, lay still on the battlefield of Gettysburg, warmed by their own blood and the stifling hot July sun.

"Oh, dear God! Help me!" Jonathan wailed.

The scene was pathetic. Death surrounded him. But in this moment, he only saw his father and Henry lying still, peaceful. They would *study war no more*.

Jonathan spent a sleepless night, the first in almost two years without his father and Henry. He was lifeless. Empty and lonely. But in the small hours before dawn, he gave in to exhaustion and fell asleep on the ground. This Gettysburg battle was far from over. He still had fighting to do, and he needed the two hours of sleep.

∽

Barksdale's brigade arrived with McLaw's division after the first day of battle. It was July 2. The plan from General Robert E. Lee was for Longstreet's Corps to maneuver into position and attack northeast up the Emmitsburg Road to disenfranchise the Union left flank. Barksdale's area of the attack placed him at the most relevant point in the Union line set tenaciously at the peach orchard where Jonathan had found Henry's body. At about 5:30 in the evening, Barksdale's brigade burst from the woods in a spectacular assault, smashing the brigade manning the peach orchard line, wounding and capturing the Union brigade commander himself. Some of Barksdale's regiment turned to the north and wreaked havoc in another Union division, causing them to withdraw, some as far back as Seminary Ridge. Others of the combined regiments went straight ahead.

So few of the Mississippi Forty-Second were left. Heth's Division charged the hill, heroically led by Ambrose P. Hill. Jonathan looked to his left and in a moment of time that brave Mississippi fire-eater, William Barksdale, fell.

"Oh, dear God!" Jonathan cried out. "Not General Barksdale!"

General Lee had called William Barksdale *My Mississippian*. And now he was down, bleeding profusely. He was dying.

∽

July 3, 1863

The air was thick with the gray dust of gunpowder from the Union cannons, and like a curtain on the finale of a paradoxical tragedy written and produced by the devil and his demons, smoke from the cannons rolled up on the ridge, exposing the Union soldiers. But they faced the bravest, most splendid army of Rebel soldiers that ever lived, standing shoulder to shoulder a mile and a half end to end, the hot July sun's rays bouncing off every squirrel rifle as though each had been polished the night before in preparation for a pass-in-review parade. Amish men riding along the Emmitsburg Road in their carriages got out and bowed to the ground, praying for men on both sides, for this was the third day of carnage. It must come to an end.

Jonathan stood with his countrymen, his rifle drawn and ready. He waited. Impatiently. In the steaming hot and humid July sun, he waited, wiping sweat out of his eyes with the sleeve of his ragged Confederate uniform. And then the nod. Longstreet to Pickett. And in that instant, Pickett's men charged the hill, screaming the blood-curdling Rebel yell. Brave men, their dignity and strength pressed to the breach, fell like autumn leaves, blood running freely down the hill. Gettysburg, Pennsylvania was a trough.

Jonathan Payne shouted the Rebel yell as he charged the hill, thousands by his side dropping like flies. His thoughts were of his father and Henry. They were dead. His father, shot through with a Minié ball to the chest and Henry, shot down and run through with a saber. He had to fight this battle for them. Their blood was in the trough and still warm on his hands, and their bodies lay in a shallow grave on the wheat field.

He could see everything with horrifying clarity from the side of the hill. Men falling on his right, on his left. Before him, behind him. Screaming, bleeding. Kemper wounded and down. Garnett, already wounded in the leg, gallantly riding his horse in the charge, certain death, and it was so. Armistead, mortally wounded. Semmes, mortally wounded. A bloody mess.

And in that moment, Jonathan took a rifle shot to the head. Just a scratch, he hoped, but blood gushed down the side of his face blurring his vision. He fell to the ground like his father had taught him, grabbed a bandanna from his knapsack, and wiped the blood from his eyes. He tied the cloth around his head and tightened his cap over it. And then he took a rifle shot to his left arm. His wounds were enough to anger him, to torment him into wishing he were dead, yet he was very much alive. It didn't hurt. Nothing hurt, not externally anyway. It was all internal. He must snap out of it. No more thoughts of his father and Henry. Not in this moment. He must think of his mother and his brothers. Of Cassie. Of home.

He reached the crest of the hill, slashing Federal soldiers with every move of his body, screaming the Rebel yell, and they fell one by one, the grotesqueness of the next few minutes seared into his consciousness. He took a saber slash through his leg. He grabbed the rogue Yank, pulled him from his horse, and, with his long bowie knife, put an end to his savagery forever. But he was a savage himself. This bloody war needed to end on the ridge. The country—both countries—had gone mad, and in madness had taken every young southern gentleman with it.

Jonathan's head was spinning, not just from the loss of blood, but from the wretchedness of the hour. Out of ammunition, he raised the butt of his gun and slashed every Union soldier who crossed his path. His father had told him to finish this fight and go home. Oh, dear Lord, how he wanted to go home and fall into his mother's arms. He fought tirelessly until the battle ended. In just fifty minutes it was over—the bloodiest battle ever fought was over. Pickett's charge was now history.

General Lee, riding alone, passed to the front, mourning his dead and imploring his good men to rally. His officers, those who were left, did the same at the rear. Bravery on the ridge had never been equaled. But the fight was lost. The enemy, whether out of fatigue or out of downright respect, stopped in their tracks. They did not follow the brave Rebel soldiers beyond their works. Enough was enough.

When General Lee passed by him, Jonathan removed his hat and bowed as low as he could in respect. Somehow a simple military salute was not enough. He bowed a second time for Henry, who loved his Commander in Chief with a passion.

Night fell and the wounded, battle weary Mississippian made his way through a crowd of soldiers to reach his commanding general, the President's nephew.

"General Davis, sir," Jonathan said, hard saluting his commander.

"Yes, son?"

"Permission to speak, sir."

"There's no need, Jonathan. Is Doc Whitaker still alive?"

"No, sir. He took a rifle shot to the head in the railroad cut. McAllister and I buried him after I buried my father and Albert Henry. General Heth knows, sir."

"Dear God!" he said, aghast at the carnage the railroad cut had wreaked, and he was responsible.

Jonathan could not speak. There was no need to place blame. General Davis had no way of knowing that the railroad cut was a Megiddo, a canyon with little chance of getting out once the Yanks knew they were in there.

"Then clean and bind your wounds, son, and go home," said General Davis.

"You've lost enough in this war to last a lifetime. Take the memory of your father and your brother and go. God speed. I'll never forget you, them, and your sacrifice for the Confederacy. Jeff Davis would be proud of the Mississippi Forty-second. Such brave men, *Our Mississippians*. The bravest I've ever seen. I'll take care of mustering you out."

"Yes, sir. Thank you, sir."

A final salute, and Jonathan dragged his weary, wounded body to the rail station where he sat on the ground until morning. Sleep never came, for the *what-ifs* began to run through his head.

His father and Albert Henry had gone with some of Heth's Division to look for shoes. Apparently, Henry had not found his size, for he died wearing old worn-out shoes that had more holes than leather. But when Jonathan found him lying under the peach tree, draped around his neck and tied together with sturdy shoestrings, was a nice new pair of boots—not Henry's size, but Jonathan's. Henry had bought his brother a pair of boots. He had sacrificed, and out of respect and love for him, Jonathan would never be able to wear those boots. He had gently placed them across his brother's chest and shoveled on the dirt.

What if General Davis had not led them into the railroad cut?
Chances are they would have all died at Longstreet's nod today.
But who could have known?
Who would ever know?

God knows best. He was somebody's love,
Somebody's heart enshrined him there;
Somebody wafted his name above,
Night and morn on the wings of prayer.
Somebody wept when he marched away,
Looking so handsome, brave and grand.
Somebody's kiss on his forehead lay,
Somebody clung to his parting hand.

Somebody's watching, and waiting for him,
Yearning to hold him again to her heart,
And there he lies—with his blue eyes dim,
And his smiling, child-like lips apart.
Tenderly bury the fair young dead,
Pausing to drop o'er his grave a tear;
Carve on the wooden slab at his head,
'Somebody's darling is lying here.'
                              A Richmond Lady

Chapter 32
Faithful Sons

It was a hot Mississippi morning. Humid. July 4, 1863. Independence Day, but with no reason to celebrate. Isaac Payne rode through the familiar hill town, dismounted, and tied Glory to the hitching post. He wiped the sweat and tears from his face, and walked up the steps to the old doctor's office. He needed Doc Malone to accompany him to bear the hideous news to his mother. He couldn't do it alone.

The heady fragrance of sweet jasmine and honeysuckle followed him to the second floor of the building where Doc lived and had his practice. It was a beautiful building, stark white and ages old, surrounded by magnolia trees that were there long before Isaac was born. The blossoms opened with a lemony fragrance. The essence of Mississippi. Another light scent drifted across that end of town. The white flowers on the privet that grew thick between Doc's building and the general store and post office, a nostalgic sweetness that Isaac had known all his life. Now, it all meant nothing, for he was steeped in a gray mood that disqualified anything that bore resemblance to cheerfulness.

He and Billy, Abe, and Cliff had passed through a Confederate camp on their way home, and the news of Gettysburg was still burning in his ears. Ten thousand of their men lay dead on Cemetery Ridge, in the peach orchard, and on the wheat field. Isaac had reason to believe his father, Jonathan, Albert Henry, and his Uncle Marcellus, were among the fourteen hundred Mississippians who fell, but he had no way of knowing for sure. No wonder his father had felt the urgency to rush him from the camp that day two weeks ago, albeit he had no way of knowing what was about to take place. It was all so peculiar. His father had uncanny discernment—an uncanny relationship with Almighty God. Now Isaac wondered if life would be worth living. Everyone was gone. His father, his brothers, his friends, his fellow countrymen. How repulsive this war had become. For certain he needed Doc Malone to go home with him.

₰

That same day, a bloody, dirty, ragged veteran of the Confederate army boarded the cars in the once sleepy little town of Gettysburg, Pennsylvania, and started the long journey home. Andrew McAllister, his friend and compatriot, sat beside him. General Davis had sent him along to take care of Jonathan, ordering Andrew to return to his regiment in not more than three weeks.

Isaac should be there by now, but nothing, not even his return home, was going to ease the pain for his mother and Cassie. Their husbands lay dead and buried together in a shallow grave on the wheat field at Gettysburg. Nothing could suffice for comfort at such a time as this. Sleep deprivation and loneliness controlled Jonathan. He pulled himself hard against the side of the railroad car, protecting his wounds as best he could. The hot July wind blew harsh through the space in the slide, beating against his tear-stained face. He remembered that first ride on the cars in December 1861. It was cold then. His father and brother were his warmth, comfort and security, and he was theirs. What a sharp contrast, the cold bitter winter and the warmth of the dearest on earth to him, and a wicked hot summer blowing the scorching winds of war and the cold despondency of death with no one to comfort him. He couldn't imagine what he would do in this life without his heroes. He was not alone in the car, but unable to control his emotions, he lay prostrate on the splintered floor moaning and sobbing for his father and Henry. At last the sobs gave way to deep sleep. Hours later, he awoke to Andrew's touch.

"Jonathan, we're almost to the Tennessee border. General Davis gave me instructions to transfer in Bristol and take the cars to Chattanooga. From there we are to travel by carriage to Calhoun City and deliver this message from General Davis to Mrs. Doc Whitaker. I must say I'm not looking forward to that."

Andrew patted the pocket where he had stored the letter from General Davis.

"I know, Andrew. Nor am I."

"I'm sorry, Jonathan. I know you have sad news to deliver, yourself."

Jonathan looked up, deep furrows of pain and sorrow drawn across his once youthful face.

"My friend, sad news to live with," he said.

He dropped his head, unwilling to offload his sorrow, compelled to bear it, self-pity festering like the wounds on his filthy body.

When they arrived at the railroad station, the two ragged men stood to their feet. Jonathan took a step and fell to the floor of the car. The pain was excruciating, aggravated by the fall. With Andrew's help, he managed to step to the ground and hobble to the bench at the station.

"Stay here, Jonathan. I'll get our transfer tickets and find out when our train arrives."

When he thought about it, Jonathan was miserable. His wounds needed to be cleaned and new bandages applied, but he doubted if that would happen before he got home. My mother will do it, he thought. The stench, not only of himself, but also of the soldiers around him was sickening. He leaned back on the bench and closed his eyes. Within minutes Andrew was back with information.

"We've got to wait a couple of hours. I'm going to find someplace for you to get these bandages changed."

If he can pull that off, I'll be a contented soldier for the time being, Jonathan thought. He closed his eyes again, trying desperately to block out everything, everybody, but to no avail.

"A man is coming to pick you up on a buckboard and take you to the doctor's office. They'll clean up your wounds and put on new bandages. No charge for soldiers."

"Andrew, I'll never be able to repay you for all you've done for me."

"You're my brother," he said, tears forming in his hazel eyes. "You've been through far too much, and I'll not leave your side."

The doctor cleaned and wrapped Jonathan's wounds then padded them for the long ride home. He dropped a small bottle of laudanum into his hands and, with Andrew's help, assisted Jonathan onto the buckboard. By the time they returned to the cars, the whistle was blasting. Time to go. Scores of wounded soldiers hobbled to the edge of the cars, waiting their turn for help to board. Jonathan gazed from one pitiful sight to the next, some skin and bones. Others without arms, legs, or hands. Some blinded by exploding Minié balls. All were hurting. Some more than others, and he felt so rebuked. He still had all of his limbs. He could see. He had a friend taking care of him. General Davis had shown him kindness for his father's sake. Even the doctor had cleaned and wrapped his wounds.

A gentleman about the age of his father, maybe fifty, sat on the ground near the car they were boarding, waiting for someone to offer a hand. He would not ask. He had one leg and one arm and a patch over his right eye. Jonathan looked at Andrew. Andrew looked at him. Without a word, together and with great care, they lifted the old gentleman into the railroad car. Tears rolled down the man's cheeks as he choked out a thank you. They could see the pain in the one good eye and on the face of this Confederate soldier, this hero. Jonathan discreetly dropped his bottle of laudanum in the man's lap, and he and Andrew climbed aboard.

Jonathan stood over the gentleman a moment and softly cried, "Pa! Oh, my Pa! I would want you with no arms and no legs—"

The old man cried aloud in thanks for the gift of something that would quell the excruciating pain. Andrew cried. And soon every man, every hero, in the car was weeping profusely. The two Mississippians situated themselves against the wall of the car, getting as comfortable as possible for the journey to Chattanooga.

*

"General Joseph Davis has requested a carriage for Private Payne," Andrew said to the attendant. "It is to be charged to the Confederate States government."

"Yes, sir," he said. "I have your carriage ready. General Davis telegraphed ahead. A driver will take you to your final destination. And Private McAllister, you're to summon the driver to meet you in Grenada, Mississippi, when you're ready to return to General Davis' brigade in no more than three weeks. Here are your papers."

"Thank you, sir."

Jonathan and Andrew rode side by side in the carriage, Jonathan scarcely speaking. Suffering from sleep deprivation, he nodded and gave in. He heard the cannons roaring and sabers clanking. Men screaming. Scenes of blood running freely down the hill, flashes of his father in the railroad cut and Henry under the peach tree—lying still. Dead. Like fourteen hundred other Mississippians—they were dead. He watched from a distance as a photographer out of control, clicked on one dreadful scene behind the other. The glassy images fell to the floor and the cracked pieces stacked to the ceiling of the carriage, one by one.

Jonathan's head jerked. He yelled and flailed about, trying to push back the ambrotypes. He felt Andrew's hand on his shoulder.

"Jonathan ... Jonathan!"

The glass plates, the appalling scenes vanished. The photographs were gone. The photographer didn't exist.

Jonathan opened his eyes and for a quick minute forgot where he was.

"It was just a dream, Jonathan."

He gathered his wits and calmly asked his dear friend, "Andrew, what do you dream about?"

"I dream about the river behind my house. About naked trees in the winter. About my Mama when she was young and I was a boy. And I dream about walking home from meetinghouse on Sundays in the spring."

"You don't dream about blood or cannons or dead family members in the cut."

Andrew looked away. Tears filled his eyes.

"I wish I could dream about riding to work with Pa and Henry, talking and laughing. About fishing down on Big Creek. Frogs croaking on a hollow log. An eagle in flight. And Benjamin."

Jonathan wiped the tears and sweat from his face.

Andrew swallowed hard.

"I know, man. Is there anything I can do for you, my friend?"

"No, Andrew, I'm afraid not. Life as I've always known it—the good life—is over. No more dreams for me. From the time we left Mother and the boys and Cassie in December of 1861, life was still good, because I had Pa and Henry.

"For almost two years we slept in the same tent or on the same oil cloth under the stars; we took our meals from the same plate many times; we bathed in the same cold stream; we warmed by the same campfire. My father practically brought me back to life when I was dying of the fever. Henry has been my soul's best friend. No, there's nothing you can do. There's nothing anybody can do. The war has seen to that. This war has taken the dearest to me. It has taken my dreams and left me nightmares in return.

"The naked trees behind the ridge and on the river are gone. I don't get to walk home from meetinghouse like that any more. Whatever you find delicious in your mouth is bitter in mine. Whatever is fine to you and better than fine—then take this into your heart. Those things are gone from me. They don't belong to me anymore."

Jonathan's shoulders shook and tears streamed down his face.

"They say time heals all wounds, Jon, and you're going to have to give it some time. You'll heal from all of this. I know you. You're strong and courageous, and a southern gentleman."

"I don't know, Andrew. I used to think that of myself until the war—especially on Cemetery Ridge yesterday—turned me into a savage. I wanted to avenge Pa and Henry's blood, but I couldn't kill enough Yanks to do it. Pa taught us well why we were fighting—for the Cause, the Greater Cause. We've been defending our Confederate states, our families, and our homes. I stood there with my rifle drawn, wiping sweat out of my eyes so I could see. It was hot, blistering hot. I wondered what was keeping Longstreet, but he must have been thinking he was leading us to the slaughter. And when he nodded to Pickett, I charged that hill to take vengeance for Pa and Henry. Is that wrong, Andrew?"

"Why, no! That's exactly what I was doing if you want to know the truth. I charged that hill with you, thinking about Captain Payne and Henry and Doc Whitaker, and all our friends from Calhoun. Listen, Jonathan, war is hellish. It takes a man's sensibilities—temporarily. But you just wait. All the good things your ma and pa taught you are going to come back to you when you turn down the Payne road. I can pretty much promise you that."

"Andrew, you're a good friend," he said.

The driver stopped the carriage, hopped down from his perch, and stuck his head in the window.

"We're going to stay the night in the livery stable in this little town. We'll leave early in the morning. There are blankets under the seats, so feel free to stretch out as best you can. I'll see what I can find us to eat."

"Thank you, sir," they said.

"Andrew, I'll be so happy to peel this wretched uniform off my body. I need to burn it, but I don't know if I can bear to part with it," Jonathan said. "I'll feel naked without it. It's been like a second layer of skin. Why, I believe part of it is stuck to me."

"I'm with you on that, Jonathan. Maybe we can at least cut the buttons off and save them for souvenirs."

The boys laughed, deciding it was good for the soul.

"Jonathan, you know, one of the greatest men that ever lived on earth was killed in this war just a little over a month ago."

"Stonewall Jackson."

"Yes. Did you hear anything about his last days, the mourning and the burial service?"

"No, I didn't, Andrew. Did you?"

Jonathan leaned back and adjusted a blanket under his head. Andrew did the same.

"Well, I was sitting around a campfire with Jed McGrew just a few weeks ago and he told us the whole story as it was passed down to him. There was not a dry eye in the camp. It was like a church meeting."

"I'm sorry I missed that."

"You were at your post, Jonathan."

"I want to hear the story. Would you tell me?"

"Sure."

The driver brought food and the boys, hungrier than they realized, scarfed it down. It had been several days since they had eaten. Food was not available to them, but never mind that, since Gettysburg, they had no appetite.

They finished the tin cups of hot coffee and lay still on the blankets on the small floor space of the carriage. The moon beamed across the night sky, and the stars cast a mere twinkle of light through the bare windows. It might have been less than fair to enjoy a balmy night, far and away from the roar of cannons, the cry of men screaming, falling, dying.

Andrew began his story.

"Chancellorsville was brilliant. The victory was ours, and Jackson, that brave soldier of the South, could hear the fight raging from the couch where he lay dying. He heard the suffering screams of his soldiers who carried on without him. It pained him to know their condition and what he could have done if circumstances were different. If he had just one more hour with them, he could cut off the enemy, fiercely repulsing them, obliging them to surrender with no alternative. We all know he would have done that. And from his deathbed, with only moments left, he undertook to commission General Rhodes to Major General for his bravery in early May. He took no thought for his dying self, just his men.

"But Jed told the deeper story of Stonewall Jackson's character, of how he would cry out on the battlefield, '*Thy will be done, O Lord!*' And he did it with a calm and quiet decisiveness. He told how his Christian character was unmistakable when he was in the thick of battle and how, when he would raise his hand toward heaven, the men of his command would take off their hats and pass the word down the line, 'Silence! Old Stonewall's going to pray!' God Almighty, help me, I can't tell this without crying."

Jonathan didn't care if Andrew could hear him sobbing. He just didn't care. Andrew choked back his own tears and continued his story.

"His wife told him the doctors were giving him just a short time to live. He said, 'Very good, very good; it is all right.' And a little bit later, when she told him again the doctors said it wouldn't be long, he said to her, 'It will be infinite gain to be translated to Heaven and be with Jesus.' Man, talk about dying grace! Jed said the general had always desired to die on the Lord's Day, and at daylight, which was Sunday, he wanted to know what provisions had been made for the men to have preaching. He was told they would have preaching, and it satisfied him. In his last two days, he was delirious, giving orders as though he were on the front line. It was sad when he said, 'Let us cross over the river and rest under the shade of the trees,' like it wouldn't be long, and then he called for Major Hawks to send forward provisions to the men. On May 10, his last words were, 'A. P. Hill, prepare for action!' and in a few short minutes, Stonewall Jackson crossed over to the other side.

"In his last words, he addressed A. P. Hill—our corps commander. General A. P. Hill. Can you imagine the action he saw when he stood in the presence of God Almighty? 'Prepare for action!' And there he was entering the gates of heaven. Why, Jonathan, I think that's exactly what your pa did, and I wouldn't be surprised if old Stonewall was there to greet him when he arrived, maybe along with thousands of other Christian men who died in the past three days at Gettysburg. When you come to think about it, heaven must be fast filling up with soldiers from both sides."

"Andrew, thank you for telling me that splendid story. I needed it. I've been bitter these last few days, and it has done me no good. I wondered how I could face my mother, but now I have the answer."

"That's what I was hoping to hear you say."

"What about his funeral, Andrew?"

"Well, they took him to the Governor's House in Richmond, draped his coffin in white, and kept his body in state that night. And, Jonathan, get this, the next morning, two of Pickett's regiments with arms reversed and some other dignitaries walked in front of the coffin. I find it eerie that Pickett mourned and accompanied General Jackson's body, not knowing what he would face at Gettysburg just weeks from then. Anyway, Jackson's war-weary horse followed the procession with the last boots he wore draped across it, followed by men of his brigade that were yet alive, though wounded and bleeding. Behind them were Generals Longstreet, Elzey, Winan, Kemper, Garnett, and other dignitaries. Some of them were his pallbearers. You know Kemper and Garnett were killed at Gettysburg yesterday. And then for hours on end, thousands passed by, paying last tribute to our fallen hero.

"It brings tears to my eyes, knowing we were so closely tied to that noble general. How do we ever get over something as somber as this?"

"I don't think we can," Jonathan replied. "I'm not sure I want to."

"Me neither."

"Doc Malone is going to have to get Rev. Banks to help him bear all the dreadful news—to Rev. Davis' wife, Jim Stewart's family, Jethro Parker's pa, and then there's Captain Savage—and to any of the others who died in the railroad cut and on Cemetery Ridge. All these families have to be told."

"Yes, I know, but I think I can tell my mother, now. She must hear it from me. I'll have to break the news to Grandpa and Grandma Church about Marcellus. They got him, Andrew. Those old Yanks took him prisoner and he was wounded—bad. Knowing him, he would rather have died in the railroad cut or on the Ridge than in that enemy prison at Point Lookout, Maryland. I fear he won't last long."

"I'm afraid you're right, Jonathan."

"Andrew you've helped me a lot. Between you and the old man in the railroad car, I'm convinced I've been selfish, and I'm ashamed."

"You have no reason to be ashamed. And, Jonathan—will you go with me to tell Mrs. Doc Whitaker?"

"I'll be glad to."

☙

Morning came. The Mississippians woke to the clop of the horses in unison. A swirl of dust rose up around the carriage wheels. Every part of Jonathan's wounded body ached. There had been a time on the Ridge when he wished for death, but it had not come for some reason—for some insane reason he was spared.

Chapter 33
Infinitely More Precious

One Year Later 1864

Watermelons lay ripe on the ground and tomatoes hung thick on the vines. Corn tasseled on the stalks, and young tender ears filled out the shucks, ready to be pulled. The maple trees by the sides of the turn rows rustled in the early morning breeze, and the mockingbirds, awake and chirping, searched for the morning dew on the leaves. Jonathan could do most anything with the help of his cane, and he and Isaac pulled four large watermelons and laid them at the end of a row then began gathering the tomatoes and squash. When the basket was full of fresh vegetables, they trekked to the back porch of the cabin and laid them out for their mother. They took off their muddy shoes, and joined the family around the breakfast table.

"Ma, we're expecting a big fourth of July frolic you know," Jonathan said. "Guess we can still celebrate what Grandpa did for us not too many years ago. We're going to plop Lee in front of one of those big watermelons and split it open."

"I have a feeling he will know exactly what to do with it," said Cassie.

She smiled at Jonathan, and his eyes locked on hers. He sat at the head of the table, holding Lee on his lap just like his father had always held Samuel. But Sam was four years old and one of the big boys now. He had his own place on the bench beside Joab. Ben's place in times past.

"Joab, are you about ready to ride?" Isaac asked. "I've got your horse saddled."

"Yep, just got to finish m' coffee and get m' shoes on," he said.

Jonathan chuckled, still finding it hard to believe Joab was fourteen years old. A real little man with a raspy changing voice. He was Isaac's age at the time the men went to war.

Rachel and Cassie stood with pride on the porch and watched the three Payne men ride off together.

☙

Fall 1864

From the front room windows, Rachel looked out across the ridge thinking about Thomas. Dear God, how she missed him! Everything about him. And though she hurt desperately, she hoped the memories would never fade. His face was etched there, as fresh as the day he went to war. As real as the day she held it in her hands, trying to commit to memory everything about it. The war was still raging, and Isaac had joined the cavalry just weeks before. He was off with Lee's Army of Northern Virginia somewhere. She prayed to God this war would be over before Joab was old enough to join. She never expected it to last this long. None of them did. She had begged Jonathan to talk to her about his father's last moments. She knew Thomas died in his arms, he dug the grave and buried his father and Henry together, and one day Jonathan would talk about it. He needed to talk, and she needed to hear. Perhaps soon he would be able to. She would let him be until he was ready.

She walked out on the porch and searched the tree line, wishing to see Jonathan and Henry riding over the ridge together, loaded down with fish out of the stream, but that was never going to be. Lee would never know his father, and Cassie would live the rest of her life with a broken heart. She walked to the giant oak midway up the hill and stopped to brush the leaves off Ben's grave, tears streaming down her face. She touched the wood carved marker Jonathan had made before he went to war and ran her fingers across his name. Benjamin Payne. Borne Up By Angels. She had endured pain and sorrow enough to last a lifetime and she was not yet fifty. But then, God had extended his favor, for she had Jonathan, Isaac, Joab, and Samuel. Cassie had come into her life at just the right time, and now there was Lee, who brought them joy unspeakable. He was Henry made over. Rachel had memories that were infinitely more precious than one could imagine. And she could hear the voice of her beloved husband, saying,

I want you to take special care of yourself and the children. When I think of the distance that we are apart, I feel that I would much rather be

there with you. I want you to recollect that life is uncertain and death sure, and if I should never be permitted to see you again, it is my wish that you should train our children up in the way that will be pleasing in the sight of the Lord that their last days may be their best days.

☙

Spring 1865

The South had seen success and failure, enough carnage to last a lifetime, battles won, battles lost. There had been sunshine and rain, fog and more rain, snow knee-deep, and mud to their knees, sickness and disease, and death at every turn; and each new day brought hope or despair, the inconsistency enough to drive both sides insane.

The affluence of the Confederacy, what was left of it, was pulled threadbare when word came that the Alabama was lost. And Sherman took Atlanta. The Battle of Petersburg broke the back of the Army of Northern Virginia. And A. P. Hill fell at Petersburg. The Payne men had loved A. P. Hill, holding him in highest honor, a real hero who fought to the bitter end with unsullied courage.

The Confederate Capitol took the deathblow in early April 1865, some evacuated and then mayhem set in. It was early on a Sunday morning, a beautiful spring day, when President Davis, sitting on his reserved church pew, received the word. It spread swiftly through the city, disrupting Sunday services and all other goings-on. Many of Richmond's citizens were in disbelief, calm, indifferent. Then reality hit like a ton of bricks, typical of how this war affected the South. Thousands prepared to leave along with the government. The banks doled out legal tender then buried what was left on the grounds of the Capitol. As if the Confederate dollar would ever again amount to anything. When night fell, looters began their unthinkable mischief. Men and women frantically packed their belongings, showing little emotion, for they were in shock. Some left, some stayed. All wept at some point. The beautiful city could no longer be described as such.

And then the news rang out over the half burned Richmond and cities all across the war-torn South.

Lee surrendered.

Four years of anguish had ended.

The cause was lost, all hopes crushed, dead, like so many of the South's noble warriors.

☙

Jane Bennett Gaddy

April 10, 1865

Isaac rode with the last of his company to Appomattox, Virginia, not knowing what to expect. He waited outside the perimeter for word. Enlisted men were not allowed to be present on the streets of the Court House area. Only commanding officers.

He was emaciated, not unlike all the other southern patriots. He dismounted and lovingly patted his sorrel mare. She was his only earthly possession besides his weapons. His only connection to home. He gripped the bridle and pressed his face to her neck. Glory herself was but skin and bones. He wished he could look up and see his father and his brothers riding up to join him. He was homesick. He needed his mother, Jonathan, Cassie, and the boys.

A mere remnant of his brave generals accompanied General Lee—Longstreet, Heth, Gordon, Wilcox and a few others. That they made it 'til the end was amazing. So many were dead. When the surrender papers were signed and the white flag of truce raised, southern soldiers stacked their arms and gave over their personal effects, saluted their commanders, and with sadness that beggared description, they walked away. Officers alone were allowed to keep their side arms and their horses, but there was no way Isaac Payne would leave Appomattox without Glory, nor would he part with his Yankee saber and rifle.

The ragged war-weary veteran, with April's breeze blowing softly across his youthful face, turned and slowly rode away, west, southwest toward Mississippi. The faithful son was going home.

༄

December 1865

Snow clouds rippled across the western sky with promise of a few flakes before long. Jonathan sat alone on the front porch swing, shivering yet not wanting to go inside out of the bitter cold. He reached in his pocket and pulled out the letter he had read time and again. Henry had put it in his haversack before Gettysburg. Jonathan had not found it until the day he emptied out the old bag and that was days after he got home. The haversack hung across his chest for weeks, the letter pushed to the bottom, and he never knew it. He heard his brother's voice.

Somewhere in Pennsylvania
June 15, 1863

Jonathan, my brother,

Some days I have thoughts that we might not make it back to Calhoun alive, and God miraculously delivers us out of the enemy's hands. Some days there is hope. But then I surrender my thoughts, for some days, there is the reality I may not see Cassie again and never my son, Lee. My selfishness overpowers me and I dare not give in to death and defeat. How foolish of me. My days are numbered and God knows best how to deal with the likes of us. Jonathan, on my best day, I'm not the man you are. You're my hero, the brother most men never have the extravagance of knowing. You have always given in excess, expecting nothing in return. I have never known a day when I didn't love you with undying devotion. In return for what you have given me, I am asking one last promise of you. Take the dearest to me. Take my wife. Take my son. Love them as your own. Do for them what I cannot do. Be to them what I cannot be. Do it without guilt and without trepidation, for you are worthy of such love as they will give in return.

And in so doing, I charge you to ensure their safe arrival in heaven with you, where I will meet you just inside the gate. Until that glorious day, may God Almighty see you safely home to Calhoun County to a love most splendid. Forever your faithful brother, Albert Henry Payne

Jonathan thought how life had pulled its punches. He had changed, finally learning that men do weep. He had never been able to read this letter without crying, and he had shared it with no one.

"Jon?"

"Oh, Cassie. You're quiet as a little mouse. I didn't hear you," he said, slipping the paper back into his pocket.

"I believe you were deep in thought."

"Come, sit with me."

"I brought us a blanket. Choctaw, of course."

Cassie draped the blanket over Jonathan and sat down beside him. She couldn't help noticing the tears on his face, but she said nothing about it.

"They're the best."

"Well, I'm sure this one is yours."

"I'm sure they're all mine."

Cassie laughed. "I like your scarf," she said.

"My mother made it to replace the one I wore out on the battlefield," he said. "I like yours."

"She made mine, too, of course. I like mine better."

"Red's a good color for you. It looks splendid with your brown hair and blue eyes. Henry used to say you had dark brown hair the color of coffee with just a touch of sweet cream."

Cassie turned her face. He saw the tears she tried to hide.

She was beautiful, and he loved her immensely. He always had. It was time he told her. He nervously clutched his cane in one hand and pulled the scarf across her shoulder with the other. He stared at her. And she gazed into his faded blue eyes.

"It hurts even now."

"The war, Jon?"

"No. To look at you. It hurts to look at you, Cassie."

"I don't understand."

It was a fragile moment. They were two fragile human beings. Circumstances had made it so. But Jonathan owed Cassie an explanation. He couldn't expect her to understand and he was going to struggle to reveal his innermost thoughts. To say the unsaid.

"Cassie, it hurts to look at you because for a long time I couldn't. You were Henry's wife. He was the one who courted you and married you. Not me. I know this doesn't make sense, but I have to explain it the best I can. I thought from the beginning that Henry had heaven laid at his feet. I was happy for him, yet sad that you weren't mine. I didn't covet my brother's wife, not for a moment, but I knew God had found favor with him for he had your love and devotion.

"Now, Henry's gone, and I feel horribly guilty. I'm alive. He's dead. He had to leave you and Lee."

"Jon, I was aware that you never even looked at me, before you left for the army. I thought for a long time you didn't like me. That maybe you were angry because I took your brother. But then it didn't matter, for you and your father took my husband and went off to war. Isn't it funny the thoughts we have that couldn't be farther from the truth? That take us to moments of despair and even speculation?"

"Yes, it is. Six months ago, I couldn't have sat here and talked to you like this. My life changed at Gettysburg. In that pathetic moment, hatred and rage and hurt fell on me. I hated Lincoln and Hooker and Meade and Grant and Sherman. I hated the entire northern army. I wanted to kill every Yankee I could get my hands on. I hated what they did to my father and Albert Henry and to our country. And then, on the ride home, Andrew McAllister told me some things. He helped me more than he will ever know. He had the wisdom of an old man, and he was just a kid like me. But if it hadn't been for him, I would have given in to the rage within me."

"I'm glad you were able to leave it out there in the past where it belongs, for you have never displayed that rage since you've been home. And I'm glad you came home. For a few weeks, we thought all of you were dead. It's been hard. I miss Henry as Rachel misses Thomas, but I'm happy you are alive and well and that you show a measure of happiness."

"Cassie, when Pa was dying in my arms, I promised him I would take care of Mother and the boys and you. He made me promise to help raise Lee."

"And you're doing a great job of all of that, Jon."

"But, Cassie—"

"Yes, Jon?"

"Well, it's been well over two years now. And would it be—"

He stumbled over his words and hesitated.

"Yes, Jon?"

Cassie smiled and her eyes glistened with tears.

"What I'm trying to say is … will you … will you marry me, Cassie? I promise to take care of you and Lee and to love you both for the rest of my life."

"Oh, yes, Jon!" Cassie said, and then she hesitated.

"What is it, Cassie?"

"I … I think Henry … I think he would want you to take care of Lee and me. Knowing him, he would want us all to be as happy as we can in spite of all the heartache, and we've all had enough to last a lifetime."

In that moment, Jonathan took her in his arms and kissed her hair. The letter was safe inside his pocket and he would not show it to her. Likely not ever.

"How about spring of 1866? And Andrew must be here. Andrew McAllister will come. And Duncan Jamison. And if Isaac can gain a little weight back, enough to fill up a suit of clothes, he can be my best man."

Laughter rang out across the hills of home, delighting the deer that played by the brook and the snowbirds that flitted about from one pine branch to another. Rachel pressed her face to the windowpanes and smiled. Snow began to fall in huge flakes and blow across the front porch of the Payne cabin.

Epilogue
In Some Golden Age

The Civil War, the War Between the North and the South, the War for Southern Independence some called it, but it was all of those. Some hold firmly that the slavery issue was the root, but there was a Greater Cause. Some say economic rivalry between the industrial North and the agricultural South was just cause, but there was a Greater Cause. Most agree that many factors, not just one, contributed. The Blue and the Gray each fought and died for what they were sure was right. They fell in blood-drenched ditches, no matter what color the uniform. But the Greater Cause revealed a gallant display of men, young and old, giving up all they held dear, losing legs, arms, eyes, and many giving up their lives for what they knew in their hearts to be right. Whatever the cause, so be it. It ended at Appomattox Court House in Virginia almost four years to the day of when it began.

Robert E. Lee stood for gallantry, morality, and devotion to the South, fighting with every fiber of his being in opposition to the tough, hot-blooded, cigar chewing U. S. Grant and high strung, volatile William T. Sherman, who marched across the South, burning everything in his path. The South boasted of Thomas J. "Stonewall" Jackson, an infantry genius, lover of the Bible, and Nathan Bedford Forrest of Mississippi, said to be the greatest cavalryman of the Civil War. And Pierre Gustave Toutant Beauregard, the romantic Creole general who gave command for the attack at Fort Sumter under the leadership of Jefferson Davis, President of the Confederate States of America.

The great southern generals fought against all odds, with an army of fewer than one third that of the North. Against a well-fed, well-clad group of Union soldiers who turned tail and ran at the first sight of blood—to begin with. But the South taught them how to fight. By example. How to stay the course. Union soldiers stood amazed at the young sharpshooters who could scream the bloodcurdling cry of war and come out victorious time and again. They beat the South simply by the strength of numbers. And there was a time, during the lull of battle, that both sides would exchange pleasantries, shake hands, share food, and help bury the dead of the enemy. A strange phenomenon, this country at war with itself.

It started April 12, 1861, when southern artillery shelled Fort Sumter in the harbor of Charleston. It ended four years later. On April 9, 1865, Confederate General Robert E. Lee surrendered his ragged, exhausted army to General Ulysses S. Grant at Appomattox Court House in Virginia. The other Confederates followed behind when they knew the war was over.

For the Payne men, it was too late, for their blood flowed red to the Potomac. Only Jonathan came home. Rachel, her remaining boys, and Cassie had only memories of last words before their loved ones left Calhoun County that day in December of 1861. Memories of holding them tenderly, wishing, hoping, crying, begging for just one more hour with them.

∽

My story is fiction. The following address by Dr. John L. Girardeau, Presbyterian Minister, delivered at the Magnolia Cemetery in Charleston in 1866 in memory of the Confederate dead—is not. It is eloquent, to the memory of the Gettysburg dead, and when I read it, I did so for Thomas Goode Clark, my great-great grandfather, and his sons, Jonathan and Albert Henry, whose *blood was poured out like water* on July 1 and 3, 1863, for in giving all they had, my forebears—my heroes—*descended to the tomb* but not in vain. And for Marcellus Church, who was wounded at Gettysburg but died in a Federal prison at Point Lookout, Maryland. And for Isaac Clark, who made it home from the battlefield, but who waited his time, joined the cavalry and fought valiantly in the Civil War. Unlike his father, brothers, and uncle, Isaac came back, alive and well and raised his family at Slate Springs, Mississippi, when the war ended. This, too, is in loving memory of the faithful son.

> *Whether they were right or wrong in the prosecution of the contest which cost them their lives, the men whose sunken graves we repair, and whose memory we honor, died for us. We can never, never forget that they were sacrificial victims on the altar which we helped to rear, and that their blood was poured out like water in defense of principles which we avowed, and which we counseled and exhorted them to maintain to the last extremity. For that cause which we as well as they regarded as the*

exponent of constitutional liberty, and which, during its protracted and agonizing struggle for existence, we loved with a passionate intensity which no words can express—for that cause these men encountered every hardship, underwent every privation, and freely sacrificed their lives ...

The blood, the precious priceless blood of our brethren, may seem to have been drunk up by the earth in vain—but whatever of truth, whatever of right, whatever of pure and lofty principles there were for which they contended and for which they died, may, in another day, in some golden age, sung by poets, sages and prophets, come forth in the resurrection of buried principles and live to bless mankind, when the bones of its confessors and martyrs shall have mouldered into dust.

At this same spot, when the dead were being re-interred from Gettysburg, he ended his address ...

Heroes of Gettysburg! Champions of constitutional rights! Martyrs for regulated liberty! Once again, farewell! Descend to your final sleep with a people's benediction upon your names! Rest ye here, soldiers of a defeated— God grant it may not be a wholly lost—Cause! We may not fire a soldier's salute over your dust, but the pulses of our hearts beat like muffled drums, and every deep-drawn sigh breathes a low and passionate requiem.

Memory will keep her guard of honor over your graves; Love will bedew them with her tears; Faith will draw from them her inspiration for future sacrifice; and Hope, kindling her torch at the fires which glow in your ashes, will in its light, look forward to a day when a people once more redeemed and enfranchised will confess that your death was not in vain.

☙

And so ... my heart beats like a muffled drum as I think of how it might have been and I lay an imaginary wreath upon their graves, somewhere out there on that Wheatfield or on Cemetery Ridge, or perhaps in the Peach Orchard or in the marshy place. It matters not, for God knows the precise location of their dust, and at the resurrection, we will glory in his infinite creative, for he will gather us together and we will nevermore part.

Notes

I am most appreciative for information gleaned from numerous sources. While mine is not a history book, I poured over historical writings, documents, essays, Civil War pamphlets, and encyclopedias in search of accuracy of chronology and events of the war; however, many authors saw the war differently and wrote their accounts accordingly. Some writings were in opposition to others. Some accounts were slanted toward the North, some toward the South. Since I'm a southerner, and some of my ideas came directly from the letters my forefathers wrote, obviously, my novel is slanted toward the South, and I make no apologies for my bias. It was my best effort to let the Clark family live on vicariously through the characters in my story.

My best and most splendid resource was the personal files, essays, books, photos, paintings and various other memoirs of Charlie Clark, who has lived his entire life within ten miles of where T. G. and the boys lived when they left to go to war.

Since most of the other accounts and writings were compiled in the late 1800's, permission to quote is not required. Credit is given below for anything I have quoted or to which I have alluded.

Blackburn, George A. *The Life Work of John L. Girardeau*, D.D., LL.D, late Professor in the Presbyterian Theological Seminary. Columbia, SC: The State Company, 1916. Excerpts of his address delivered in 1866 to the Civil War dead and the Gettysburg heroes.

Gordon, John B., Confederate Army General. *Reminiscences of the Civil War.* New York: Charles Scribner's Sons, 1903.

Jones, J. W., Dr. *Life and Letters of General Robert E. Lee.* The Neal Publishing Company, 1903.

Putnam, Sallie B. *Richmond During the War, By A Richmond Lady.* New York: G. W. Carleton & Co. Publishers, 1867.

Sykes, Winnie Hellums. *Dear Margery*, compiled in 2004, not copyrighted. Excerpts of the Clark letters used by permission of Charlie Clark, Calhoun County, Mississippi. Original letters are archived at the University of Mississippi, Oxford.

CPSIA information can be obtained at www.ICGtesting.com
Printed in the USA
LVOW132059130313

324156LV00002B/149/P

9 780595 527922